Ft. Lupton Public & School Library

3 3455 02412 5194

PRAISE ~~FOR THE~~

MRS. FRUGALICIOUS SHOPPING MYSTERIES:

Black Thursday:

"A fun and savvy mystery."

—*Booklist*

Eternally 21:

"A character whom readers will be pleased to follow."

—*Publishers Weekly*

"Maddie's coupon-clipping tips are seamlessly incorporated into the well-constructed mystery, which provides a series of stunning twists that will leave readers eager to see what will happen to Maddie in the next installment."

—*Booklist*

"Never has coupon clipping been so fun or harrowing. Fast-paced, entertaining and filled with twist and turns, *Eternally 21* will save mystery readers money and make them lose sleep as they cheer for formerly wealthy turned frugally funny Maddie Michaels. With colorful characters and an engaging heroine, this series debut will leave cozy readers clamoring for more."

—Joelle Charbonneau, author of the Rebecca Robbins and Glee Club mysteries

OTHER WORKS BY LINDA JOFFE HULL

The Big Bang (Tyrus, 2012)
Eternally 21 (Midnight Ink, 2013)
Black Thursday (Midnight Ink, 2014)
Frog Kisses (Literary Wanderlust, 2015)

Sweetheart Deal

*A Mrs. Frugalicious
Shopping Mystery*

Sweetheart Deal

Linda Joffe Hull

MIDNIGHT INK
WOODBURY, MINNESOTA

Sweetheart Deal: A Mrs. Frugalicious Shopping Mystery © 2015 by Linda Joffe Hull. All rights reserved. No part of this book may be used or reproduced in any manner whatsoever, including Internet usage, without written permission from Midnight Ink, except in the case of brief quotations embodied in critical articles and reviews.

FIRST EDITION
First Printing, 2015

Book format by Teresa Pojar
Cover design by Lisa Novak
Cover illustration by Bunky Hurter
Editing by Nicole Nugent

Midnight Ink, an imprint of Llewellyn Worldwide Ltd.

This is a work of fiction. Names, characters, places, and incidents are either the product of the author's imagination or are used fictitiously, and any resemblance to actual persons, living or dead, business establishments, events, or locales is entirely coincidental.

Library of Congress Cataloging-in-Publication Data
Hull, Linda Joffe, author.
  Sweetheart deal / by Linda Joffe Hull. — First edition.
      pages ; cm. — (A Mrs. Frugalicious shopping mystery ; #3)
   ISBN 978-0-7387-3491-0 (softcover)
  1. Murder—Investigation—Fiction. I. Title.
   PS3608.U433S94 2015
   813'.6—dc23
                                2015027010

Midnight Ink
Llewellyn Worldwide Ltd.
2143 Wooddale Drive
Woodbury, MN 55125-2989
www.midnightinkbooks.com

Printed in the United States of America

For Andrew, Evan, and Eliza

ONE

THE SCENARIO WAS SUPPOSED to be straightforward: I, Maddie Michaels, AKA online blogger Mrs. Frugalicious, and, most recently, matriarch of the Reality Channel's newest offering, *The Family Frugalicious*, was in beautiful, coastal Mexico to tape a sun-soaked, south-of-the-border, budget-destination wedding episode of my show.

Considering our arrival had been delayed by a freak ice storm that left us stranded for a day in Houston, and the fact that I was there to play savings-minded matron-of-honor for producer Anastasia Chastain's televised nuptials, I knew better than to expect a relaxing, uneventful stay at the beach gazing out at the impossibly azure waters of the Mayan Riviera. Really, given the tumultuous events of the last year,[1] it was crazy to expect things to go smoothly at all.

---

1. Including but not limited to my financial newscaster husband losing all of our money in a Ponzi scheme, my transformation from well-heeled housewife into reality TV's Mrs. Frugalicious, a series of savings-related scrapes, and two murders.

"I'm not feeling so well," my husband[2] Frank said, rubbing his sit-up flat stomach as we, the Family Frugalicious, pulled up to the grand columned portico of the Hacienda de la Fortuna a full twenty-four hours after we were due to arrive.

Before I could reach into my purse for a furry Tums, our director Geo appeared at the passenger window.

"Finally," he said by way of hello, running his hands through his shoulder-length hair and leaning into the resort's official SUV to hand me the day's schedule:

11:00 a.m.: Arrival of travel-weary but excited Michaels clan.

11:05 a.m.: Enter hotel, comment on beauty and charm of lobby.

11:07 a.m.: Introduction of hotel staff.

11:15 a.m.: Appearance of Anastasia Chastain and wedding planner for "chance" greeting.

"Holy moly," I said, continuing to scan the first of two single-spaced pages. "Is all of this just for today?"

"All we could do yesterday were visual shots and a few cut-ins of the bride and groom, so we have to make up for lost time," Geo said, snatching the schedule and motioning our driver to take another spin around the circle so the cameras could document our "spontaneous" arrival. "Starting now."

Luckily the kids were enthusiastic about their new status as reality TV personalities, so oohing and ahhing for the cameras while re-arriving once or twice for our beach "vacation" was hardly a problem. Their enthusiasm made the larger problem—that Frank and I were over and done, married in name only, and even that solely for the sake of the show—somewhat easier to conceal. As far

---

2. So to speak—see next footnote.

as they and the network knew, we'd reconciled our various issues[3] and arisen from the ashes new, improved, and full of value advice for our viewers.

We'd sailed through the small amount of shooting involved in pulling together the clips from my Black Friday murder misadventure for our pilot. We'd adjusted quickly to a crew wearing backward baseball caps and cameras strapped to their shoulders making themselves comfortable in our house and everywhere else we needed to go.

I questioned, however, just how we were going to keep up our charade under the watchful eyes of our children, our producer bride, and a wedding's worth of guests.

Nevertheless, we managed to kick things off with big smiles as we stepped out of the car, entered the opulent lobby of the Hacienda de la Fortuna, and stepped over to our mark in front of a second camera.

"Wow!" Frank said, turning on the charm despite rubbing his stomach. "What a place!"

"Totally cool!" said our teenage son FJ, a younger, sandy-haired clone of his handsome father.

"Where's the pool?" asked my college-coed stepdaughter, Eloise.

"The website said there are like five of them," added Trent, our other son and FJ's identical twin. "Not to mention the beach!"

"I expected it to be beautiful and fun here," I agreed as I took in what felt like a football field's worth of marble, gleaming chandeliers, scrolled ironwork, dark wood, and opulent colonial plantation charm. "But I had no idea it would be this elegant!"

---

3. Not only his personal indiscretions, but also his creative solution to keep me in the fold by orchestrating a television deal for us as a *family* whereby we pretended to be happily married in order to foot the bill for our children's college education and restore his tarnished image, thus re-ensuring our financial future.

On cue, a handsome Hispanic man with a slim physique joined us.

"I am Enrique, the general manager of Hacienda de la Fortuna," he said, offering a fetching smile and a handshake. "*Mi casa es su casa.*"

"*Muchas gracias,*" I said, in my best (but still faulty) Spanish.

Enrique gestured behind me. "Allow me to introduce some of the staff assigned to making sure your stay is an exceptional one."

I turned to find a line of employees clad in the same peach, white, and chocolate color scheme of the lobby.

"You've already met Felipe," he said, as our chatty, grandfatherly driver rushed in from outside and joined the group.

"Is all that Mayan sacrifice stuff he told us about on the way from the airport really true?" Trent asked.

"No one knows more about this area than Felipe," Enrique said with a nod, before moving on to the gentleman to Felipe's right. "Next we have Jorge, our concierge. Beside him is Benito, our head chef, who is putting the finishing touches on a special menu for a private dinner we've arranged for your family on Sunday night."

"Sounds wonderful."

"It will be," Benito said, with no trace of humility. "I assume you're all open to local—"

"Maddie! Frank! Kids!!" Anastasia Chastain—blond beauty, bride-to-be, and all around savvy, type-A producer—came rushing across the lobby trailed by three women who looked too much like her not to be her sisters. She enveloped me in a huge hug. "I'm *so* relieved you're finally here! I've bitten my nails down to the quick worrying about the safe arrival of my favorite family. Wondering when, if, you'd actually—"

"Mother Nature was giving you the gift of the inevitable wedding glitch early, before things really got underway," said an attractive woman in official garb, joining the group.

4

"This is Elena, the resort's wedding planner," Anastasia said, as though anyone that self-assured, pretty-if-severe-looking, and bearing such a firm handshake could be anyone else. "And these are my sisters, Susan, Sara, and Sally."

I gave each sister a hello hug despite Anastasia's warning that they'd likely be slow to warm up because of dismay over her choice of me as matron of honor. It was a decision she'd made partly for the sake of this special episode of *The Family Frugalicious*, but mainly to keep from having to pick any one of her sisters over the others.

"I'm sorry the delay threw things off schedule," I said. "What can I do to help make sure the wedding goes off without any more unintended hitches?"

"Just be at the rehearsal at five sharp," Elena said.

"Cut!" Geo said. "Let's set up for the next shot."

"Good, because I think I'm about to die," Frank said, rushing off for a nearby *baño* while Elena, Anastasia, and most of the staff scattered in various directions.

"I didn't think that was supposed to happen until you were down here for a day or two," Trent remarked. "Must have been that breakfast burrito he ate at the airport."

"This is not good," Geo said, tugging at the chin of his hipster beard. "We're behind schedule as it is."

"I'm sure Frank will be back in a few minutes," I said. "He was fine until we drove up."

"I guess I'll have you do a pre-cap[4] while we wait to do a second take," Geo said, reaching into a nearby folder and handing me a piece of paper. "The Hacienda de la Fortuna has a few things for you to say."

---

4. An interview of a reality show participant before or early into a major event that captures the excitement and anticipatory giddiness.

"Okay," I said, looking over a list of "candid" talking points penned not by me, but by a *Family Frugalicious* staff writer. "But I don't even have time to memorize—"

"We have cue cards."

"Do I at least have a few seconds to freshen up?" I asked, glad I was learning to expect the unexpected enough to leave Houston in a sundress (albeit beneath my down coat), but wondering just how harried I looked after a mostly sleepless night, the flight, customs, an hour drive to the resort, and the shock to my hair and skin of the bona fide humidity lacking back home in Denver.

"You have a wardrobe change in fifteen minutes," one of the assistants said.

"Into bathing suits, I hope?" Eloise asked. "Please say you plan to tape us spending the afternoon hanging by the pool and ordering smoothies or something."

"Or something," said a young man who appeared beside her. "At least for you and your brothers."

"Meet Ivan," said Enrique. "Head of activities."

"Hi," said Ivan, whose official garb was clearly at odds with his light brown dreadlocks, nose ring, and the sea turtle tattoo on his bicep. "Nice to meet all of you."

"You have no accent," Trent said.

"I grew up in California," Ivan said with a dimpled smile. "But my heart is here in Mexico."

"This does seem like a pretty chill place," FJ said.

"There's definitely a lot to see and do," Ivan said. "Like spending this afternoon at one of the nearby cenotes."

"*Cenotes?*" Trent asked.

"Beautiful, clear, freshwater sinkholes where we can swim and snorkel."

"Sounds cool," FJ said.

I waited for the inevitable sniff and brush-off from the typically high-maintenance Eloise.

"Are there snakes or anything creepy-crawly there?" she asked.

"I'll make sure there isn't."

"You sure?"

"Positive," Ivan said. "And I'm sure we have a picnic lunch already packed for you and your brothers."

"Okay." Eloise smiled. "Sounds like a plan."

The next thing I knew, the kids and company were out the front door of the hotel and I was sitting on a barstool in front of another, pretending I wasn't reading off the aforementioned cue cards:

"We're here at the beautiful Hacienda de la Fortuna for my producer Anastasia Chastain's wedding! I was thrilled when Stasia asked me to be her matron of honor and Frank to be the best man. Being the frugal shopper I am though, I have to admit I had a few second thoughts about the cost of traveling and staying at an all-inclusive resort…"

Geo signaled for me to smile.

"Boy, was I surprised to find out just how wrong I was! By following a few simple tips, here we are enjoying affordable paradise—all five of us!"

Anastasia gave me a thumbs up from across the lobby.

Considering her wedding and our lodging had been comped by the hotel, I felt a stab of consternation wondering what tips I could possibly be about to give. Luckily as I began to recite them, they all seemed to be pretty much Budget Conscious Travel 101:

1. Instead of going on two different family getaways this year, make the wedding part of an extended family vacation or your own second honeymoon—you'll save on everything from air-fare to hassle!

2. Set a price alert as soon as the couple sets the date and book your flights when a sale pops up.

3. Most resorts offer great block rates for bridal parties. Here at the Hacienda de la Fortuna, for example, rooms booked for special events are up to 50% off!

4. All-inclusive means that your meals, beverages (including cocktails), and even some activities are included in the price. Plan sightseeing trips off the resort property between meal times when you can, or order box meals from the hotel so there will be few additional costs.

Nothing the show's writers had come up with served to promote the resort in any unexpected way. Not until the next tip, that was ...

5. One way to get the most value out of your next resort-style vacation is to sign up for the vacation ownership presentation. Here at the Hacienda de la Fortuna, for example, they offer incentives like upgraded rooms simply for agreeing to give them ninety, no-obligation minutes of your time!

I was prompted to smile once again.

"Cut," Geo said.

"We're pushing the resort's timeshare presentation?"

"Providing promotional consideration."

"Like an infomercial?"

"Like a reality show about bargain hunting that, to add to its overall appeal, is helping viewers navigate the ins and outs of vacation ownership," Geo said, sounding just a little more impressed with himself than usual.

"Okay…" I said, but suddenly I was distracted by the appearance of a man that could only be described as tall, dark, and *muy guapo*.

The next thing I knew, he was standing beside me in the bar/ makeshift set area and the camera was rolling again.

"I'm Alejandro," he said, looking that much more chiseled, broad, and altogether attractive up close. Even his peach hotel-issue polo shirt and tan khakis looked somehow suave. "And I've been looking forward to spending the afternoon with the famous Mrs. Frugalicious."

TWO

"I'm sorry your husband is feeling under the weather," Alejandro said.

"Me too," I said with crossed fingers. I wouldn't wish stomach discomfort on anyone, not even my all-but-former husband. However, I wasn't entirely unhappy about having my own private tour of the hotel property. Especially since Alejandro, with his thick brown hair, light brown eyes, and just shy of full lips, was the closest I was going to come to a date until Frank and I could officially un-couple.

But just then Frank reappeared from the men's room looking downright pasty. He seemed to regain a bit of color as he introduced himself to naturally bronze Alejandro, who, as I suspected, ran the vacation ownership operations for the resort. Frank, who made it a point to always be camera-ready, appeared to be on the mend while we did the necessary extra takes, had a quick *story day* wardrobe change, mulled over a script for the segment, and strolled across the lobby for the camera, past the veranda where the rehearsal dinner was to take place. We made our way over to the poolside café.

Frank did his part, admiring the grounds and abundant grandeur of the hotel. One glance at the pan of refried beans bubbling at the lunch buffet however, and whatever color had returned to his face drained.

He rushed away once more.

Alejandro and I found ourselves dining alone. We indulged in a pleasant poolside lunch of shrimp quesadillas and I had my first of what threatened to be a weekend's worth of the Hacienda de la Fortuna's signature *bottomless* mango margaritas.

The drinks went down a little too easily as Alejandro shared details about his youth, graduating with honors from the Universidad Autónoma de Somewhere-in-Mexico and working his way up in the resort business. His relaxed style and easy laugh had me revealing not only a few tidbits about my life and family, but comfortable enough to recite a cue card–prompted vacation ownership wish list I hadn't created. Thankfully it was both reasonable and accurate:

A place to create family memories…
Somewhere we'll look forward to returning year after year…
Has to be by the beach…

I wasn't sure whether it was Alejandro's charming manners—starting with whether I wanted to sit in the sun or shade—the way the staff seemed to be at extra attention in his presence, his seemingly earnest interest in my growing notoriety as Mrs. Frugalicious, or those delicious margaritas, but the camera crew seemed to vanish. Despite the multiple takes, out-of-sequence shots, and other assorted realities of reality television, we might as well have been all alone together as we ventured back indoors for a whirlwind tour of everything from Sushi Especia, one of the six internationally themed,

11

on-premise restaurants, to Serenidad, the plush state-of-the-art spa and fitness facility. More impressive than the various amenities were the guest rooms—all suites, and all boasting living rooms filled with designer furniture and bathrooms filled with marble fixtures and high-end appliances.

"Our beds have high thread count Egyptian cotton sheets and your choice of pillows," Alejandro said with a wry smile as he followed me into the bedroom. "And a specially made mattress so comfortable that guests often claim they've never enjoyed anywhere they've spent the night more."

I willed myself not to think about how long it had been since I'd actually *enjoyed* spending the night in my own bedroom.

Much less anywhere else …

The remainder of the tour was something of a blur as we wove around the never-ending mosaic-lined swimming pools featuring everything from submerged chaises to swim-up bars, past the championship golf course, and out to a stretch of soft white sand that looked out onto the impossibly blue waters of the Mayan Riviera.

"Delightful," Alejandro said. "Yes?"

So were the undertones of his spicy yet subtle cologne as I followed him into the resort sales office.

Vacation ownership at the luxe Hacienda de la Fortuna had to come with a steep price tag, so I expected to see a room full of uncomfortable presentees, all seated in defensive positions, looking nervously at one another, arms and legs crossed, the women clutching their handbags, and the men looking down at their feet. Instead, prospective buyers seemed downright relaxed as they sipped on cocktails, nibbled on snacks, and chatted with well-dressed salespeople.

As Alejandro led me toward his office on the other side of the sales floor, he stopped to check in at various conversation clusters.

"How has your experience with us been so far?"

"Wonderful," said an older lady. "Antonio here is taking wonderful care of me."

Antonio, who looked like Alejandro's slightly swarthy brother, gave her a playful wink. "Tell me, are you staying in an ocean or courtyard room?"

"Courtyard," she said.

"How about we upgrade this fine lady so she can enjoy the view?" he said.

"Done," Alejandro said.

"Wow," she said. "Thank you."

"Wow is right," I said, after watching Alejandro proceed to authorize a free boat tour pass for one family and stop to pour a congratulatory glass of champagne from the signing bottle of another on our way to his glass-walled office. "I can't imagine how this could be any more—"

"Pleasant?" he asked as he motioned me to sit and an assistant appeared with snack and beverage cart. "That's how we roll around here."

The presentation itself lasted far longer than it was supposed to, but the time somehow flew by as I sipped on a fresh margarita. Alejandro covered everything from a brief history of the resort to a detailed explanation of the exchange program that allowed owners to trade their vacation time at Hacienda de la Fortuna with resorts all over the world.

"Certainly in Hawaii and the Bahamas," he said, recounting the spots I'd mentioned over lunch as destinations I most wanted to visit.

"So I can trade my week here for—?"

"A romantic getaway to Bora Bora," he said. "If that's what you desire."

I looked down and fiddled with my ring so neither the camera nor Alejandro could see my expression. "I can't imagine anyone desiring anything more than what you're offering here."

"I'm glad you feel that way," Alejandro said.

"I guess it all comes down to cost..." I mumbled, "versus benefits."

"Which we have in abundance," he said.

I looked up and our eyes met again.

Alejandro pulled out a pad of paper and a pen. "Given everything you've told me about your lifestyle and vacation habits, I hope you will allow me to presume that your family would be most interested in a three-bedroom unit you'd use for two weeks a year?"

"Theoretically," I said. "But—"

"You don't usually get away for two consecutive weeks and, because of your schedules, it's hard to know exactly when you'll be able to take that time off?"

"Exactly," I said, impressed by just how attentive he'd been and how fuzzy I was starting to feel. "And depending on—"

"A price that would satisfy the very bargain-wise Mrs. Frugalicious?" he said, jotting down a number on the notepad, which he proceeded to slide across his desk.

"Wow!" I said, putting down my drink and confirming the lack of zeros on the page. "This is all it costs for two weeks a year in a three-bedroom unit?"

"I've quoted the bottom-line price for what are known as floating weeks, which will exclude certain high-traffic times of the year, but yes."

"But—?"

"What point would there be in playing price games with you, of all people?" he asked. "We both know the true investment lies in the vacation—the fun and memories created by spending time in any number of great places we can offer you as a vacation property owner."

"True," I managed.

"How about I give you a few minutes to think it over?"

"That would be great," I said, picking up a conveniently placed calculator and pretending to crunch a number or two of my own.

"Cut," Geo said.

We set up for the shot again, and once again I found myself sharing *my* cue-card prompted thoughts:

"Like most people, I agreed to this whole timeshare presentation business for the perks I was promised in exchange for ninety minutes of my precious vacation time. I mean, what are the chances that I, Mrs. Frugalicious, would spring for such a big-ticket item without doing extensive background research first? Here's the thing, though . . ."

I read the next line I was supposed to recite: *This feels like it may be too good a deal to pass up!*

I signaled Geo to stop shooting. "Hold up."

"What is it?" he asked.

"This all looks great and everything, but I haven't done any real research on timeshares and—"

"One step ahead of you," he said, handing me an article entitled *Ten Tips for Your Timeshare Presentation*. "Look it over and let's get on with it."

I scanned a few of the bolded points:

—Even though you may have agreed to the timeshare presentation simply for the perks and upgrades, take the tour with sincere interest.

—Location is key. If you plan to trade or exchange timeshare locations, especially in desirable areas, you need to own in an area that has high year-round, global demand.

—The average timeshare purchase is roughly $15,000 to $20,000. Upscale units are in the upper $20,000s to low $40,000s. There's also an average yearly maintenance fee that can run anywhere from $250 to $1,000.

—Assume approximately 20 years of use and determine the true cost per week by adding annual fees to annual amortized cost, factoring in the number of weeks per year.

"This is informative," I said, noting that I was supposed to, *ask questions so the salesman recognizes you're too savvy to fall for anything short of a great deal.* "But I should still do some more in-depth research if I'm actually going to go ahead and sign something."

"No need," Geo said. "The timeshare was pre-negotiated as part of the deal we made with the resort."

"I still have to pay—"

"Nothing!"

"W-What?"

"Just another benefit of being the star of *The Family Frugalicious!*"

"Oh," I said.

"More like, *olé!*"

With that, Alejandro stepped back into the room, champagne bottle in hand, and the camera was back on.

"Ready to celebrate?" he asked, with an expectant smile. A smile shared by Geo, the cameraman, the cue card holder—everyone.

Everyone but me.

All I had to do was sign on the (inevitable variety of) dotted line(s) that would materialize before me and we would own two weeks of paradise.

In perpetuity...

And all for the unheard of price of absolutely nothing, assuming the annual maintenance fee was included.

But, as light-headed as I felt from the alcohol and the possibility of having my own free dream-vacation spot, I couldn't sign up for what seemed to be the most satisfying of frugasms[5] without making sure I wasn't violating the greatest commandment of bargain shopping first:

If it sounds too good to be true...

"I'd like to think about it[6] for a little longer," I said, with what I feared was a bit of a slur.

"No!" Geo mouthed, shaking his head furiously. "No!"

"You've done a wonderful job," I said to Alejandro. "But, to be honest, I haven't had a chance to do my due diligence."[7]

Alejandro looked puzzled.

---

5. Self-explanatory, but an especially satisfying deal.
6. Whether you actually plan to purchase the timeshare or not, don't ever accept the first price offered. *I'd like to think about it* and/or a *no* or two for the record is your most effective bargaining tool to assure the best price.
7. If you are indeed interested in vacation ownership, be sure to do your research first. Don't allow a persuasive salesman to tell you what you want and for what price.

"I'm afraid there are just too many people who rely on the quality of my advice where deals are concerned."

"I see," Alejandro said.

I waited for a *but...*

But how about one week a year instead of two?

How about a two-bedroom unit every other year for even less?

Of course, he couldn't possibly offer me anything more favorable than two free weeks a year, including a trade option with properties all over the world.

"I just need a little more time," I said, looking earnestly at Alejandro before he could come up with a rebuttal. "How about we plan to meet again after I've had time to do a little more research and can provide my Frugarmy with enough information so they too can make their best deal?"

Geo threw his hands in the air. "Cut!"

———

The *situation*—as it was deemed by Geo, who was ranting into the phone before I could even apologize—was handled by stationing me behind Alejandro's desk to surf the web. While Geo and the camera crew assuaged their irritation with a snack break, I was instructed to absorb timeshare ownership information to my heart's content.

That, or fifteen minutes—whichever came first.

Luckily I managed to take in a fair bit of knowledge:

Only buy a timeshare if you expect to hold onto it. Timeshares are not real estate investments and typically don't appreciate. In fact, de-

preciation is the norm, so it shouldn't be considered a financial invest-ment but an investment in your future vacations.[8]

Don't kid yourself that the presentation will last a mere 90 minutes. Plan on 3 hours and know you'll likely need the patience of Job.

If you can, pay in cash. The interest rates on timeshare mortgage loans are typically higher than traditional mortgages.

And one particularly interesting additional fact:

If brand-new isn't of paramount importance, skip the developers altogether. You can buy a timeshare for a fraction of its initial value through an owner or resale site.

I'd managed to read most of the Federal Trade Commission's webpage about buying and selling timeshares as well as a sticky note on the monitor that said, simply, *Mrs. Frugalicious!!* when Frank burst into the room and closed the door behind him.

"You're feeling better?" I asked, suddenly feeling worse.

"What choice did I have?" His expression was a mixture of irrita-tion and concern. "Why on Earth would you balk about—?"

"Committing ourselves to another piece of community prop-erty that will just need to be split up as soon as this show is over?" I whispered.

"Easily split into one week for each of us."

"In the meantime, it's our job to give sound financial advice and bargain tips."

"Like, *if someone offers to give you a free timeshare, sign the paper-work ASAP?*"

---

8. If you buy a timeshare today for $20,000, use it for the next twenty years and sell it for $10,000, is this really loss? Probably not if you add up your hotel receipts over the same twenty-year period.

Before we could hash it out any further, all three kids *just happened* to appear in the lobby of the timeshare office, their camera crew trailing behind them.

"The cenotes were *awesome*!" FJ exclaimed as they joined us in Alejandro's office.

"You wouldn't believe how amazing they were," Trent added.

"And we met another kid from Colorado there." FJ smiled. "Liam."

"He's Anastasia's sister's kid," Trent said.

"And he seems really cool," FJ said.

"Great," I said.

"We had the best day," Eloise said. "Like, ever."

At least their enthusiasm, unaided or abetted by the use of cue cards, was clearly authentic. So was the cameraman's interest in Eloise—more accurately, in getting footage of Eloise in a red-checkered bikini top and short shorts as she sashayed across the room, plopped down on the couch, and attempted to tame her trademark Michaels curls into a ponytail.

She smiled. "Ivan says he's taking me to the beach tomorrow before the wedding."

"He's taking all of us," Trent said.

"Liam says he's going to tag along too," FJ said.

"The bodysurfing is supposed to be amazing here," Eloise said.

"I thought you hated bodysurfing," FJ said.

"Used to," said Eloise, who tended to despise anything athletic. "I'm broadening my horizons."

"You're obviously enjoying yourselves," Frank said.

"Totally," Trent said.

"Definitely," FJ added.

"I already love this place," Eloise said wistfully.

"Good," Frank said. "What if I told you we're going to be spending a lot more time vacationing here in the future?"

"Say what?" FJ asked.

Frank put his arm around my shoulder and smiled broadly for the kids and the camera.

"Your mother and I will soon be the proud owners of two glorious weeks a year here at the Hacienda de la Fortuna and a whole host of partner resorts across the globe."

"Probably," I added, despite the rolling camera.

THREE

THERE WAS NO DENYING the sheer beauty of what was to be the new site of our annual vacations. Given the startling turquoise ocean backdrop where Anastasia would say her I dos and the equally scenic beachfront spot where Geo sent us to shoot a pre-rehearsal segment about destination weddings, it was difficult to argue that a timeshare here was anything but a tremendous boon. Particularly when a seabird swooped in behind us and a gentle breeze rustled the scrim behind the cabana where we'd been seated to share a few tips.

Still, I couldn't help but feel more than a little railroaded.

"I really can't pretend I'm paying a good price for something that's free," I said as we awaited Geo's cue.

"Not free, Maddie," Frank said, finger gelling his hair. "Any perks we get while working are simply additional income. It goes on our taxes and everything." At my wide-eyed look, he added, "Relax, Maddie. They're including a cash sum to cover the income tax."

"Hmm. But if we're promoting something as a bargain for our viewers, we have to be able to stand behind the deal."

"Sure, but without throwing off the whole production schedule in the process," he said. "The only time they can squeeze in the signing segment now is on Saturday at the crack of dawn, before the postwedding brunch."

"Assuming I agree to it."

"Maddie, there's no downside."

"Not so far." I sighed. "I just wish I'd have known the plan so I could think about it ahead of time."

"Welcome to reality TV," Frank said.

"Exactly," Geo said, appearing beside us. "Ready to roll?"

Frank nodded for both of us.

Geo said "action" and despite the beginnings of a mild tequila headache, I had no choice but smile and launch into my spiel:

"When Anastasia told me she had her heart set on a budget destination wedding, I figured there would be little in the way of bargains or discounts. I quickly learned that opulent and outrageously priced are not necessarily synonymous—not here in beautiful Mexico, anyway."

Frank nodded. "I sure wish we'd have thought of having our wedding at a place like Hacienda de la Fortuna. Don't you, Maddie?"

"I do," I heard myself say as I glanced over at the Cala de la Boda, a picturesque cove bordered by mangrove trees that was reserved for weddings and other events.

I peered around the reflectors at Anastasia and her groom, Philip, who stood together in front of a second camera crew having a prearranged, but no less touching, private moment together beneath the wrought-iron wedding arch. Serious, graying at the temples, and usually distracted by his job as acting chief of the South Metro Denver Police, Philip looked giddy and downright boyish as he planted a kiss on Anastasia's cheek and surveyed the scene.

"I can't imagine a more romantic setting," I added.

A golf cart with the Hacienda de la Fortuna roulette wheel logo pulled up via a foliage-obscured access path. Elena, the wedding planner, slid out of the passenger side and approached the happy couple complete with her clipboard, no-nonsense up-do, and take-charge stride.

"Be sure your venue comes with an onsite wedding planner," I continued. "Her services are often included in the deal you've negotiated with the hotel, or they can be for a small additional cost. A competent wedding planner will save you big money and bigger headaches by knowing everything from the rules about getting married in their country to the best local suppliers for extras not provided by the hotel."

I paused for a moment as a second golf cart arrived and Elena consulted with workers who began to unload the Lucite chairs Anastasia had added to her wedding package.[9] As they arranged them in key spots for the rehearsal, Anastasia's sister-bridesmaids appeared at the Cala de la Boda in camera-friendly jewel-toned sundresses.

They were joined by the parents of the bride and groom. Behind them, two groomsmen materialized, both in Bermudas but wearing solid, bright polo shirts.

Elena—ever camera-ready in her brown skirt, peach hotel-issue blouse, and perfectly coiffed French Twist—glanced in our direction and waved us over.

---

9. Wedding packages typically include significant built-in discounts. While some people feel hesitant about the potentially impersonal feel of a prearranged package, remember you can always customize by adding on a few signature extras.

"One thing's for sure," I said, wrapping up, "the wedding planner here at the Hacienda de la Fortuna has proven to be not only invaluable, but on anything but island time ..."

———

"Remember, everyone ..." Geo announced, "just be natural."

"I'm a little nervous," whispered one of Anastasia's sisters—the one I'd quickly come to think of as Hair, due to her thick, lustrous, honey blond tresses.

Given the sisters had largely interchangeable names and looked like not-quite-perfect versions of the bride, I'd named each of them for the one feature they shared with the all-around-stunning Stasia.

"Forget about the cameras and focus on the beautiful occasion you've come to celebrate," I managed before the word *action* filled the air.

Sister Number Three, Body, who shared Anastasia's flawless figure, but little of her composure, seemed to freeze. She remained that way for both takes of everyone introducing themselves.

We're Anastasia's parents.

I'm David, Phil's friend.

I'm Philip's mother and this is his stepfather ...

"Who are we still missing?" The wedding planner asked, her accent somehow adding to and softening her authoritative edge.

"No one, now," Philip said as a short, homely, balding man materialized from the footpath and joined the group.

"Everyone, this is my pal Steve. He'll be officiating."

"Sorry folks," he said. "I forgot to mention I was with the wedding party before I got caught up in a high-octane timeshare—"

"*Atención!*" Elena said, not allowing his arrival to disrupt the flow. "Bridesmaids to my left, groomsmen to my right. Immediate family, please be seated on the appropriate side of the aisle."[10]

Anastasia and Philip gazed lovingly at each other while everyone fell in as requested.

Elena scanned the group, giving each and every person a thorough twice-over.

"Sara," she finally said, having (admirably) memorized everyone's names.

Body took a step forward.

The other sisters seemed to nod as Elena pointed to blond handsome Dave, the groomsman, and paired them off together.

"Of course," Hair whispered under her breath.

"What do you mean?" I asked.

Before she could answer, Elena called her given name (Susan), assigned her to Philip's brother, and motioned for me to join best man Frank.

Who I'd once thought was *my* best man.

Once the pairing off was complete, we stepped into our familiar, time-honored roles, following the detailed processional instructions. "Ladies, walk slowly but to the beat of the music. Once Maddie takes her place, the music will change, everyone will stand, and Anastasia and her father will start down the aisle …"

The cameras—one trained on Philip, the other on Anastasia—captured both perspectives of their final practice run, then veered

---

10. Another advantage of utilizing a wedding planner—the bride and groom get to focus on each other and no one else (the made-for-tv matron of honor, for example) is forced to take on the bossy bad guy organizational job.

onto me and then Frank, respectively, as I pretended to accept the bouquet for the ceremony run-through.

And Frank glanced lovingly in my direction as though blissfully reliving our own trip down the aisle.

I'd sworn to myself I wouldn't cry another tear over the circumstances that obligated us to break our *until death do us part* vow, namely his cheating, but with the combination of palpable love between the soon-to-be-newlyweds and our faux reality, my eyes began to sting.

"Marriage..." Face (Sally, by process of elimination) sighed. "If only it was half as romantic as the wedding."

I bit the inside of my cheek and tried to will away the sudden throb at my temples while Elena detailed the particulars of the service itself, introduced the couple as husband and wife, and instructed us to begin the recessional.

The headache spread across my forehead. By the time Frank slipped his arm through mine and we made our way away from the marriage altar, I winced not only from the symbolism but from the sensation that my scalp was shrink-wrapped around my head.

"You two are as cute together as the bride and groom," said an elderly woman who was part of the crowd gathered just out of disruption range to watch the wedding rehearsal shoot.

"We love you, Mr. and Mrs. Frugalicious!" said her companion, a red-haired woman I'd seen around the resort.

"That's me!" Frank said, leaning in to give me a kiss on the lips for our fans. "Mr. Frugalicious."

———

"No cameras?" A familiar voice asked from behind me as I headed for the suite to grab an Advil or three.

I turned to find Alejandro leaning against the rails of a nearby footbridge, looking every bit as long, lean, and downright handsome as he had that morning.

"Camera-free moments are few and far between," I said, feeling flushed and slightly flustered. "I was just heading to my room to get something for my headache."

"Too many margaritas?"

"Something like that."

"Doesn't that make me at least partially responsible?" he asked with a sympathetic but playful smile.

"There's just been a lot going on today."

"Maybe I can save you a few minutes of rushing around," he said, already taking me by the hand. "We have a fully stocked first-aid drawer in our offices."

"I've already been enough of a bother," I said as we headed back over to the vacation sales office. "And I'm sure you're anxious to get home to your family."

"Not at all," he said, opening the door. "On Fridays, I usually stay late to complete paperwork. Particularly when we've had a good week."

"No thanks to me," I said. "We're likely to be signing before the end of the weekend, it's just that I have a responsibility to my viewers to—"

"No explanations necessary." He smiled. "I wasn't looking to make a profit on your deal anyway," he said, leading me into the breakroom, where he reached into a drawer, grabbed a bottle even I could read (*Ibuprofeno*), and poured a few into my outstretched palm. "Not financially, anyway."

"*Gracias*," I said.

"Thank *you*, for bringing your show down here to our resort," he said. "If everything continues to go this well, the payoff will be even better than I imagined."

"I can't take much, if any, credit," I said. "My producer had her heart set on a destination wedding episode."

"And a stunning wedding it's going to be," he said, looking out a window that happened to overlook the Cala de la Boda, where much of the group stood finalizing the last of the details with Philip and Anastasia.

"She is going to make a beautiful bride," I said.

"With beautiful bridesmaids," Alejandro added.

"Anastasia's sisters are all very pretty," I said as he led me over to the water cooler beside the front door. "Each in her own way."

"Not as pretty as you," he said. Our fingers touched as he handed me a cup of cool water.

"Thank you," I managed, my cheeks suddenly on fire.

The waning light shimmered in his deep brown eyes as he led me back outside. "Maddie, I—"

"Maddie!" Frank materialized from around a stand of Tecate Cypress at exactly the key moment yet again. The clatter of equipment and voices filtered through the humid breeze from the pathway behind him.

"That's my cue, I'm afraid," I said as Geo and some of the crew met up with Frank.

"*Buenas tardes*," Alejandro said, greeting them all with a friendly nod that belied nothing of whatever it was that had just happened between us.

Which was…?

I couldn't help but notice that Alejandro wore a gold bracelet on his wrist, but no wedding ring to match.

"We need both of you at the rehearsal dinner in ten," Geo said, motioning the crew to continue on toward the private dining area off the main lobby.

"No problemo," Frank said, checking his cell phone—or rather, checking his makeup, hair, and teeth in the selfie picture mode. "Maddie, I thought you were headed back to the room before dinner started?"

"I was," I said, "and then I ran into Alejandro …"

———

My cheeks still felt flushed as I stood beside a buffet table covered in brightly colored platters offering everything from enchiladas de rojos to shrimp posole.

Not as pretty as you …

"You ready to roll, Maddie?" Geo asked.

I'd assumed Alejandro's initial flirtation during our meeting, timely and flattering as it was, was simply salesmanship he was playing up for the camera …

"Maddie?"

I nodded, took a deep breath, and forced myself to focus on reality—or my TV reality, as it were—by smiling and delivering my rehearsal dinner spiel:

"The pre-wedding dinner provides an opportunity for the bride and groom to thank everyone involved with the wedding. In general, the guest list includes the wedding party and their dates or spouses, immediate family, and anyone else participating in the ceremony. It is customary, but not required, that you invite extended family and out-of-town guests."

I plucked a giant strawberry from the top tier of a "cake" constructed entirely of fruit, took a dainty bite, chewed, and swallowed.[11]

"At a destination wedding, however, 'all-inclusive' applies to more than just the food and beverages. Since your guests are travelling a great distance, everyone who makes the trip should be invited to all the events that take place over the course of the weekend. While this may seem costly, remember, the reduction in the overall number of people who actually attend typically more than makes up for the added cost per person."

As the camera shot switched to the buffet table, the veranda filled with partygoers, and the beginnings of what promised to be a spectacular sunset, I stole a glance out past the scrolled iron railing, and across the lush grounds, toward a single light in the window of the vacation sales office.

What was it Alejandro was planning to say before Frank had interrupted him?

I think you're one of the most attractive women I've met in years…
I know it's wrong, but I can't help but wish you were single…
I haven't stopped thinking about you all day…

Despite feeling more jangly than hungry, I piled my plate high with assorted *especiales de la casa* and started for the head table, where Anastasia and Philip were dipping chips into the Hacienda's signature guacamole and feeding them to each other.

---

11. Many of the customs we associate with a stateside wedding translate to foreign locations, but not all. Flexibility about traditions—like a groom's cake made of fruit and at the rehearsal dinner instead of the reception—is key.

"Look," Frank said as soon as I took my place beside him and the crew had given us the go-ahead for the next scheduled shot. He flashed a handful of tickets. "Tickets to the eco water park for the whole family!"[12]

"What an incredible thank you present!" I said, amazed not only by Anastasia's ability to pay next to nothing for her wedding, but her dual-purpose gift of a bathing-suit clad day at the local eco water park—just the wedding party, the camera crew, me, and my middle-aged body. Oh joy.

"We're all going to go on Sunday!" said groomsman Dave, who flashed a charming smile in shapely Body's direction.

As soon as we were finished eating, Face stood. She waited for the chatter to die down and announced that each of Anastasia and Philip's siblings planned to share some stories to ensure the bride and groom "had all the facts" about their soon-to-be spouse.

"I'll start," Hair said, tucking her blond locks behind her ears and smiling in my direction, as if to say she'd heeded my advice about ignoring the cameras. Her voice was a little shaky just the same. "Philip, I hope you're prepared to always look your best, because Stasia is a stickler about grooming those around her. One time, she even used pomade on the cat and trimmed his whiskers. He was banging into walls for a week."

One by one, each of the siblings stood, and with varying degrees of trepidation, began to share tales of their own:

"Phil once told me that thinking about your muscles will make you stronger."

---

12. Instead of the usual pearl earrings for the bridesmaids and mono-grammed flasks for the guys, a destination wedding can provide the unique opportunity of the gift of sightseeing or an outdoor experience for your attendants, often at discounted group rates.

"Do not, I repeat, do not so much as *suggest* to Stasia that there are 'alternate' ways to load the dishwasher."

"I hope you're prepared for the fact that you're going to have to cut the crusts off big, strong Phil's sandwiches."

As I laughed along at their funny, insightful, sometimes TMI observations and comments—*Phil says it's an odd-looking inconveniently placed chest mole, but don't be surprised if one of your children inherits his, how shall I say, third nipple*—I noticed half the faces in the crowd also looked familiar from the afternoon timeshare presentation.

Which got me thinking about Alejandro. Which got me thinking about the way our eyes kept meeting and the flirtation that seemed to slip so easily into the conversation. I knew he was trying to sell timeshares, but ...

As Face wrapped things up with a teary story about all four sisters getting their ears pierced together, Steve, the minister, stood and pinged his water glass.

"We've heard a number of insightful stories about Anastasia and Philip as they progressed on their paths to each other ..."

Was there a real spark between Alejandro and I, or was I so rusty, not to mention entrenched in being Mrs. Frugalicious, that I'd over-interpreted our flirtation to the point where I felt like I'd landed in the first few pages of a romance novel?

"I thought we'd cap off the evening by asking this question of you, their happily married friends and family," he continued. "What is the secret to marital longevity?"

There was a brief silence and then hands went up all around the veranda.

"Never go to bed angry," someone at a back table said, kicking things off.

"Fight fair!"

33

"Learn to say 'yes, dear'!"

"Embrace each other's imperfections."

I suddenly felt a lot less like I'd been dropped into a bodice ripper and a lot more like I was trapped in a straight-to-DVD movie when someone else added, "Marry the right person in the first place."

Particularly when one of the cameras zoomed in on our table just in time for Frank to wink at me, look up at Anastasia and Philip, and pronounce, "Make romance a priority."

Both of the boys groaned in unison.

"Gross," Eloise added.

The crowd laughed, clapped, and cheered as Frank lifted his glass and I stood beside him for a toast to romance and marital bliss.

———

Our on-camera fauxmance continued as the rehearsal dinner wound down. The kids, now including Hair's teenage son, Liam—a trim, well-groomed boy of about sixteen—went off to movie under the stars at the outdoor El Teatro de Fortuna, and I followed Frank back to our suite. With a few soundbites along the way about the beauty of the evening and the glow of the handsome, soon-to-be wedded pair, we retired to our bedroom.

"What's with that kid hanging around FJ all night?" Frank asked.

"He's Anastasia's nephew."

"He seems kind of . . ."

"Kind of what?" I asked. "He's nice, polite, and—"

"Doesn't seem very sports-minded, if you know what I mean."

"Sports-minded?" I said, avoiding where Frank might be trying to go with the conversation. I began to pluck the decorative pillows off the bed and arrange them in an orderly line down the middle to separate the *his* from the *hers* side. "I guess I don't know what you mean."

Frank paused as if thinking about what he would (but likely shouldn't) say next. He thought better of it and headed for the bathroom instead.

Relieved I'd managed to avoid yet another go-nowhere conversation about Frank's concerns over what he termed our son's "potentially artistic tendencies," I turned down the comforter. As I tugged at my corner of the sheets, I spotted a pale peach rectangle sticking out from underneath my pillow.

The toilet flushed and the sink began to run.

I pulled out what turned out to be an envelope with the hotel logo in the upper corner and *Maddie* written across the front.

Frank emerged from the bathroom just as I was ripping it open. "What's that?" he asked.

"Note from housekeeping," I mumbled, figuring it had to be.

"Say anything interesting?" he asked, lumbering past me to his side of the bed as I removed a single sheet of paper from inside.

"Nope," I managed. "Just one of those 'we care about the environment so please conserve linens and towels' messages."

"Gotcha," he said, falling into bed, not noticing that my voice had cracked. Or that I was lying.

The note, while written on the resort stationary, contained a very different message than the one I heard myself telling Frank.

And it definitely wasn't from housekeeping...

What are the chances you can tear yourself away from your official obligations tomorrow evening and join me at the Poolside Bar? Say, 9 p.m.?

—A

FOUR

I SPENT MOST OF the night plucking proverbial daisies: Maybe Alejandro meant to address the note to both of us. Maybe it was a Freudian slip that only my name was on the front of the envelope. Perhaps he sent notes to all potential-but-reluctant timeshare owners inviting them for a cocktail and ours had somehow slipped beneath the pillow.

I tossed, turned, and finally dozed off, but I woke up again not long after the first rays of sun glinted off the ocean. I glanced over at Frank, now snoring softly in his familiar (though no longer endearing) snort-puh pattern. Too keyed up to go back to sleep myself, I tiptoed out of the bedroom for a cup of tea and a peek at the day's call sheet.

My very full schedule started with *8:30 a.m.: Yoga* and was broken down in a seemingly endless list of pre-, during-, and postwedding shots, including everything from *Discussion of discount table centerpiece options* to *Teary-eyed toast.* My eyes were drawn to the bottom of the sheet, where I couldn't help but note that the last entry of the day was *8:30 p.m.: Dance with Frank.*

As in, just in time to make it to an engagement at, oh, 9 p.m. at the Poolside Bar?

Frank woke soon after I did and immediately left for his *8:15: Massage with fellow groomsmen*. The kids set off to the beach, and I headed down the hall toward my first task of the day.

"You need more towels, Señora Frugalicious?" Zelda, the floor manager, offered when I found her in the housekeeping supply room

"I'm good, thanks." I smiled back. "But I do have a question: Did you or someone on your staff happen to deliver a note to my room last evening?"

Zelda nodded. "*Sí, Señora.*"

"I found it in the weirdest spot."

"Under *la almohada*?" she asked, then thought for a moment. "The pillow?"

"Yes," I said, my heart suddenly thumping.

She smiled. "I always do what Señor Alejandro tell me to do."

———

"Joe-gah," said the attractive, raven-haired, spandex-clad yoga instructor, "is jour oasis of peace, tranquility, and calm."

With the camera trained on her from the rearview of my sorry excuse for a Downward Dog, I couldn't say I entirely agreed.

"Breathe deep, relax, and clear jour cluttered mind ..."

Having left housekeeping with a fresh piece of stationary, an envelope, a complimentary pen, and the knowledge that Alejandro had specifically asked that the note be placed under my pillow, I somehow couldn't manage a single breath that could be called relaxing.

And there was no clearing my hoarder's paradise of a mind.

Alejandro had to be trying out some kind of high-level sales technique on me. What other reason could there be for an extremely handsome man who could have practically anyone he wanted to pursue a woman on vacation with her *loving* spouse? That was, unless he really was attracted to me, sensed there were plot holes in the Frugalicious happily ever after, and just decided to go for it. After all, it was no secret that Frank and I had weathered our fair share of marital woes. And, given the high-profile nature of our careers and the murders I'd been involved in solving, the details of our lives were easily available to anyone who was curious enough to type *Mrs. Frugalicious* into their browser. Still, Alejandro was bold, unbelievably so, to have a note delivered to the room of a very married woman, asking her to meet him for a drink.

The fact he'd actually gone ahead and done it sent an involuntary and not entirely unpleasant shudder through me.

It wasn't until the shoot finished with me rolling up my yoga mat and offering a few tips about vacation exercise classes[13] that I began to feel ever so slightly Zen. While I couldn't possibly meet up with Alejandro, I couldn't help but fantasize, if just for a moment, about returning someday for a sun-and-fun week in his tall, dark, and handsome company.

Instead of heading directly to the spa locker room for a shower before I was due in makeup and hair, I took a quick detour to the

---

13. All-inclusive doesn't just mean food and drink. Many resorts are also all-you-can-exercise by offering world-class fitness centers and classes for beginners on up. Never tried Pilates or yoga? What better way to check it out than for no additional cost (and no risk of embarrassment at your local gym)?

vacation ownership office and, with a touch of regret, slid a short note of my own in the mail slot for Alejandro:

Chances are slim, I'm afraid.

————

"Look who's glowing almost as much as our bride," Geo said, joining me in the spa lobby.

"I must be flushed from yoga," I said, thankful our makeup artist was busily brushing finishing powder on my once-again warm cheeks. "Haven't done it in a while."

"You should," he said, with an uncharacteristic smile. "It clearly agrees with you."

Despite somewhat mixed emotions about nipping the Alejandro situation in the bud, I couldn't help but agree that the attention put a little extra spring in my step. A spring I needed for the next few hours posed in front of various locations, discussing overall costs:

Destination weddings are a great deal for the bride and groom, who will save on just about everything including the final tab since many guests send a gift instead of making what they assume will be a costly trip.

And the nuts and bolts of planning:

While the best specials and discounts for destinations are during off-peak seasons, it's a good idea to look into less-traveled U.S. holiday weekends like Mother's Day, Fourth of July, and Halloween, when resorts, especially in the Caribbean, tend to offer some great deals.

I did an overview of floral options at various price points to highlight that less was often more when Mother Nature was handling the bulk of the decorating: *Even though you'll need bouquets for the bridal party and perhaps a few accents, there's no need for a big floral budget when you get married in a scenic locale. If you're flexible and allow the florist to use local blooms instead of expensive imported flowers and consider less-expensive centerpieces like shells and sand or tropical fruit centerpieces, you'll not only save, but stun your guests with natural beauty.*

I even sampled the evening's fare ahead of the actual reception: *A $30,000 stateside wedding for a hundred guests in a major city would likely include a plated chicken or fish meal, a limited open bar, a serviceable DJ, and standard wedding cake. Here at the Hacienda de la Fortuna, the same money gets you a multi-course feast, Mariachi band, tequila tasting at the open bar, and late-night dessert bar.*

By the time I'd finished, it was time to meet up with the other bridesmaids for *Makeup, hair, and pre-ceremony bonding with the bride.*

"All you'll need to do is read off the cue cards while the hotel stylists get the other bridesmaids ready," Geo said as I changed out of my raspberry satin, halter-style bridesmaid's dress and back into a fluffy white hotel-issue robe to pretend I was getting ready along with my fellow bridesmaids in the salon.

As *Family Frugalicious* hair and makeup people finished touching me up and headed into the bride's room to start on Anastasia, Geo handed me a photo of a pretty model with the very same flattering up-do I was sporting, complete with curly loose tendrils. "Hold this up to your face on my cue."

"Great," I said, following him into the salon to greet the bridesmaids—Body in a massage chair soaking her feet and hands in preparation for a mani-pedi, Hair in a stylist's chair in front of a large mirror, and Face beside a big makeup kit with the Hacienda de la Fortuna roulette wheel emblazoned on the side.

After our hellos, the manicurist took a seat on her low stool and Geo pointed me to my mark.

The camera began to roll:

"While having your bridesmaids do their own hair, makeup, and nails is obviously the most cost-effective way to primp for a wedding, most brides prefer to have a professional on hand for the big day." I paused while the camera zoomed in on the hotel hairdresser, who'd begun to run her to fingers through Hair's lovely honey blond tresses. "The thing is, hair and makeup can be a tricky proposition when you're talking destination weddings. Assuming you don't have a trusted stylist who would love a free trip in exchange for glamming up the wedding party, you will likely be using a local referred by your wedding planner."

Geo gave me a thumbs up as I continued.

"If so, be sure to check references from other brides, try to meet with whomever you're planning to hire for your event beforehand, and, ideally, bring along a visual of what you want to look like on your wedding day."

As I held up the photo of my hairstyle, a curvaceous little woman in sausage-tight leggings came tottering past me. There was no missing that she'd coordinated her heavy eye shadow with her aquamarine pants and her lipstick with the fuchsia flowers dotting her top.

"*Hola*," she said, stopping beside Face and extending her hand. "I do your makeup."

"Okay..." Face said, returning her handshake and looking anything but okay.

"How you like?" the makeup artist asked.

"As subtle as possible?" Face asked, pleadingly.

Hair looked equally nervous as her stylist began to tease the back of her hair. "Me too," Hair added.

"*Sí*," one woman said.

The other nodded with seeming nonrecognition.

As the camera zeroed in on the four sisters, I stepped over to Geo. "Do you think they know what they're doing?"

Geo smirked. "Depends on your definition of *subtle*."

The makeup woman clicked open a case, pulled out what looked like a putty knife, and set to work on Face, who now looked downright petrified.

Along with her sisters.

"And action!" Geo announced.

Face clasped her hands as if in prayer and closed her eyes.

Out of the corner of mine, I noticed Jorge the concierge standing silently in the doorway of the salon. My resident butterflies began to flutter as he waved a peach envelope in my direction.

"Thank you," I mouthed silently as I stepped over and accepted the note.

"*De nada*," he whispered.

Suspecting otherwise, I followed him out to the spa lobby, waited for him to head back down the hallway, opened the envelope, and read Alejandro's response:

Don't be afraid.

———

I wasn't exactly afraid, nor was I entirely surprised by Alejandro's persistence. After all, tip number five on the timeshare handout Geo had given me told viewers to *expect them to keep offering deals too*

42

good to turn down,[14] to which I was to keep repeating *I'm not sure* and *we're just not ready.* The scenario seemed to apply to both time-shares and forbidden romance.

Face, however, was terrified.

Not to mention, terrifying.

"OMG!" she said, opening her eyes to lids and lips that had been colored raspberry to match her bridesmaid's dress. She began to wave her hands. "*Rojo? Nada!* No!"

The camera stopped rolling, the makeup lady was led away, and Face launched into a teary OTF[15] about looking like a streetwalker for her sister's wedding.

"How bad is it?" a *Family Frugalicious* staff makeup artist asked, appearing beside me.

Before I could respond, she'd not only taken a peek and answered her own question, but was rushing in to offer assistance.

Luckily Face only had to suffer through two teary takes before being restored back to her beautiful self.

For the next two and a half hours, I was so immersed in shooting segments related to destination wedding prep that I gave little thought to much of anything beyond the "surprise" lunch delivered by Chef Benito, the seamstress who had to be brought in posthaste to repair a torn seam near the zipper of Anastasia's vintage designer

---

14. Sales reps know that persistence is essential to making a sale. It is their job to say or do whatever it takes to overcome your objections until you *see* how great the product is for you. A rep wouldn't have a job for very long if he or she took a single no for an answer.

15. OTF (n) On the Fly: An impromptu interview of a reality show participant intended to capture emotions and actions in the moment.

dress,[16] and the teary moment when Anastasia's parents entered the bride's room and saw their stunning daughter in her wedding finery. It wasn't until my own personal *2:30 p.m.: Matron of honor bonding moment with bride* that I had time to consider how staged certain moments of the day felt.

As we hugged and Anastasia thanked me profusely for coming up with the idea of a destination wedding (even though she had) and working so hard to make it so *surprisingly* affordable (also her doing), I found myself wondering how Alejandro could have known I would be the one to actually find the note he'd put under my pillow in the first place.

It wasn't hard for housekeeping to figure out who planned to sleep on which side of the bed—Frank had his prescription on his nightstand and I had placed a tube of hand cream and a magazine with an article about couponing on mine. But how could anyone be sure Frank wouldn't turn down the covers first? Frank, who'd be obligated to at least threaten to beat the daylights out of anyone who dared to leave such a note for his wife?

Maybe I was a little more flirtatious than I should have been, and maybe Alejandro was a lot more forward than your run-of-the-mill ladies man, but, somehow, it didn't seem likely that he could he really be so immediately lovestruck.

Or stupid...

---

16. Tips for saving on your wedding dress: 1. Look in stores and on the Internet well in advance of your wedding for sales and specials. 2. Consider a used dress from a consignment shop—but be sure the price is at least 50% below market and examine it thoroughly for stains, tears, and odors. 3. Nontraditional dresses work well for more casual weddings and cost a fraction of the price. 4. Borrow your dress from a friend or relative—your something borrowed will have that much more meaning.

Then again, this show was centered on us as a wholesome, frugal family, and this episode in particular was about the blissful, blessed sanctity of marriage. It was one thing for the show's handlers to mess with a little makeup or even a dress seam to make a point; a secret cheating subplot written in by someone to spice things up didn't make sense.

Not demographically, anyway.

Still, I wasn't keen on watching an upcoming episode filled with Frankenbites[17] of me looking like I'd fallen victim to Alejandro's not-at-all uncertain charms while poor born-again-innocent Frank looked on helplessly.

I grabbed a pen that had been conveniently left on a table outside the salon, scrawled a message of my own on the backside of the note, and headed down the hall before the ceremony started to give it to the concierge to return to Alejandro:

I'm afraid that I'm a happily married woman.

———

Given the show was less about the wedding "reveal," and more a how-to about putting on a discount destination wedding, there was only one lovely, stunningly scenic, tear-rending take of the ceremony itself. Everyone flawlessly executed their parts, from Elena giving last-minute directives to the bridal party strolling in perfect time with the

---

17. Frankenbite (n): an edited reality show snippet that splices together several pieces of a various interviews, conversations, and interactions into a single seemingly blunt or revealing clip. Potentially made to manipulating viewer perceptions of the participants involved.

harpist's strums. Even the seabirds somehow cawed more softly and the turquoise waves lapped especially gently in the background.

As Anastasia, gorgeous and resplendent, strolled down the aisle on the arm of her father and joined Philip beneath the altar festooned with locally sourced flowers, love infused the light breeze. With all teary eyes trained on the clearly besotted couple, I felt much less like the de facto maid of honor in a reality show spectacle and a lot more like a costar in a magical, romantic movie.

By the time the minister announced Philip and Anastasia as husband and wife and invited them to share a kiss, I'd even begun to believe in the potential sanctity of marriage once again. So much so that as I walked down the aisle on Frank's arm, I felt, for the first time, as if our strained and tenuous balance as faux spouses could actually give way to a successful on-screen partnership as Mr. and Mrs. Frugalicious.

My tranquility continued through the pictures and into cocktail hour. And it might have lasted through the evening had I not spotted Ivan the activities director, whose current number-one activity seemed to be courting Eloise. He smiled and she waved me over to where the two of them stood beside a palm tree at the edge of the veranda outside of the dining area.

"Ivan just told me there are going to be fireworks later on tonight down at the beach," Eloise said.

"We have a pyrotechnics expert on staff that does them the first weekend of every month," Ivan said, as if to explain that the fireworks were not just of the romantic variety.

"It's okay if I go," Eloise asked, looking moony-eyed, "right?"

"As long as the reception is over and Geo doesn't need you or us for anything."

"It won't start until dark," Ivan said.

"And there's nothing on my call sheet after eight p.m.," Eloise added.

"Then great," I said. "But don't stay out too late. We'll probably have an early call in the morning."

"So we're getting the timeshare, aren't we?" Eloise asked, smiling at Ivan.

Bothered that I hadn't researched as much as I'd have liked to, but promising myself I'd provide the Frugarmy with a thoroughly researched blog before the episode aired, I nodded.

"Yay!" Eloise said, throwing her arms around me. "I love this place!"

"Which reminds me …" Ivan said.

My heart skipped a beat once again as he reached into his back pocket and pulled out a sealed peach-colored envelope.

"Alejandro told me to give this to you."

———

"Frank?" I whispered as we finished shooting our *5:00 p.m.: Stolen postwedding kiss.* "Have you ever mentioned anything, even in passing, to anyone about our marital situation?"

"Course not," he said. "Why?"

The truth wasn't a particularly sensible option at the moment: *That note last night was actually from Alejandro wanting to have drinks with me. Which leads me to wonder if …?*

"No reason, really," I said, hastily concocting a white lie and thinking about the contents of his most recent note: *It's just a drink …* "It's just that I overheard someone on the crew saying something about a marriage of convenience or something and I was a little concerned they might be talking about us."

"As though our situation is convenient?"

"Good point," I said, and proceeded to play dutiful matron of honor and loving wife to the best man through dinner and a seemingly endless round of toasts.

"Susan and Michael look like chickens doing a mating dance out there," Face said as she, Body, and I, sat together observing Hair and her hubby out on the dance floor. "Don't you think?"

"Maybe they'll get some new moves when they get a gander of how embarrassing they look on TV," Body said.

"Not as embarrassing as the whole world seeing you in that god-awful eye shadow and lipstick," Face said.

"I don't think your sister and her husband look all that bad, but I have to admit, that was quite a makeup job," I said rubbing my blistered, slightly pink feet.

"Stasia said it wouldn't be that bad, but—"

"You knew?"

"Pretty good acting, huh?" Face asked.

"She warned us that television is *visual*," Body said. "And to expect examples—"

"To pique and maintain viewer interest," Face finished. "Starring me."

"I see," I said, my blood pressure suddenly ticking upwards once again.

Just then, the music shifted from Michael Jackson's "Rock with You" into something a little more sultry and a lot more stripper-esque. Dave, the handsome groomsman, started across the dance floor toward Body.

"This weekend is turning out better than I expected!" Body said.

As Dave reached out his hand and led Body out on the dance floor in full view of the camera, I breathed a sigh of relief.

I knew Anastasia well enough to know she wasn't averse to a little drama, nor to doing whatever it took to frame a story. I also knew *The Family Frugalicious* was her brainchild. It made sense that she'd tipped off her sisters about piquing viewer interest without telling them exactly how it would be done. It also made sense that Anastasia wouldn't let get herself hung up on drama unrelated to the overall vibe of the show.

I allowed myself to believe exactly that through my scheduled dances, as the bride and groom pressed cake into each other's faces, and while I watched from the sidelines as the single women collected for the bouquet toss.

It wasn't until Anastasia checked to see if the cameraman was ready, took a peek over her shoulder, and heaved the flowers into what seemed to be Body's direction that I began to wonder again.

Particularly when the bouquet went over her sister's head and landed directly in my hands.

With Geo's wry smile from beside the camera, I looked across the pool toward the lights and music coming from the bar area. No way was I falling into the trap of being caught on tape with Alejandro, but I had to find out just exactly what his intentions were—and if they were even *his* to begin with.

Besides, I needed a fresh drink.

I scanned the area. One camera crew was over at catering, a second was following the boys around on their quest to *meet cute señoritas* (as suggested by Frank and embraced primarily by Trent), and the third was set up by the bar where Philip, Frank, and the groomsmen were scheduled for an *8:40 p.m.: Celebratory tequila shot.* I seized the opportunity to approach Alejandro early by excusing myself to "freshen my lipstick."

I'd crossed the dance floor and was on my way to the ladies' room by way of the Poolside Bar when "Crazy Little Thing Called Love" ended.

The DJ spoke into the microphone in a lilting accent. "Brides-maids and groomsmen, if you would please proceed to the Estanque Reflectante for an evening group photo."

"What a perfectly glorious day," Frank said, his breath smelling of garlic and tequila. "Everything's gone exactly as planned."

Speak for yourself, I thought. He wrapped an arm around my waist as though we were alone and unaccompanied by the camera that had trailed him over to me. He led me away from the answers I sought at the Poolside Bar and toward the smallest, most intimate of the Hacienda de la Fortuna's five swimming pools.

We were halfway across the footbridge when a horrified, high-pitched shriek filled the humid evening air.

Anastasia's sisters, who had rounded the bend to the pool area ahead of us, joined the chorus.

Seeing as I'd been part and party to not one but two murders in the past year, I shouldn't have been all that shocked. But with the silhouette of a body floating facedown in the moonlit, Olympic-size reflection pond, I let out a scream of my own.

Particularly when I spotted the telltale Hacienda de la Fortuna polo, khakis and, the thick brown hair fanning out in the water.

Alejandro.

FIVE

ONCE AGAIN I FOUND myself staring into the gruesome face of death as an off-duty, whistle-less, *salvavida* dove into the pool, towed Alejandro to the side, and began to administer CPR on the pool deck.

That all-too-familiar sick feeling engulfed me like a weighty blanket as I stood helplessly among the unfamiliar swirl of rescue personnel that materialized around us. While the *paramédicos* set about the awful business of trying to revive Alejandro and the *policía* did whatever it was they did in such a situation, the cameraman who'd followed Frank and I from the reception area captured the awful tableau.

Complete with proper lighting even, thanks to the wedding photo shoot that was supposed to have been taking place.[18]

---

18. Because of the additional costs associated with outdoor lighting, reality shoots are often limited to daylight to keep within budgetary guidelines.

Anastasia immediately (albeit proverbially) traded her veil for her television journalist's cap and took over directorial duties for Geo, who I'd last seen headed for the crew buffet.

Instead of morphing into reporter mode, Frank pulled me in close. Then again, we were on camera and he had the all-consuming goal of polishing his tarnished image as respected family man.

A half hour earlier I'd have thought the mere idea that I could, once again, be suspecting Frank and/or Anastasia of being involved in a murder impossible. Beyond farfetched. Then again, a half-hour earlier I was merely concerned that I was being set up (and not in the right way) with a man who was now utterly lifeless.

As one of the *paramédicos* shook his head in recognition of the futility of his efforts, I wondered what might (or might not) have happened had I agreed right away to meet Alejandro for a drink. A twinge of guilt added a twist to the already numbing cocktail of shock and horror I found myself drinking in great gulps.

Would he still be alive if I'd been there?

"What are the police saying?" I asked Philip as he joined up with us after conferring with the officers on scene.

"They spoke so fast I couldn't really keep up with the Spanish." Philip, whose job as the acting chief of the South Metro Denver Police had him at the scene of tragic incidents on a daily basis, seemed as shell-shocked as anyone.

"Terrible," Frank said, wiping a tear from his eye. "Just terrible."

Face, Body, and Hair stood on my other side huddled together, shaking their heads in unison.

"I can't believe this," Face said, her perfect makeup streaked with tears.

"We were supposed to meet with him tomorrow," Hair wailed into her husband's shoulder.

"This is definitely not how things were supposed to happen today," Body added, as Dave the handsome groomsmen slipped a comforting arm around her shoulder.

As they continued to hug and weep, there was no denying that things had definitely taken a truly disturbing turn.

But was it a completely unexpected turn?

Seeing as Frank had been the one who'd talked me into expanding my horizons beyond the relative obscurity and safety of the cyber world and into the great unknown of reality TV, and there was no denying that *The Family Frugalicious* had been partly his idea to begin with, wasn't he as likely to be in the know about any story line detours as anyone else on set? While I couldn't blurt my growing irrational fear that Alejandro's death was somehow connected to the show, I needed to gauge his reaction with a question or two.

"Frank," I whispered, my heart suddenly thumping as the police began to tape off the area to keep back the hotel staff, wedding guests, and assorted onlookers who'd begun to filter onto the pool deck as word of the incident spread around the resort. "How do you suppose this will affect the shoot?"

"What do you mean?" he asked, his eyes downcast, ostensibly because Alejandro was being placed on a gurney.

"I mean, Alejandro was part of the story line, wasn't he?"

"How can you think about that at a time like this?" he said, dramatically. "It's sick."

I couldn't have agreed more. Nauseating as the whole situation was (including Frank's too noncommittal to be entirely noncommittal answer), I didn't feel like I was truly going to throw up until fireworks began to light up the night sky and bursts of color reflected off the white sheet covering Alejandro's body.

Over the boom and crackle of exploding pyrotechnics, I swore I could hear someone from the behind me say, "Money shot!"[19]

---

19. Money shot (n.): Pivotal footage that provides an episode's dramatic climax.

SIX

Following routine questioning by the police and the conclusion of whatever was left of the wedding reception, Frank and I collected the boys, confirmed Eloise was still being squired around by Ivan, and returned to our room.

"Exhausted and emotionally drained," or so he said, Frank headed for the bedroom, tossed a few pillows between our sides, and passed out immediately.

I was as weary and tired as I'd ever been, but my head was spinning. According to the employees gathered poolside, there'd never even been a near drowning at the Hacienda de la Fortuna, much less a fatal one. Could it be any coincidence that my arrival coincided with a visit by the Grim Reaper? Or that a person with whom I was connected (or who might have liked to have been connected with given the opportunity) was the Reaper's target?[20]

---

20. Seeing as I'd been obliged to investigate the untimely passages of both a haughty sales clerk who'd falsely accused me of shoplifting and a seemingly discontented member of my Frugarmy in the past six months, it was hard to dispute the fact of my proximity to death.

Upset, sleepless, and sure I wouldn't be able to relax entirely until Eloise came back to the room, I waited for Frank to settle into sleep. With his first set of rhythmic snores, I slipped silently out of my side of the bed and out into the living room. Specifically, to the couch beside the coffee table where I'd left my computer.

With all the research I did as a matter of course for each and every bargain-hunting expedition or question posed on my blog, there was one thing I'd never researched before I signed on the dotted line:

Reality television.

In fact, I'd gone into the whole experience with a healthy appreciation for DIY shows on the home and garden channels as well as equal parts fascination and disdain for the celebrity, dating, and lifestyles of the rich-and-freaky shows. Mostly, I'd agreed to star in *The Family Frugalicious* trusting that the concept of our show was everything Anastasia and the network execs said it was: a slice-of-life reality show about a bargain-conscious family on the hunt for the best deals for themselves and their viewers.

My growing concern was that I should have pinned down an exact definition for *slice-of-life*. Did that also include *sudden death*?

I Googled the phrase "How is reality TV made?"

Along with the how-to blogs for would-be producers and descriptions of how to become a contestant on various types of reality shows were numerous articles about the "realities" of reality television.

The driest but most damning simply asserted:

Reality television shows notoriously depict their topics in artificial, deceptive, and even fraudulent ways. Not only are participants coached and story lines generated ahead of time, but scenes are routinely edited and/or re-staged for the cameras in order to slant content. Many reality television shows are de-

signed to humiliate and exploit, while others make celebrities out of untalented people who do not deserve fame. Most shows glamorize bad behavior, materialism, and personal failings.

The site included terminology I had never heard in the short time I'd been a member of the reality TV world, but that sent an eerie chill down my spine. E.g.:

Date producer (n): A specialist who orchestrates reality dating shows. Job description includes coaxing confessions, cultivating jealousies, and ensuring alcohol flows so contestants will make essential "miscues" like hooking up, revealing intimate details, and otherwise behaving inappropriately.

Another website featured an article written by a former producer entitled, "Get Real Before You Try Out for Reality TV." The author, now an accountant in Chicago, listed five facts about his job on set:

1. Everything you see is preplanned. We wrote the storyboard and we worked out what the story was going to be. We thought of it as dropping guinea pigs (contestants) in an obstacle course we had built to watch how they navigated the various issues.

2. It was my job to make the participants upset with each other by dropping little hints and asides. In fact, that was the whole point. Film a show where everyone gets along and there's nothing to watch.

3. Everyone is edited into a specific character. The editors make you into whoever they want you to be.

4. The primary goal was to make a big story line from the littlest of tense moments.

And, most ominously:

5. The concept we sold to the audience wasn't necessarily the concept we sold to the participants.

I'd already seen about as much as I could take when a final blog post caught my eye: "Unreal: My Brief Foray into Reality TV."

As I read the story of an attractive blond aspiring actress who thought she was accepted on a reality show about young people and their job struggles, I was certain I was in deeper than I ever realized.

The woman "Michelle" thought a mistake had been made when a production crew showed up at her apartment, handed her a script, and told she'd be starring in a makeover show. Before she could ask any questions, the camera was rolling and she realized that she was expected to play a stereotypical party-girl version of herself. A girl in need of a style update.

Unlike me, Michelle quickly overcame her misgivings and decided the situations the producers presented were so far from her real self that no one who really knew her would believe she'd act that way. She watched the producers do their thing and realized she *got* that they were just trying to make the most interesting show possible. In fact, she decided that improvising every scene—from a meltdown over a haircut (which was just extensions attached to her real hair) to pushing around a clerk while shopping for designer duds for her dog was simply good acting experience. She even took it in stride when a dark-haired member of the crew was sent to get his back waxed so they could pretend the strips were her leg hair.

As I read the conclusion of her story, in which Michelle recounted how the friendly crew was genuinely concerned for her and her well-being during the entire process and how they went out of their way to make her feel talented and invaluable, even apologizing for having to fake situations, I couldn't help but feel worse than I already did. Would Michelle have been smart enough to know she was supposed to play along the moment Alejandro began to flirt on the timeshare tour? Surely *she* wouldn't have protested his advances to the point where producers on her show might possibly feel as though they had to goose the story line along with something dramatic, like, perhaps, a sudden death?

I shut my computer and leaned back against a throw pillow while I awaited Eloise's safe return, closing my eyes against the throbbing headache that had returned with a vengeance.

———

"I need for you to scream," Geo said from under a raspberry beret. He straightened the bow tie of his coordinating tuxedo. "With conviction."

"What's my motivation?" I heard myself ask.

He looked over at a receiving line where Frank checked his face in his cell phone and proceeded to congratulate the bride. Instead of kissing her cheek, he sunk his teeth into her face.

"Here's your Frankenbite," he pronounced with satisfaction, smiling for the camera beside him.

"Isn't being stuck married to that husband of yours motivation enough?" Geo asked.

"He won't be her hubby for long." Alejandro, who was floating in a nearby pool, raised his margarita glass. "Not if I have anything to say about it."

"I have the ultimate say," Geo said. "So scream. Both of you."

I opened my mouth and tried, but no sound emerged.

A deathly gurgle emerged from Alejandro.

"Can't save him now," shouted Anastasia's sisters, who had materialized poolside.

They began to throw dollar bills into the water at Alejandro, who'd rolled over and was floating face down, margarita glass still in hand.

"Money shot," one of them sang.

A door creaked open and a policewoman appeared. Her nametag read OFFICER MICHELLE.

"You should have played along," she said, shaking her head. "That's the reality of the situation."

"Vérité," Frank said with a grin. "It's all about ratings, in the end."

I began to cry. "This isn't how it was supposed to—"

"Whose fault is that?" Geo asked.

"Maddie's!" everyone cheered in unison.

"No!" I finally managed to scream as Officer Michelle began to shake me.

"Maddie?"

I opened my eyes.

"Maddie?" Eloise was tapping me gently. "I think you were having a bad dream."

"Definitely," I said. But as I got off the couch and headed for the bedroom, I was more afraid of what "reality" would bring.

SEVEN

DESPITE THE UPBEAT CLASSICAL guitar music, fanciful papier-mâché vegetable centerpieces, and specific instructions for all guests to dress in colorful, casual attire for the cameras, a pall permeated the postwedding brunch.

Not only did the waitstaff look pale and stony-faced, but as I stood in the buffet line, it was clear that word of Alejandro's fate had spread to anyone who had missed the disquieting news the evening before.

I can't believe something like this happened while we were dancing the night away...

I had a feeling it wasn't entirely safe to come down here...

I can't imagine how horrified Anastasia and Philip must have been when they went to take pictures and found that poor man...

One of the servers dropped a fresh chafing dish full of chorizo into the heated steamer tray with a heavy plunk.

"Why didn't you say anything to me when I got in last night?" Eloise whispered from beside me as we neared the fresh fruit and pan dulce table.

"I didn't want to bring down your evening with bad news," I said, ever more concerned about just how bad the news would turn out to be. Particularly after Frank got up early and reported that the day's call sheet had *TBD* written across the front as well as lines through *Timeshare contract signing* and shots of us *Lounging and swimming* in the very pool where we'd all witnessed the gruesome discovery of a man who might have been my dream date in another life.

"I have to admit, it really was an awesome night," Eloise said, the same lovesick smile plastered across her face that had kept me from saying anything about the incident last night. She helped herself to assorted melon, an *empanada de piña,* and two aptly named *novias* (brides). "We watched the fireworks from a cliff overlooking the resort and then we went on a really long walk down the coast."

"I'm surprised you didn't see any police activity when you came back up from the beach."

"We came back onto the property by one of the other pools, but it was quiet as could be," Eloise said. "I wonder if he knows yet?"

A server sniffled as she added a helping of huevos rancheros onto Eloise's outstretched plate.

The waiter next to her shook his head.

The subdued hush that permeated the banquet room was temporarily broken by hoots and clapping as the bride and groom made their entrance with camera crew in tow. They raised an imaginary toast to the crowd and began to work their way through the gauntlet of congratulatory hugs and good wishes.

They'd about reached the first buffet table when Enrique, the general manager, appeared from behind the swinging kitchen doors.

With an efficiency that belied his rumpled polo shirt, the heavy bags under his eyes, and the whiskers on his face, he nodded to two staff members. As they set about preparing plates with a little of everything, he beelined over to the bride and groom and escorted them to their reserved table for two at the front of the room.

Seconds later, the waiters appeared with full plates and placed them on the table. As soon as the happy couple was seated, Enrique took a couple of steps over to the hostess desk that had been turned so it functioned as a perfect makeshift podium. With all eyes on him there was no reason to tap on a glass or otherwise quiet the room beyond clearing his throat.

"*Buenos días, señores y señoras.*" He waited while everyone put down their forks and the room stilled completely. "As many of you are aware, there was an incident here at the resort last night." His voice cracked. "In fact, it was the most tragic event that has ever taken place here at the Hacienda de la Fortuna."

He waited for the inevitable chatter to die down.

"Naturally, there has been a lot of concern and speculation among our guests and staff as to the nature of what happened." The room fell dead silent as Enrique pulled a tissue from his pocket, blew his nose, and took a moment to collect himself.

"A valued member of the Hacienda de la Fortuna family, who some of you had the pleasure of getting to know, was found last night in the Estanque Reflectante." He waited for the gasps to die down before continuing. "The police conducted a thorough examination and have determined that, unfortunately, Alejandro had far too much to drink."

"Word is his blood alcohol level was up there," one of Philip's police officer friends whispered from me beside me.

"I'm afraid he passed out, fell in the upper pool, and floated down under the bridge into the adjoining pool," Enrique said, bowing his head as he relayed the story. "It is the most awful of tragedies."

EIGHT

So the local police had determined that Alejandro had died via accidental drowning, and Philip's assorted law enforcement pals all seemed to concur:

I'm glad I'm on vacation because I hate dealing with drownings—those telltale glistening eyes always creep me out.

It's the wrinkled skin that gets me.

Lucky he wasn't there longer than an hour or so. Have you seen how the skin on the hands and feet start to come loose like gloves and socks?

While I wasn't exactly relaxed about the whole thing, I felt somewhat relieved when Geo handed out a new call sheet.

"We were up all night strategizing and revising the schedule in light of everything that's happened."

"No swimming?" Trent asked.

"That wouldn't be in the best of taste, seeing as they're holding a poolside wake today," Eloise said with sniff. "Now would it?"

Frank looked out the floor-to-ceiling windows and up at the gathering clouds. "Lighting's not great, anyway."

I forced myself not to react to Frank's insensitive comment as I read through the call sheet. Not only had the timeshare signing and the swim shoot been canceled, but the revamped plan had us venturing off the hotel property entirely and heading into the nearby resort town for a newly created segment called "Bargaining, South-of-the-Border Style."

"This makes sense," I said, nodding as I read.

Geo smiled sympathetically in Enrique's direction. "And it makes sense for all of us to get off the property to give the hotel staff some time to mourn without all the extra commotion."

———

The shopping excursion, as it turned out, was for not just our family and the crew, but for all the wedding guests. We would pile into buses for an afternoon in town, followed by happy hour at a local cantina.

Before we left, however, tradition (and the call sheet) called for the time-honored tradition of showering the new couple with prosperity, fertility, and good fortune by dousing them in birdseed[21] before they left for a water's edge bridal suite at Casa Armonia, the Hacienda de la Fortuna's sister resort ten miles down the coast.

The production assistants corralled everyone and had them stand together under the front portico of the hotel just in time for the getaway car, a white limo, to pull up.

---

21. Rice fell out of favor when it was erroneously rumored that if birds ate the rice, it would expand in their stomach and kill them. Given the fact that birds eat dried rice, corn, and other grains from fields all the time, this turns out to be an urban myth.

Geo directed me to the limo door to deliver an impromptu tip about asking for complimentary car service when booking a bridal suite not only in Mexico, but anywhere in the world.

Anastasia and Philip appeared in the doorway just as I finished.

The crowd, eager to give the bride and groom a proper on-camera send-off, did a great job of providing the local birds with plenty to snack on for the next day or two.

As Philip paused for man hugs with his groomsmen, Anastasia's sisters encircled her like schoolgirls for a group good-bye.

Just before they slipped into the limo together, Anastasia gave me a big hug.

"Are you doing okay?" she whispered. "I haven't had a single moment to check in with you."

"I'm fine," I said, adding a smile in the midst of the on-camera pomp and circumstance.

"Really?" she asked. "Because I'm not sure I would be—not given everything you've been through over the past six months."

While it wasn't like I'd had any time to process how I really felt, something about her earnest expression gave me an extra dash of comfort.

"I can't say it hasn't been upsetting," I said. "But I don't want to let an unfortunate accident mar what has otherwise been a wonderful celebration."

"I knew you were going to be a total pro," she said, her voice cracking as she gave me a hug. "Thank you for being the best matron of honor ever."

Other than a look I thought I saw pass between Hair, Body, and Face, it felt like one of the most genuine moments I'd experienced since I'd been down in Mexico.

The moment the limo was out of camera range, a sightseeing bus pulled up and we were off on an afternoon getaway of our own.

On the way into town, Felipe, our resident driver, provided color commentary:

This area, known as the Riviera Maya, was an important commercial and religious center for the ancient Mayans from about 1000 to 1550 A.D. Tulum, a Mayan fortress which many of you will get a chance to see over the next few days, was the most important population center from this era, but there were other key towns such as Xaman-Ha, now known as Playa del Carmen, where we are headed right now...

Despite the wealth of facts and figures, there was no missing the lack of inflection in Felipe's voice, or the breaks he took, setting down his handheld speaker to blow his nose.

"My apologies," he said at one point.

"No explanations necessary," Geo said, patting him on the shoulder from his seat beside me in the front row. "We all understand."

"I saw Ivan just before we left," Eloise said from across the aisle where she sat beside Frank. "Did you know they're setting up his body by the pool and taking turns keeping his soul company because he can't be alone until he's buried or something?"

FJ and Trent, seated across from her, rolled their eyes at their sister's sudden in-the-know status.

"Interesting," Trent deadpanned.

"Totally," FJ added.

Liam, seated behind them, smiled conspiratorially.

"I mean, the whole thing is awful and everything," I heard one of Anastasia's other sisters whisper. "But if the pools are going to be closed and the staff is falling apart, maybe they should think about switching all of us over to the hotel where Stasia and Philip went."

"Or give us some sort of credit or something," another one said. "For our trauma and inconvenience."

"Seriously," the third said. "The only thing that hasn't been rescheduled was my timeshare presentation."

"Charming, aren't they," Geo whispered almost inaudibly in my ear. "Like Cinderella's wicked stepsisters."

"Here we are," Felipe announced. "The shopping, restaurants, and nightlife all center around Fifth Avenue. Meet me back here at eight p.m. In the meantime, I wish you many bargains."

———

"Bargaining, known here in Mexico as *el regateo,* has been an essential part of the business and social fabric for centuries," I stated for the camera, curious locals, and the tourists who'd gathered to watch us outside a colorful knickknack shop. "Knowing when, where, and how to engage in negotiations can be a little tricky, especially for us foreigners, but here are a few dos and don'ts to help you on your way."

"Great," Geo said. "Now it's time to have some fun."

And despite the somber circumstances that had us in town, Geo and the crew managed to pull together a surprisingly lighthearted shoot.

The first camera segment was set up in front of a jewelry vendor where Eloise was already browsing, her face frozen in the snooty scowl she normally reserved for low-end shoe stores.

"How much?" she asked in English waving a pair of hoop earrings.

"Twenty American dollars," the owner finally said, but without making eye contact.

"Ten," she said.

"Nineteen," he said.

"For a junky pair of earrings?" she sniffed. "They don't even look like real silver."

He shrugged. "That's the price."

"Perfect!" Geo said, stopping the action as soon as the vendor turned away from her. "Now, Maddie, you give some tips and then we'll redo this whole scenario again the right way."

The merchant, who seemed to be attracted to my stepdaughter's assets, if not her attitude, sidled up beside her while Geo directed me to a spot where I was surrounded by stores and colorful merchandise.

As he was about to cue me to speak, I saw a woman standing in the midst of the crowd and found myself drawn in (much like a bull) by her traditional white top with red embroidery and matching bright red full skirt. Something about the pleading look in her eyes told me she wanted or needed something—likely to sell a few or all of the sombreros she was peddling.

"And action!" Geo said.

I quickly decided I would ask Geo to include her in one of the upcoming shots, smiled in her direction, and began: "In the more traditional parts of Mexico, almost everything is bargained for, but in the modern or tourist areas, the rules become less clear. Permanent storefronts and food sellers traditionally maintain fixed prices, but vendors on foot, in markets or booths, or at tables generally welcome bargaining. Another clue can be the presence or absence of price tags."

Before I could start on the actual tips themselves, Trent and FJ bounded up as if the cameras weren't there.

Liam watched from outside the shot.

"*Hola*," FJ said to the owner.

"*Hola*," he smiled, leaving Eloise's side and appearing on camera once again. "*Cómo estàs?*"

"*Estoy bien, y tú?*" FJ answered in his best high school Spanish.

"Mom would like this," Trent said, holding up a turquoise bracelet that had, in fact, caught my eye. "Don't you think?"

"I don't think we'll have enough money to buy it," FJ said with a sigh. "It looks pretty expensive."

"*Cuánto cuesta, por favor?*" Trent asked.

"Twenty-five dollars American," the vendor said in English.

"I'm afraid that's just too much," FJ said, also in English.

The vendor smiled, stealing a glance at Eloise's legs. "How much can you spend?"

"Fifteen dollars," Trent blurted.

"Fifteen dollars?" the vendor said, sounding insulted by the mere mention of such an unthinkable price.

"I know it's worth more than that," FJ added, brushing a humidity-curled lock of hair out of his eyes. "But it's all we have on us."

The boys looked convincingly disappointed as Trent returned the bracelet to its resting spot amongst a group of similar baubles.

"I can tell you are nice boys," the vendor said, lifting the bracelet by the clasp. "Fifteen is okay."

"Really?"

As the vendor nodded, Geo nodded in my direction to finish my spiel.

"You are likely to have the most success and fetch the best possible prices by following a few simple guidelines," I said, noting that the sombrero lady had, unfortunately, disappeared before I could help contribute to her daily earnings. "First, if you can, make a little small talk in Spanish as a show of respect. Second, keep a positive attitude. Bargaining is a friendly game of skill and wit, and you'll catch more bees and lower prices with honey. And lastly, don't insult the merchandise unless there is truly a flaw for which you are asking a discount. It's okay to say something's too much, but you are better off addressing your lack of willingness to pay the asking price than discrediting the item itself."

In a manner uncharacteristic of our usual hectic schedule, Geo and the crew took their time setting up interesting and colorful spots for the remainder of our afternoon bargaining shoot. Like somewhat normal tourists, we took our time with on-camera bargaining, pointing out pitfalls.

Frank was sent into a hat store with a roll of bills and instructed to say, "I only have two hundred pesos," but pull a 500-peso note out of his wallet to highlight a big bargaining faux pas.

The boys did a setup in a shop full of key chains, coffee mugs, blankets, and assorted local merchandise. They asked what they could get for a dollar, and I added a bit of color commentary while they transacted their deals.

"There are no fixed rules about where to start your initial low bid. The trick is to know what you are willing to pay and then try to make that price your mid-point between the initial asking price and your first offer."

Eloise had the best poker face and Frank the worst, so they were sent off together—Eloise to specifically act lukewarm over a leather bag she really wanted, and Frank to gush over a belt and buckle he just had to have for an upcoming Western-themed fundraiser we were scheduled to emcee together.

I was enjoying both of their admirable acting jobs. Eloise examined the bag for quality before negotiating the price, and Frank balanced out his natural tendency to be impulsive by warming up the store owner with some friendly chitchat. In fact, I'd relaxed enough to set aside some of the tumult of the past twenty-four hours when Hair, Face, and Body chanced into the T-shirt shop beside the leather goods store where we were doing our shoot.

"So two-faced," Geo whispered from beside me, glancing over at them. "Or three-faced, I guess I should say."

"How so?"

"For one thing, they act all happy when they're really jealous and pissed."

"That she got married?"

"That she's a star, you're a star, and they're just extras," he said. "In their sister's wedding, no less."

While Frank and I were friendly with the bride and groom, I was well aware that our primary qualification as matron of honor and best man was that their gratis wedding was taking place on our reality show and thus needed to include us in key roles.

"Stasia asked me to be matron of honor, in part, so she wouldn't have to pick one of them over the others and cause a rift."

"No doubt," he said. "You ready to wrap up this bargaining segment?"

As I nodded and got into place, I forced myself to ignore the three sisters, who were huddled together and whispering once again.

"Where appropriate, venders expect and welcome negotiations," I said. "When incorrectly approached, bargaining can not only be fruitless, but downright offensive."

Eloise, who'd been negotiating a price for her handbag, shook her head and began to walk out of the store.

"Don't be afraid to walk away if you cannot reach a price you are happy with," I said, watching her go. "This is an expected move and vendors will often respond with a new offer, either now or the next time you stroll by. If not, you know that they have given you the final price and you can take it or leave it."

Before Eloise made it out of the shop, the vendor had, of course, accepted her new price. The camera rolled as she turned back to finalize the transaction.

"Just as a note, backing out of a sale once a price has been accepted is considered extremely rude."

As I wrapped up by explaining that bargaining is truly a cultural experience and that one shouldn't deny a vendor the chance to show off his or her bargaining skills, the owner of the leather store came over to me.

"*Gracias Señora*. It is most helpful and enjoyable to have tourists who understand the way things are done here."

"*De nada*," I said, distracted by a flash of red from just outside the store. I looked to see if Sombrero Lady had chanced by again, but it was, as I'd just said, *nothing*.

"I imagine it was a relief to get away from the Hacienda de la Fortuna for the afternoon," he said shaking his head. "Awful."

"You heard about what happened?"

"My sister works up at the resort."

"We came into town to give everyone a break from dealing with guests so they could mourn privately."

"Tequila." He shook his head once more. "It's the devil's drink."

———

"The store owners were all so nice," I said, over guacamole, chips, and the cold cerveza I'd ordered in lieu of anything containing tequila. "The man in the leather place actually thanked me for taping in his store."

"They seem to love having your show down here, Mrs. Frugalicious," Liam, whom FJ and Trent had invited to sit with us, said.

"Everyone loves their fifteen minutes of fame," Frank said, pointedly not looking in Liam's direction.

"The exposure has to be good for their business too," I said, giving Frank a warning stare and noting that Hair, Face, and Body were seated right in front of the camera assigned to do random shots (as it were) from inside the cantina while the entire wedding party enjoyed tapas, cocktails, and some decidedly loud 1980s pop music.

The waitress came by to offer refills.

"Any reason why we can't, you know, enjoy a local cerveza in the company of our parents?" Trent suggested with a little wink. "I'm technically almost old enough down here."

Frank winked back. "Nice try."

"Especially since he doesn't even like the taste of beer," FJ said.

"Oh but he definitely needs a prop to attempt and fail to meet girls in a real live bar," Eloise added.

Trent smiled. "*Me encantan las señoritas.*"

"Atta boy," Frank said too loudly, patting both boys on the back and pretending to push his beer in Trent's direction.

"Need I remind everyone we're shooting a family show that takes place in the States, where you're not even close to technically old enough?"

"I wish we didn't have to stay here until eight," Eloise, who *was* of legal age in Mexico, sighed. "With everything that's going on, I don't know when I can see Ivan, except for tonight."

"How do you know he's available tonight?" Frank asked.

"He's been texting me," she said, unable to contain her smile.

"You are aware that we don't have an international data plan, right?" I asked.

"My bad," she said, with a giggle. "I'll pay the extra charges."

The boys rolled their eyes once again at their sister and the knowledge that Frank, who had a notorious soft spot where his daughter and her expenses were concerned, would forget about her financial misdeed as soon as it was time to put the monthly check into her account.

Not wanting to play wicked stepmom and chime in, nor further condone Eloise's ability to wrap Frank around her finger, I excused myself and headed to the ladies' room.

"I gotta go too," Eloise said over the beginning bars of "Girls Just Wanna Have Fun."

We got up and followed the sign to a hallway in the back of the cantina, but instead of an interior bathroom along the back wall, we proceeded through a door and found ourselves in an interior courtyard overlooked by three or four stories of apartments.

"This is kinda weird," Eloise said as we followed yet another sign to a small freestanding building that housed both men's and women's rooms that were apparently shared by a number of the local storefronts.

Ignoring the dripping sink, the hum of an automatic hand dryer stuck on low, and a not-quite-fresh odor that bode poorly for the condition of the stalls themselves, we each set about doing our business. I was finished and unlocking the stall latch with a tissue from my pocket when a flash of red once again caught my eye.

I opened the door to Sombrero Lady standing in front of the sink. Facing me.

"*Hola*," I said, somewhat startled.

"*Hola*," she said in return, but with a seeming sense of urgency.

Unlike my boys, I'd taken French in school and basically only knew how to say hello, good-bye, and order to my heart's content off a menu in a Mexican restaurant. Everything else required assistance from cue cards, a member of the camera crew, or a dictionary.

"We're already done for today," I said, far too slowly and loudly, making a motion like I was operating an old-time camera. "Um, finito…?"

She shook her head. "*No* finito."

"I'm glad to buy some of your sombreros," I said, wondering just what it was she wanted. "*Cuanto sombreros?*"

"No," she said definitively. "Big *problemo.*"

"Sorry?" I said. "My *español* is *no bueno.*"

She motioned me closer, then whispered in my ear, "Alejandro."

"Alej—?" I started to say, then stopped as Eloise emerged from her stall.

"Everything okay?" she asked.

"Fine," I said.

The woman shook her head as Eloise started for the sink.

"What?" I managed.

"*Fue asesinado,*" she said, starting for the door. "*Fue asesinado!*" And then she disappeared as quickly as she'd appeared.

"What was that all about?" Eloise asked.

"She was looking to get on camera," I said, unsure exactly what the woman had said but sure Eloise, who'd barely gotten a C in high school Spanish, would have no idea what the words meant. "And some money for the stuff she's peddling."

"Oh," Eloise said, rubbing her hands under the ineffective hand dryer. "I mean, I love it down here and everything, but you have to admit, it really is different."

"No question," I said, washing my hands and pulling my smart phone out of my purse. Pretending to check for messages, I consulted the Spanish/English translation app I'd installed on my phone before the trip and keyed in my best guess for her words. A few tries led me to a rough translation:

He was murdered.

NINE

"I COULD REALLY USE a cup of coffee," I said the moment we arrived back at the hotel. It was the only thing I'd said during the ride back from town. "Care to join me, Frank?"

Without waiting for his answer, I grabbed his hand and led him toward the kiosk in the middle of the lobby. I took the liberty of ordering us each a café con crema, accepted both cups from the barista, and led us over to a table and chairs. Specifically, a secluded table where no one was close enough to eavesdrop.

"Listen," I said, "I've been through far too much from you to put up with any more lies, deceit, or, for that matter, petty nonsense."

"Oookaaay..." Frank said, assuming his de facto *bad dog* face.

"I agreed to this whole reality TV business because it made sense to get back on track financially, and to make sure there was money for the kids' education. I'm even willing to admit there was some ego involved since I created Mrs. Frugalicious in the first place."

"Of which you should be proud," he said.

"I'm not entirely proud that I agreed to do this show under dubious pretenses." I sighed. "And if I had known how dubious the premise really was …"

"What do you mean?"

"Cut the bullshit, Frank."

Seeing as I rarely swore, Frank sat up straighter in his chair.

"You get a mystery stomach ailment just in time for me to spend an afternoon alone with Alejandro, but reappear the moment I hesitate to sign the paperwork. You materialize once again, and with a camera crew, just before Alejandro asks me out."

His surprise looked vaguely genuine. "He asked you out?"

"Wasn't that part of the story line all along?"

"Not that I'm aware of."

"Are we going to continue to pretend you knew nothing about the note he left under my pillow that you conveniently didn't find or ask about, and that asked me to meet him at exactly the time he was found floating in the pool?"

"I didn't." Frank looked truly shocked now. "The only Alejandro story line I knew they were adding was the whole timeshare element that would plump up the episode and promote sales for the resort. I was told to be scarce so the segment could focus on Mrs. Frugalicious during the timeshare presentation, and to reappear when you started to balk, which you inevitably would."

Having been fed more than a few true untruths over the last year, I could only shake my head. "Seriously, how stupid do you think I am?"

"Apparently not as stupid as me," he said, his face draining of color under his burgeoning vacation tan. "I didn't expect to have to face the thought of you dating for quite a while."

"You should have thought of that before you—"

"I know," he said, shushing me. "I know."

The awful silence that permeated so many of our conversations over the last year fell between us once again.

"So you didn't hear anything about a romantic complication?" I finally asked.

"Not a word," Frank said, adding, "I swear."

"And you didn't say a single thing about our marital situation to anyone?"

"Why would I?" he asked, his tone somewhat convincing for the first time in a long time. "It would compromise everything I'm trying reestablish with viewers by doing the show."

"Don't you mean *we*?"

"*We*," he said. "Sorry, I'm just trying to get my head around all this."

"Me too. Especially with a suspicious death in the mix."

"Maddie, Alejandro's death was an accident."

"Just like the pallet of toasters that crushed Cathy Carter turned out to be on Black Thursday at Bargain Barn?" I asked, referencing my last inadvertent sleuthing assignment. "Or the salesgirl who dropped dead in front of me at the mall last summer?"

Frank looked startled. "What the—?"

"I'm not sure, but when I went to the ladies' room at the cantina, a woman I'd seen selling sombreros during the shopping segments followed me in to share a very unsettling message about Alejandro."

"Which was?"

"*Fue asesinado*," I said, repeating her words.

"Meaning what?"

"He. Was. Murdered."

"Oh shit," said Frank, who did swear, but primarily only when he pretended to tinker at his garage workbench. "Not again."

"Exactly."

TEN

"You okay, Mom?" the boys asked after Frank set off on what we agreed would be a very clandestine preliminary fact-finding mission and I made our way back to our suite.

"I'm just really tired," I said to the boys before heading off to lock myself away in the master bathroom for a long soak.

I was also anything but okay. At least I wasn't entirely alone in my concerns this time around; Frank had listened intently while I recounted my findings about the realities of reality TV. He admitted that a certain amount of story manipulation was, in fact, par for the course. While he didn't believe anyone associated with our show could be behind anything truly sinister, he did agree there were "issues" to look into and that we shouldn't worry the kids until we figured out what they were.

If only Sombrero Lady had stuck around another minute, I could have sent Eloise on and figured out how to bridge the language barrier long enough to find out what the woman thought she knew and why she felt the need to tell me.

If it turned out she was right, and given that *The Family Frugali-cious* had been sold to the network on the strength of the pilot, which featured me as a savings sleuth who survived death while sniffing out sales, wasn't it logical to presume the show might actually involve me solving crimes?

Crimes that would be supplied as necessary?

A long, soapy bath did little to ease my sense of déjà vu. Particularly with the melancholy mixture of music and mourning filtering through my open window from the spontaneous poolside *velatorio* (wake) that had started as we left the hotel that morning and seemed to be building steam as the night wore on.

I finally forced myself out of the bathtub, slipped on a robe, and went out to the family room to grab a bottle of water in advance of what was threatening to be another sleepless night.

"I mean, I didn't bring anything fancy and black to wear," Eloise said as she, Frank, and the boys stood huddled around the next day's call sheet.

"We just wear the suits we wore yesterday," Trent said. "Right?"

"I hate going to funerals," FJ said.

"We're going to the funeral?" I asked.

Frank nodded. "To pay our respects."

"Okay," I managed, despite the frenzied flutter of butterflies in my stomach. "When is it?"

"Ten a.m.," FJ said.

"Tomorrow?"

"Management doesn't want to delay, and Alejandro's whole family lives nearby, and it is Sunday, so it all just makes sense," Eloise said. "At least that's what Ivan told me."

"And because we're leaving tomorrow," FJ said.

"Which means our trip to the water park is canceled," Trent said, grumpily.

"Worse," Eloise whined, "I have no time to find something to wear."

"Wardrobe will come up with something for you," Frank said. "Apparently Mexican funerals are a big deal and we need to look—"

"They're going to shoot footage of Alejandro's funeral?!" I asked, warning bells now clanging in my head.

"Alejandro and timeshares were part of the story line," Frank said.

"I see," I said, giving him a look that said I didn't see at all.

The second the kids dispersed, he motioned for me to follow him back into the bedroom.

"I ran into Geo in the lobby right after you left to go back upstairs," Frank said, closing the door behind us. "He handed me the call sheet and told me were going to shoot some footage at the funeral."

"And what did you say?"

"What could I say?"

"Were you able to ask him anything about anything to do with—"

"Not without clueing him in that we might be suspicious," he said. "But the more I think about this, the more I believe there has to be a completely logical explanation for wanting to film the funeral."

"Which is?"

"For one thing, the resort has a potential PR nightmare on their hands, and they insisted we shoot the funeral so the public can see how much they care about their employees," he said. "Besides, our concern will make us that much more sympathetic to viewers."

"And none of this makes you feel like the tail is wagging the dog?"

"Maddie"—Frank put his hands on my shoulders—"you have my promise: we are going to get to the bottom of whatever is or isn't going on."

"Okay," I sighed.

But was it? Not only were promises and Frank something of a juxtaposition, so was the jarring reality that he and I were suddenly, once again, legitimately united as a *we*.

ELEVEN

Unfortunately, I'd all but come to expect attending unexpected funerals for people I'd just met. Somehow though, willing away the rubbery feeling in my legs while we entered the candle-and-flower-filled church to view Alejandro in his final resting position was not at all how I'd anticipated spending this particular south-of-the-border Sunday.

"I feel so awkward being here," I said, watching Frank wipe away a showy tear while we made our way past the cameraman lurking behind a carved wooden pillar in the simple but stunning local church.

"It's good public relations all around."

"I guess," I said. "Everything feels like it's happening so fast."

"Here in Mexico, we bury loved ones as quickly as possible," Felipe, our ever-informative driver and guide said from behind us. "When someone dies, we gather everyone immediately, and the body goes into the ground within forty-eight hours."

"I don't know about this..." Eloise said approaching the open casket. She was initially pleased at the prospect of clandestine screen time in the sexy-yet-somehow-appropriate black cap-sleeved, v-back dress that wardrobe had shown up with for her to wear. But as soon as she neared the body, she squeezed her eyes shut, paid her respects, and disappeared.

I couldn't say I blamed her. I could barely force myself to look at the ghoulish, gray-skinned remains of the vibrant and handsome man who'd been sending me flirty notes not two days earlier.

More difficult was the idea that my mere presence in his world might have been the cause of his untimely demise.

Thank you for bringing your show down here to our resort, he'd said. *If everything continues to go this well, the payoff will be even better than I imagined.*

Or so much worse.

"Can you believe people are taking pictures of him?" FJ whispered from beside me.

"It's our way of remembering the departed," Felipe explained as a couple other mourners followed suit. "The photographs are considered a tribute to the rite of passage."

"Kinda cool when you think about it," Trent said, eyeing the body as well as the rosaries, books, poems, and assorted belongings surrounding him in the casket.

The crowd, already speaking in low tones, fell completely silent as a woman dressed in black appeared in the central doorway of the church sanctuary, her face concealed by a sheer black veil. A moment later, she was joined by Enrique, who was looking more ashen than he had when he'd addressed the wedding guests at yesterday's brunch.

As they strode together to the front of the church, our eyes met for the briefest of moments. I realized I hadn't recognized who she also was because her beautiful brown hair tumbled past her shoulders instead of being slicked back in a tight French twist.

Elena, the wedding planner.

I was about to ask Felipe if she and Enrique were a couple when the crowd parted and Elena reached the coffin. She tucked a photo underneath his folded hands, touched his undoubtedly cold, waxy cheek, and her legs buckled beneath her.

Felipe, along with a couple of other mourners, rushed to her aid.

The next thing I knew we were being guided to VIP seats in view of the camera and away from anyone who could have answered my latest in a growing list of questions.

The ceremony was something of a blur as Elena was revived and seated between Enrique and the town mayor in the front row along with family, key members of the Hacienda de la Fortuna staff, and other local dignitaries. The padre made his way toward the front of the sanctuary with the usual pomp and circumstance. I knelt when everyone else knelt, stood when everyone else stood, and said amen when I was supposed to. I even sang along, to the extent I could, with the Spanish versions of some familiar hymns. As the service continued, I noted that everyone I'd met since arriving was in attendance, from the yoga instructor to a doe-eyed Ivan, who kept stealing gazes at Eloise. I also spotted familiar faces from our afternoon in town, including the manager of the cantina and two or three shop owners.

As the padre spoke about the fullness of Alejandro's life and his success as a sales manager, and quoted beautiful and hopeful passages from the bible in both Spanish and English, the giant lump that was lodged in my throat threatened to choke me. I scanned the pews, trying to make eye contact with the numerous women who matched the description of Sombrero Lady (short, stocky, and of indeterminate age) in the hopes one of them would return my eye contact and meet up with me later for a detailed explanation of her suspicions.

No such luck.

The mass concluded with the sprinkling of holy water on the coffin. Before there was time to get up and stretch our legs, a Mariachi band appeared to accompany us, our ever-discreet camera crew, and the rest of the mourners to the burial site.

It wasn't until we'd arrived at the cemetery and assorted family members were in the process of saying their final good-byes that I caught a glimpse of the photo tucked under Alejandro's crossed hands.

A photo of Alejandro and Elena standing together, his arm draped around her shoulder.

I stepped back over to Felipe, who happened to be standing not far from Frank.

"So tragic," I whispered, my eyes on a once-again sobbing Elena.

"Incredibly," Felipe agreed.

"Were Alejandro and Elena a couple?" I finally managed to ask.

He nodded. "But it was complicated."

Somehow, whatever so-called complications there were did nothing to make me feel better about his passes at me. Particularly given the realities of the situation.

Before I could mull that over much, the coffin was closed and the burial got underway. Individual prayers were said, the padre led the group in a communal rosary, and relatives went up to throw handfuls of dirt on the coffin. Even the lead police officer on the case shuffled up and tossed in his own handful of dirt.

"Is it customary for the police to come to the funerals of the victims they investigate?" I asked.

"It's best not to question these kind of things too much," Felipe said in the most hushed of tones.

"Because?"

I expected a long-winded response about tradition and small-town life in Mexico.

"*A lo hecho, pecho,*" Felipe said instead, dabbing a tear from his eye. "What's done is done."

TWELVE

"I THINK FELIPE IS suspicious about Alejandro's drowning too," I whispered to Frank as he led me back toward the hotel SUV that had taken us into town for the funeral.

"Why? What did he say?"

"I asked why the policeman was at the funeral, and he told me it was best not to question things. And then he said, 'what's done is done.'"

"Interesting," Frank said. "Definitely."

But before I could elaborate on just how definitely interesting I thought it was, Geo rushed over to us from the rented equipment van parked behind the SUV.

"Who's going to explain to me why neither of you bothered to fill me in on this *fue asesinado* business?"

"How did you …?" Frank asked, his smooth newscaster voice cracking and trailing off.

Geo glanced in the direction of my stepdaughter, who stood a little too close to Ivan under a nearby tree. "The appearance of a mysterious lady with sobering information does tend to leave one's children understandably concerned."

"Eloise…" I heard myself say.

"Eloise doesn't even speak Spanish," Frank added.

"Apparently she remembered the word *asesinado* from a skit she did in high school," Geo said.

Of all the things for Eloise, who wasn't necessarily known for her acute mind or elephant-like memory, to remember, the Spanish word for *murdered* had to stick with her?

"Seriously." Geo folded his arms across his chest. "Why didn't one of you two tell me about this right away?"

"I—*we*—thought we'd ask a few questions and see why someone would say such a thing before getting everyone else all up in arms," I said quickly and making confirmatory eye contact with Frank. "Particularly the kids."

"Hard to get much past your brood," Geo said far too meaningfully for my taste.

The rubbery feeling in my legs travelled throughout my body.

"So, what did you find out when you started asking questions?" Geo asked.

"Uh, I…" I stammered.

"We haven't heard much of anything," Frank interjected, not mentioning my recent interchange with Felipe.

"Well, I'm sure the woman was trying to get on TV," Geo said definitively. "They always are."

"Exactly," Frank agreed.

"But maybe you should look into things a little further," Geo went on.

"What?" Frank and I asked in unison.

"Make a few inquiries," he said, with what could only be described as a smirk.

"But—"

"What will viewers think knowing Alejandro died and we simply packed up and left without looking into any unanswered questions?"

"They'll think it was an accident, since that's what's on the official report," I said, still wondering if I was really hearing what I thought I was hearing.

"Maddie…" Geo took my hand and held it in his slightly damp palms. "These days you're almost as much a sleuth as you are a savvy shopper."

Desperate as I was to gauge his reaction, I didn't dare glance over at Frank. "I doubt we'll be able to find out much before we leave tomorrow," I said. "Most of the people we'd probably want to talk to will still be at the wake."

"But not all," Geo said.

As Felipe—who was just out of earshot but well within collusion range—flashed what should have been a comforting smile, I looked into the open back door of the van and spotted the camera.

With its red light staring right at us.

Geo handed us yet another revised schedule. "What do you say we kick things off with a visit to the timeshare sales office?"

THIRTEEN

THE RESORT WAS, AS I suspected (and for lack of a better word), dead. A skeleton crew was all that remained to attend to guests while most everyone on staff still seemed to be at Alejandro's postfuneral wake. The notable exception was the resort sales office, which was not only very much open for business, but suddenly the site of our *2:00: Console grieving staff members and finalize timeshare paperwork* shoot.

"I don't find it entirely surprising that Geo wants us to look into things," Frank said as soon as the makeup artist finished touching us up, leaving us alone for the first moment since we'd been handed our afternoon schedule. "He's right that viewers will want to see us do something about Alejandro's death."

"Like ask a few cursory questions while we sign timeshare paperwork?" I said doubtfully.

"As long as we have to fulfill our obligation to the resort to promote their properties, we might as well."

"Which I assume was pre-negotiated into whatever deal Anastasia cooked up?"

"There's always a trade-off."

"Alejandro certainly paid quite a price." Any hopes I'd had, however wishful, that Alejandro really had gotten plastered and innocently drowned in the pool were suddenly circling the drain.

"If only I'd signed when I was supposed to. He'd probably still be—"

"Maddie, the timing of the signing didn't have anything to do with Alejandro's death."

"How could it not?"

"I'm one of the creators of the show. I honestly don't believe anyone associated with *The Family Frugalicious* would go so far as to—"

"Create a plot angle that had me falling for a tall, dark, and handsome timeshare salesman?"

"So you *did* find him handsome!"

"Frank." I resisted a sigh. "The point is, I refuse to sign the contract, and the next thing I know, I'm getting secret notes from a man who ends up dead at exactly the time he proposed we meet. A man whose death we are now investigating."

"This whole sign-and-snoop scenario is—"

"A setup?"

"Exactly," Frank said. "Why on earth would anyone from the show have us look into things if they were somehow involved?"

"This is going to be great!" Geo said, popping his head through the door. "We've got cue cards, but we're going for authentic here, especially where the sympathy is concerned."

"Ratings maybe?" I whispered in answer to Frank's question.

"The ratings are going to be thru the roof for this episode," Geo said, confirming my worst suspicions.

"May I help you?" asked the receptionist. She had the wooden tone of an on-camera first-timer, but the fake eyelashes, glossy lipstick, and heavy-handed eye shadow job of a true professional like Esmeralda, the Hacienda de la Fortuna makeup artist.

"We're here to finalize our resort ownership paperwork," Frank said.

"And your name is?" the receptionist asked.

"Maddie," I said. "Maddie Michaels."

"As in Mrs. Frugalicious?" she read with enthusiasm, but straight off the cue card.

"And her husband, Mr. Frugalicious," Frank added.

"I'm Beti," she said, and picked up the phone to let someone in the back know we were there. "Welcome to the vacation sales office."

"We're so sorry for your loss, Beti," Frank said the moment she'd hung up from announcing our arrival.

"Thank you," she said and reached for a tissue.

In the awkward silence that followed, I looked around the sales office. Unlike the upbeat enthusiasm of a few days earlier, a stifling pall permeated the place. Behind the glass walls of the nearby children's lounge, however, a bumper crop of kids seemed to be gorging on treats, toys, and video games.

"You're busy today," I said, ad libbing as instructed.

Beti nodded.

"I'm surprised you're even open."

"Saturdays and Sundays are always our busiest days of the week," she said. "And we were closed this morning for the funeral, so everything got pushed back to this afternoon."

Geo cued the cameraman, who turned the camera toward the door to the sales floor just in time to capture the Alejandro lookalike assistant manager emerge with a solemn smile.

"The show must go on," Beti whispered. "Or so our new manager says."

"Is he Alejandro's replacement?"

"Antonio's been the assistant manager for almost as long as Alejandro's been here."

And, voilà, I'd been fed my first bona fide name for my not so bona fide suspect list.

Antonio.

And he even had a textbook motive as a long-suffering second fiddle.

"Welcome," Antonio said, still looking more slick and slightly lower rent than Alejandro. His smile was nowhere close to reaching his eyes, which held both sadness and something I couldn't quite read. He shook hands, first with Frank, then me, and summoned us to follow him back.

While I expected prospective timeshare buyers to be peppered throughout the room as he led us across the sales floor, every conversation cluster was, once again, filled. But unlike Friday's festive atmosphere, the sales associates all looked dour and slightly sweaty, and the prospective owners looked tense and resigned to endure their presentations for whatever freebies they'd been offered in exchange.

Only Hair (Susan), who was there along with her husband, seemed to be enjoying the presentation.

"The paperwork is really just a formality," Antonio said, leading us toward the corner office he'd already commandeered from Alejandro. "This shouldn't take long."

I couldn't help but think about another type of formality-only paperwork: the signed, sealed, but not delivered divorce document locked in our home safe.

Home and *safe* suddenly felt like keywords.

"I'm sorry to have to bother you with this today in the midst of what has to be unimaginable grief," I said.

"Having you here is a good distraction," he said thickly, bidding us to sit in the very same chairs and handing over what had to have been the very pen Alejandro had offered.

As Frank started to sign on the variety of dotted lines with his usual flourish on the *F* and *M*, I found myself gazing at photos of what I presumed were Antonio's wife and three kids already gracing the credenza behind him.

"Did Alejandro leave behind a family?" I asked.

"Just Elena," he said, sending a jolt of guilt through me, despite any wrongdoing on my part. "Rest assured his portion of this and all commissions due to him will go directly to her."

"I'm so glad," I said, not pointing out that our particular time-share deal was gratis, and thus unlikely to result in much of a boon for her or whoever else might be named in his will. "Poor dear."

"I'm sure she'll land on her feet," he said, with a touch of what seemed like contempt. Before I could figure out a polite way to ask what he meant, he added, "Enrique's been waiting for an opportunity like this his whole life."

"Um, that"—I searched for a way to keep the conversation going so I could get more information—"sounds complicated."

Antonio wiped away a tear. "Not anymore."

Geo gave the thumbs up.

"I suppose not," I said, taking what I assumed was a hint that Elena and Enrique belonged on my suspect list.

With that, it was my turn to sign the paperwork.

"Do you have any other questions?" Antonio asked as I dotted my i's and crossed my t's.

So many, I didn't say. *Starting with, What in the world is really going on here and who, exactly, put you up to whatever it is you are and aren't telling us?*

"I can't think of anything specific right now," I said instead, feeling somewhat sorry for Alejandro now as well, but following my cue.

"If you do, you know where to find us," Antonio said, motioning for an assistant to bring in the champagne I felt certain none of us felt like sipping in celebration.

"Thank you," I said.

"Yes. Thank you," Frank said, slipping an arm around me. "We're looking forward to many happy years here as vacation property owners." He pulled me in close for a kiss. "Aren't we, hon?"

———

"Next!" Geo called out and tucked his hair behind his ears. He offered a smile that made me think of cats and canaries. "We're setting up for a poolside powwow."

"A powwow?"

"You, Frank, and the boys."

"I thought the call sheet said—"

"Whatever," he said, whisking both Frank and me out the door of the timeshare office. "The boys unearthed some extremely interesting information."

"The boys did?" I asked.

Geo directed us to the camera set up beside two chaises in a remote corner of one of the smaller pools. As soon as we arrived, a waiter handed us drinks with umbrellas and disappeared.

"Sit and look like you're relaxing, but deep in thought."

"Okay," I said, settling in next to Frank, anything but relaxed.

"And action," he said.

With that, the boys came barreling over to where we *contemplating both the beauty of our surroundings and the tragic situation,* per the cue card that had suddenly appeared beside the camera.

"You're not going to believe what we found out," Trent said with the enthusiasm of a sixteen-year-old who believed he might become a legitimate investigative journalist.

"What's that?" Frank asked.

"Alejandro didn't drink," FJ announced.

"Who told you that?" I asked, sitting up, startled the boys had stumbled upon actual information that hadn't somehow been fed to them.

"A waiter at the poolside restaurant," Trent said, puffing out his chest with satisfaction over his first official sleuthing mission accomplished.

"But I saw him drink," I said. "We had margaritas together."

"How many?" FJ asked. "Apparently he only drank when he was entertaining potential clients and kept to a strict one-drink maximum when he did."

I thought back to our poolside lunch and realized that while the waiter had ensured my bottomless margarita remained that way, Alejandro had consumed only one glass before switching to water.

"Which leads to the second big bit of information," FJ said.

Trent smiled. "Alejandro was supposedly a champion swimmer."

"By champion, you mean …?"

"I mean Olympic hopeful, or something, back in the day."

———

"First we have *chapulines*," Chef Benito said, greeting us with the appetizer course. "Prepared with garlic, salt, lime juice, and a hint of red chili powder."

"*Chapulines*?" Frank asked.

"Crickets," Benito said with smug satisfaction.

Eloise's eyes widened with horror.

"They're quite the delicacy down here."

"Seriously?" FJ asked.

"The small ones in particular," Benito said. "They're harder to catch."

"Cool!" Trent said, stabbing a couple tiny crickets with his fork and doing the honors while we watched him chew.

"Delicious," Benito said. "No?"

"Hmmm," Trent said. "Interesting."

"Cut," Geo said. "Can you do another take please? This time with the rest of you looking just a little more horrified."

"Fine by me," Trent said.

"So they're not as disgusting as they look?" FJ asked.

"They're pretty crunchy."

"I'll guess I'll try one," FJ said.

"If the boys are man enough, so am I," Frank said, giving FJ a meaningful pat on the back and holding his breath.

As the boys dug into the plate of chapulines, Eloise and I watched on in earnest revulsion.

"Now it's your turn, ladies," Geo said, satisfied with his shot of the boys gobbling down insects.

"No can do," Eloise said, looking as green as I felt. "That's not in my contract."

"Be brave," Benito said with a smile as he offered the platter to Eloise. "Señora Frugalicious certainly is."

"I am?" I asked, dreading the thought of crunchy exoskeleton.

Benito nodded. "So much more brave than anyone else around here."

I had to assume Benito had been coached to let me know he was a team player and that we could and should be open when talking to him.

"I understand Alejandro wasn't much of a drinker," I said, taking the bait.

"No," Benito said, definitively. "And he swam in the ocean almost every day."

"So you think his death was unusual?"

He looked around and lowered his voice to a whisper. "No more than his life."

Without further elaboration, the camera was back on and I was being served a spicy cricket, which, for the record, tasted nothing like chicken.

Geo was apparently pleased with my ability to feign a swallow and sent Benito back to the kitchen. Within minutes we were working our way through an unusual but delicious multicourse feast that included everything from green tomato pozole to seafood cooked in a mixture of citrus, radish, roasted cherries, onion, and coriander. Our dinner conversation, however, felt like a smorgasbord of obvious questions:

What was the story surrounding Elena, Alejandro, and Enrique?

What was truth behind Alejandro's drinking?

How did a champion swimmer simply drown?

Who was Sombrero Lady, and how did she know anything about Alejandro's death?

Why didn't almost anyone care to question what happened?

"I'm wondering," FJ said as we were midway through a dessert of dark chocolate soup, "if Alejandro didn't drink and was that comfortable in the water, how did the police explain off the alcohol in his body and the fact he drowned?"

"Yet another good question," I said, wondering exactly what Benito meant when he said that Alejandro's death was no more unusual than his life.

"Cut," said Geo, rushing back beside the camera. He'd been on the phone just outside the doors to our private dining room.

"Did I do something wrong?" FJ asked.

"Not at all."

"Do we get more chocolate soup for the next take?" Trent asked. "It's super good."

Eloise, who'd been sullen since saying her good-byes with Ivan after the funeral not four hours previously, simply sighed loudly.

"I don't think we'll need another take of dinner at all," Geo said.

"Good call," Eloise said.

"Speaking of calls, I've just gotten off the phone with the executive producers about looking further into what happened," Geo said.

I swallowed back a rising sense of dread. "Further? What more can we realistically do?" I asked.

"Look into FJ's question about police procedure, for one thing. Anastasia has already instructed a couple of Philip's officer buddies to sniff around the local police department for us."

"Great," I said.

"While you do the rest," Geo said.

"The rest?"

"All of you, as a family," Geo said with that cloying smile. "After all, our show is about the Family Frugalicious, not a police drama. Right?"

"But—"

"You've got to admit, we have developed a few skills," FJ said.

Trent nodded in agreement.

"Good," Geo said. "The new plan is to spend most of tomorrow at the water park."

"Awesome!" both boys exclaimed in unison.

"Wait," I said. "Tomorrow's Monday. We're leaving for the airport at noon."

"Not anymore."

"Really?" Eloise said with the first real enthusiasm I'd heard in her voice all evening.

"The shoot's been extended," he said.

"When are we leaving, then?"

"When we figure out what's going on around here," Geo said. "And whoever is responsible."

"But what about the hotel?" I asked, noting that Frank was not only silent, but nodding in agreement. "The resort probably won't want us here. A murder investigation can't be good for publicity and public relations."

"We'll handle the hotel," Geo said.

"Does this mean we'll get to see the Mayan ruins, and jet ski, and do some of the other stuff we were going to miss?" FJ asked.

"Already being arranged," Geo said.

"Yay!" Eloise said, looking longingly in the direction of the activities office.

"This isn't going to work," I said, silently beseeching Frank to speak up in some fashion.

"It's going to work great," Geo said. "The Family Frugalicious—frolicking and fighting crime for a few extra days in paradise."

"But school—"

"Doesn't start again until next Monday," Trent said.

"And I don't have classes on Mondays or Tuesdays," Eloise said. "If I need to miss a few classes later in the week, I'll just email my profs and tell them what's up."

At the note of excitement in the kids' eyes, I tried to swallow away the lump in my throat.

"You don't have to worry," Geo said. "Everyone will be as safe as can be."

As in, they wouldn't kill off the talent—at least not yet, anyway?

"And if things go as well as I expect," he added. "We'll have enough footage for killer two-part episode."

FOURTEEN

"IF THINGS GO AS well as he expects?" I whisper-screamed at Frank as we headed back to our suite, where the alternate camera crew was setting up for our *Family Sleuthing Strategy Conversation.* "Do you know Alejandro said the very same thing to me the day before he—"

"Maddie," Frank said, "it just doesn't make sense that they hurt Alejandro for the sake of the show, okay?"

"Or it makes perfect twisted sense," I said, peering around a clump of nearby bushes to make sure there were no hidden cameras or people lurking nearby. "Why didn't you object to this?"

"Because Geo is right," he said. "Mrs. Frugalicious investigating another murder—the ratings are going to be killer."

"I can't believe you actually said that," I said. But then I wondered how surprised I could really be given that Frank lived for ratings and fame. "Besides, we won't really be investigating. You know we'll be spoonfed who to talk to and what to say to them just like they've already done with Felipe, Antonio, Benito, the waiter the kids *coincidentally* ran into, and whoever else they've paid off."

"This is reality TV. There's no budget for that kind of elaborate subterfuge."

"You're saying they could afford to fly a cast and crew down to Mexico for what is now an indefinite period of time, but they couldn't pay off a few people for the sake of a story line?"

"Not for a *murder*."

"Whatever's going on here, Frank, we have no business getting in the middle of it."

"It's absolutely our business if making a show of our search leads to *The Family Frugalicious* becoming a huge hit."

I shook my head. We walked the rest of the way in silence until we reached the door to our building and stepped onto the elevator. "Frank, I'm not comfortable with whatever it is that's going on."

"Everything will work out," Frank said. "Trust me."

I sighed as the door slid open and we headed down the hall toward our suite. "What other option do I have?"

———

In truth, I figured I actually had two options:

1. Go to the local *policía*, beg them to reopen their investigation, and hope they'd protect us based on what I'd already heard.

2. Go along with the setup of all setups by pretending to look into things, come up with a conclusion similar to that of the local authorities, and keep out of any further trouble.

Neither option was too palatable, but seeing as our return ticket home appeared to be contingent on a TV-worthy investigation of some sort, Frank was right that we had to make a show, as it were, of narrowing down whodunit to a few likely suspects.

The kids were waiting for us and the camera was rolling as we walked back into the suite.

"Since I can't use my cell phone, I'm going to go down to the activities office to see if they'll let Ivan know I'm staying," Eloise said. "Okay?"

"Speaking of activities," FJ said, "Liam said they're having a piñata-making demonstration in the lobby."

Frank raised an eyebrow. "A piñata demonstration?"

"Why don't you go with them, Frank?"

"Cut," Geo said. "The whole point of this scene is to have you two strategizing about what you think is going down and how you're going to work together to solve the murder."

"Assuming there is a murder," I said.

"Assuming," he said with that smarmy smile. "Of course."

"We will strategize together," I said. "But before we do, I want to organize everything we've learned so far into some—"

"Spreadsheets," the kids, all of whom had grown accustomed to my methods as Mrs. Frugalicious, said in unison.

"Exactly." I certainly didn't need nor want Frank looking over my shoulder and inserting his *we're gonna be big stars* agenda into what was already likely to be a wild goose chase. Besides, a little arts and crafts with FJ couldn't hurt him in the sensitivity department. "And it really is a one-person job."

"Not a very camera-friendly one though," Frank said.

"Perhaps not," I said, hoping for a few minutes to organize my thoughts and my mental state in some sort of peace. "But it's still necessary."

"Might not be an entirely bad idea," Geo finally said.

"Really?"

"Just make it interesting, somehow."

"I'll certainly try," I said.

"Get some footage of Maddie," Geo said, pointing to the cameraman and an assistant. "Everyone else, follow me."

With assurance that I'd call everyone back to the room as soon as I had everything organized and ready to discuss, Geo, Frank, Eloise, and the boys set off toward the lobby.

Not sure how I was going to be *interesting*, I powered on my computer and gave it a go by typing out a few basic questions in a big, easy-to-film font: WHAT REALLY HAPPENED TO ALEJAN-DRO?

Tragic accident?
Murdered?

Assuming Alejandro was, in fact, murdered ...

Why?
By whom?
How?

I couldn't very well start listing my real suspects (*Geo, Anastasia, a hit man posing as a crewman, the network execs, all of the above*), so that particular spreadsheet would have to wait until I was alone for long enough to come up with a password-protected secret file. In the meantime, I created POTENTIAL SUSPECTS and dutifully listed everyone Geo had paraded by us that fit the bill and could possibly have had a motive for the murder:

Antonio—assistant manager of resort property sales.
Motive: No hope of upward mobility?

Enrique—Elena's back-up.

Motive: Alejandro's principal rival for her affections?

Elena—Alejandro's wife.

Motive: According to every police procedural on TV, the wife is the first and most logical person of interest.

Benito—chef.

Motive: Unknown.

I had to assume dinner was prearranged precisely so I would see fit to add Benito to my burgeoning nonsuspect list. Closing that file, I opened another spreadsheet and titled it EVIDENCE FOR MURDER. I keyed in the supposed facts:

1. Alejandro limited his alcohol content to one drink per day.

2. He was a strong swimmer: one-time Olympic hopeful and daily ocean swimmer.

3. Sombrero Lady's statement: fue asesinado—*it was murder.*

4. Lack of questions about "accidental" death.

I gave the camera my best pensive (or was it petrified?) look and continued to peck away at my keyboard by starting yet another spreadsheet entitled PEOPLE TO QUESTION. I figured there were four potential categories:

Resort Employees

Townspeople

Relatives

Other

The only category where I could actually begin to list anyone was Resort Employees, a heading broad enough to include everyone from the lowliest groundskeeper to the president of Hacienda de la Fortuna, LLC. I decided to start with the employees we'd been introduced to when we arrived at the resort and/or who had managed to play into my scenario with Alejandro in one way or another:

Jorge—concierge and deliverer of Alejandro's notes to me.

I moved Felipe—who, in retrospect, had likely been instructed to give us the head's up that Alejandro's demise was indeed suspicious—into my suspect spreadsheet, just because. I wrote *Unknown* for his motive.

I'd shifted back to my PEOPLE TO QUESTION list and had just typed in *Ivan—activities director and deliverer of yet another note* when the door to the suite clicked open and Eloise came bounding into the room.

Of course.

"Ivan completely switched his schedule around so he can be at the water park tomorrow," she said, trying (but unable) to contain a huge grin.

"So sweet," I said.

"Right?" she said dreamily.

"Convenient too," I said. "You'll have all day to ask him a few questions."

Her already big eyes grew huge. "You seriously want me to, like, interrogate Ivan?"

"That's why we're still here, isn't it?" I said.

"I guess," Eloise said with a sigh.

"Honey, there's a big difference between interrogating someone and asking them a few questions."

"Still awkward," she said, sounding far less enthusiastic.

"If you ask me, it gives you two something to talk about."

"Like, 'Look at that cool seagull and, by the way, do you think Alejandro was murdered?'"

"Not like that at all. Just say how weird everything seems, and mention that your parents are really upset for Alejandro's family." I grabbed a paper and pen, and listed off some conversation starters, writing them down as I went.

What was Alejandro really like?

Did he really follow his "one drink and only with clients" policy?

How was his relationship with Elena?

How is everyone taking his death around the resort?

"You want me to ask of all these?" she said, scanning the list.

I turned so the camera couldn't quite make out what I was writing and jotted down one more question I couldn't say aloud:

What do you know about the note Alejandro had you deliver to my mom?

"And whatever else you think of," I said, handing her the list. "Just don't imply or use the word *murder*."

"Whatever," she said definitively as she headed down the hall and disappeared into her room.

I entered the list into my computer, along with some additional conversation starters and questions of varying specificity and suspiciousness for Frank and the boys to use, depending on who they were speaking with. I planned to look into anything of significance using whatever means I could to keep the camera focused on everyone else before, during, and after our day at the water park.

Without any real inkling of how I might actually pull that off, I let the production assistant know I was as ready as I was going to be for our *Family Sleuthing Strategy Conversation*. Which was to say, not very. While he went to round them up and the cameraman took a fifteen-minute break, I quickly created a *real* file of potentially important details that should have been entitled SUSPICIOUS STUFF, but I hid it under the benign heading SHOPPING TIPS 101:

Alejandro's sudden and prominent appearance at the beginning of the shoot.

His unexpected flirtation and notes—where they were left, who did and didn't find them, and the means by which they were delivered.

Suspicious behavior: Anastasia/Geo/Crew

The convenient timing of Alejandro's death, i.e., moments before he'd requested we meet.

Investigation resolved very quickly and determined to be an accident by police despite suspicious circumstances. Why?

Sombrero Lady and her warning.

Funeral scheduled even more quickly. Why?

The sudden parade of naysayers and people with potential motive.

Shooting schedule extended and budget increased with a single phone call to execs about an "accidental" death.

Just before everyone returned, I wrote *To Be Continued* at the bottom of the spreadsheet, saved and closed it, and was preparing to wing a family plan for how best to proceed.

As it turned out, I didn't have to.

"Okay," Geo said, handing me piece of paper, "I've taken the liberty of prioritizing people for questioning, noted who I think should question them, and wrote some questions for you five to discuss."

Unsurprisingly, his handwritten *Persons of Interest* list and his list of questions pretty much matched the spreadsheet I'd already created. As did most of the questions he wanted us to ask:

1. What was the story surrounding the Elena, Alejandro, and Enrique?

2. What was truth behind Alejandro's drinking?

3. How did a champion swimmer simply drown?

Missing was my number-three question, for which Geo claimed he was having someone else do the legwork: *Who was Sombrero Lady and how did she know what she said she knew?*

And the all-important final question:

4. Why didn't anyone care to question further what happened?

The answer, I feared, was going to be more complicated than even my most crowded price and sales spreadsheet.

FIFTEEN

"Ready to start reeling in the big fish before we head off to the water park?" Geo asked the next morning, handing me a call sheet so jam-packed, the only thing missing was a spare moment for me to try and actually figure out what was so fishy.

I calmed the swarm of butterflies fluttering from my stomach toward my throat by reassuring myself that we wouldn't be doing anything more than following a carefully choreographed script in which we would simply be playing our assigned roles to no specific outcome other than our safe return home.

As in, *I'm not really a sleuth, I just play one on TV.*

Frank scanned his copy of the call sheet. "Enrique, huh?"

"He's in the lobby," Geo said, confirming my working theory that much more. "Waiting for you."

"And willing to answer questions?" I asked.

"Eager, actually," Geo said.

"Let's get rolling," Frank said, heading for the door of our suite.

The understanding the two of us had hammered out from opposite sides of our pillow barrier—that Frank would provide a distraction whenever possible in order for me to find out whatever needed finding out—seemed only to extend to the neon green swim trunks and oddly coordinating Hawaiian shirt he'd decided to wear to the water park.

"I thought we didn't have to do anything until breakfast," Trent said, rubbing sleep out of his eyes.

"I only need Maddie and Frank right now."

"Good, because I'm not even close to ready yet," Eloise said, holding up two tiny bikinis.

"The blue one with the fringe," the makeup artist said. "It matches your eyes."

"And we definitely want all of you looking and feeling your best today." Geo smiled his smarmy smile. "It's gonna be a long day."

———

"You watch—first we'll talk to Enrique and then, suddenly, Elena will show up," I said to Frank as we made our way down the corridor toward the elevators. "And then—"

"*Señor y Señora Frugalicious!*" Zelda, the housekeeping manager, appeared beside her cleaning cart in the hallway and hurried toward us.

"Or Zelda will turn up first," I whispered.

"You're way overthinking this," Frank said. "The cameras aren't even on us yet."

"Are you sure about that?" I asked glancing up at a strategically positioned security camera.

"*Gracias,*" Zelda said, making her way over.

115

"You're welcome," Frank said, assuming, I presumed, that she was thanking us for the tip[22] we left on the nightstand every morning since we'd arrived in Mexico.

He gave me an *I told you so* look.

"Señor Alejandro, he not supposed to be dead," she whispered breathlessly. "Not his time yet."

I gave Frank a return *I told YOU so.*

"You figure out why, no?" she asked.

Frank nodded. "We are."

"*Gracias*," she said again.

"*Es no problemo*," Frank said. "But—"

"But how did you know we're looking into things?" I asked.

She looked at me blankly as though she didn't understand a word I'd said.

"*¡Ten cuidado!*" she said instead.

————

"Zelda is dramatic and more than a little superstitious," Enrique said, as we made our way across the lobby toward a set of chocolate brown leather couches where Geo and the crew awaited our arrival. "It's just her way."

"How did she know we were looking into things in the first place?" I asked.

"We informed a few key employees so they can keep an eye out for you and your family."

22. Tipping plays a significant role in Mexico's informal, cash-driven economy. Many people leave their hotel maid a daily tip of between $1 and $5 (in pesos, of course) for each night's stay spent at the hotel.

"Do you feel we're in danger?" I asked as we were seated across from him.

"Not at all," he said with an uneasy smile. "But I wouldn't be doing my job if I didn't anticipate anything and everything in order to ensure your safety."

"Never mind my sanity," Geo said, looking at his watch and shaking his head. "Let's get rolling. We're already behind schedule."

The next thing I knew, Frank was reciting his first line: "Who do you think could have wanted Alejandro dead?"

"I spent all night awake asking myself the same question," Enrique answered, as prompted.

While he did look tired around the eyes, he'd clearly spent some of his awake time making sure his peach polo was perfectly pressed, his tan slacks creased, and his hair perfectly coiffed for his morning close-up.

"And?" I asked.

"And I honestly can't think of any one particular person."

"But you agree that Alejandro's death is suspicious?"

"The authorities think otherwise," Enrique said. "And that is enough for me."

"Why would the police so quickly determine the death to be an accident, do you think?"

"One doesn't question those sorts of things around here," he said.

"Was it true that Alejandro was a strong swimmer?"

"Very."

"And drank in moderation?"

"In recent years, yes."

"But not always?"

Enrique sighed. "I think it's fair to say that Alejandro was a man who enjoyed the good life."

"We were told that you and Elena—" Frank said.

"Grew up together." Enrique, who'd maintained perfect on-camera composure so far, looked down and away. "But it was always a given that she'd marry Alejandro."

"I apologize for my frankness," I said sincerely, despite the fact that Frank had ad libbed the awkward line, not me. "How was your relationship with Alejandro?"

"I loved him like family," he said a little quickly and without a cue card.

I decided that persistence was the only way we were going to get anything useful from the polished general manager. "Even though you were in love with Elena?"

"We both wanted her to be happy," he said.

"How is she doing?" I asked.

"As well as can be expected."

"I can't imagine," I said.

But, as I'd predicted, Elena suddenly appeared from behind the French doors leading to the corporate offices. She managed a decent approximation of looking surprised to find us in the lobby. Unlike the well-groomed Enrique, and in spite of her own usually impeccable presentation, her hair was in an unkempt bun and her uniform showed several wrinkles.

"I told her to take off as long as she needed to get her feet back under her, but she insisted on coming in to finalize details for the four weddings we have scheduled for this week," Enrique said quickly. He stood to greet her as she came over and joined our *private* conversation.

As they hugged, he whispered something in her ear in Spanish far too rapidly to even attempt to translate. She nodded in response, seemed to steel herself, and joined him on the couch to play her part in our noncandid interview.

"We're so sorry for your loss," Frank said.

"Thank you," she said in a barely audible whisper.

"I apologize for having to ask, but do you have any reason to believe there's more to Alejandro's passing than an accidental drowning?" I recited from my cue card, starting to feel more and more like a broken record.

"There couldn't be," she said and began to weep.

Enrique reached into his pocket, pulled out a tissue, and looked into her eyes as he lovingly dabbed the tears that had begun to drip down her cheeks.

"Who would want to kill Alejandro, of all people?" she whispered.

"Cut," Geo said. "Perfect."

"Señor Enrique," a front desk clerk said, appearing from behind the camera crew. "We have an issue that needs your immediate attention."

"And I'm late for a meeting with the florist," Elena said.

And in perfect suspicious fashion, they both disappeared.

———

"Really, the police didn't do much of any investigating at all," FJ said as the camera, situated on the opposite side of the buffet line, recorded us reciting our lines and filling our plates with the various fruits that would comprise our custom-blended breakfast smoothies. "What do you think that's all about?"

"I've asked a couple of Philip's officer buddies to sniff around down at the local police station," Frank said as though he, and not Anastasia, actually had done the asking.

"It'll be interesting to see what they find out," I said, confident we'd find out little or nothing.

"I hope they don't find anything out too quickly," Trent said, setting down a full plate and a Jell-O parfait from the main buffet before picking up a bowl to fill with fruit. "I mean, there's like a month of cool stuff to do down here."

"Need I remind you we're not down here just to frolic in the sun?"

"Sleuthing in the sand and surf," FJ said, delivering his line with a chuckle.

"Let's not forget someone has not only died, but was possibly murdered," Frank said.

"Was definitely murdered," Eloise said, "according to the Sombrero Lady."

"We need to find her," FJ said.

"In the meantime, we have Zelda, the head of housekeeping, who seemed to think so too," Frank said.

"What does Enrique think?" one of the kids asked, reading off a cue card that had just popped up.

"Neither he nor Elena are convinced there's anything more to it," I answered.

"She was concerned, though," Frank said.

"She's just really rattled by Alejandro's death," I said, not wanting to worry the kids. I gave Frank a look that said *Cool it.*

"Which is why we'll do what we can to shed light on what really happened before we leave," Frank added, not getting my drift.

"I mean, champion swimmers don't usually drown," Trent said, filling his entire bowl with bananas. "That's for sure."

"Anyone can drown if they've had too much to drink," I said, watching him soak the bananas in chocolate sauce. At least the murder talk wasn't affecting his teenage-boy appetite.

"But he didn't drink," FJ said, handing his own bowl and a glass of orange juice to the young man working the blender. "Right?"

"According to Enrique, he may have had a bit of a battle with the bottle," I said, over the whir of ice and fresh fruit.

"Seriously?" Eloise sniffed as Trent added peanut butter, chocolate chips, and heaven knew what else to his chocolate-covered-banana bowl.

"Are you talking about Alejandro's drinking problem?" Trent asked.

"I was referring to your breakfast, you idiot," Eloise wrinkled her nose. "It's supposed to be a healthy fruit smoothie, not a liquid banana split. How can you eat that at eight in the morning?"

"I need energy for the water park."

Behind us, the doors to the kitchen swung open and Chef Benito appeared. He barked an angry command in Spanish to a group of waiters, motioned one of them to follow him, and disappeared back into the kitchen.

"Well, Benito thinks something's not right," Trent said.

"Benito's never happy," the smoothie guy said shaking his head as he accepted Trent's concoction. "But he'd love this smoothie you've created."

"Ha!" Trent said, sticking his tongue out at Eloise.

"It'll definitely give you energy." The smoothie guy smiled. "Hopefully enough even to keep you away from the sharks."

———

"There is little to no risk of encountering a shark," Jorge, the concierge, said as everyone (except Geo and the camera crew who'd gone ahead of us to get set up) began to gather in the front lobby.

"I'm staying in the water park part," Eloise said.

"It's an *eco* water park, Einstein," FJ said. "It's all ocean."

Eloise's already big blue eyes grew huge. "Seriously?"

"There aren't any slides?" Trent asked.

"I think you'll find plenty to keep you occupied." Jorge surveyed the group, which included not only our family and most of the wedding party, but a number of other hotel guests. "Señores and Señoras." He whistled and waved his hands. "Before the bus arrives to take you to the water park, I'd like to make a few announcements." He waited for everyone to quiet down. "First, please check that you have your printed proof of purchase for your park admission."

Everyone began to dig through their bags.

"Today you will experience a very unique aquatic park. You will be swimming and snorkeling in a natural inlet, a warm mix of salt and fresh water. The inlet is filled with unique tropical fish and flora. Research is being constantly carried out to learn more about marine life and ecological maintenance of the native species. There is also the opportunity to swim with dolphins."

"Ooh!" said Body, who was draped over Dave the groomsman. "I love dolphins!"

"Most of you look to be wearing comfortable attire,[23] but does everyone have their bathing suit, extra clothes, and natural sunscreen?"

---

23. Including me, in the navy blue crochet-detailed tankini, swim skirt, and coordinating cover-up I'd picked up for a song last August, when stores are most eager to get rid of summer leftovers. Websites also have abundant inventory on sale, if you're brave enough (or standardly-built enough) to buy a bathing suit online. The second best month to buy a bathing suit is May, when prices drop because shoppers begin to spend more time outdoors and less time at their local retailers.

"Natural sunscreen?" asked Face, who was showing a lot more body than anyone else in a sheer cover-up over some sort of iridescent bikini.

"To maintain the ecological balance, the only sunscreens allowed are those that are free of environmental pollutants."

"But how do we—?"

"There are a number of different varieties available in our gift shop. You may also trade your bottle for the chemical-free sunscreen at the water park for a small charge per person and trade back as you leave for the day."

"That's pretty cool," Liam said.

"Really cool," FJ agreed.

Frank sighed under his breath. I was already wondering if it would be better to buy a bottle for the family to share or "rent" sunscreen for the day. It would depend on the per-person charge, the price per bottle, and how often we'd need to apply it throughout the day ...

"Also be sure to bring credit cards or cash with you to buy souvenirs, purchase optional activities, or buy the photos from your visit."

"What about snacks and lunch?" Hair's husband asked.

"The lunch buffet is open from eleven thirty until closing and is included in your admission, along with snorkeling gear, floating tires, and life jackets for those of you who want to wear them."

"That sounds a lot less relaxing than I expected," someone said.

"There are also plenty of hammocks and deck chairs."

"Sweet!"

"Ummm ..." Eloise said, "what about the sharks?"

"Rest assured, everyone," Jorge said as the word *sharks* echoed ominously through the lobby, "an underwater fence extends across the inlet entrance, so you're perfectly safe from seafaring predators."

As the tour bus pulled up with a squeal and a hydraulic hiss, I couldn't help but notice his emphasis was on the word *seafaring*.

Sensing an opportunity to ask a question or two without a camera or crew around to eavesdrop, I hung back while my family got in line to board the bus.

"So you're saying we should be more worried about creatures roaming the land?" I asked Jorge.

"There is abundant wildlife to spot along the trails surrounding the water park, but I've never heard of a guest encountering anything dangerous."

"That's not what I mean."

Jorge, despite his superior command of the English language, gave me a look of incomprehension nearly identical to Zelda's.

"Jorge," I asked, "do you think Alejandro's death was—"

"A tragic accident," he said, both loudly and emphatically.

"Tragic for sure, but there are a few people who seem to believe it might not have been an accident," I whispered back.

"What have you heard?" he asked.

"That he was too strong a swimmer to have drowned, for one thing."

"Tequila," he said, repeating a familiar refrain. "She whispers sweet lies."

Yeah, I'd heard that one too.

———

"*Hola*," the driver said as I boarded the bus.

"No Felipe today?" I asked.

"*Mañana*," the driver said.

Seeing as everything else had been laid out so systematically, Felipe, who'd already played his role where Alejandro's death was concerned, had to have been tucked away for a more opportune on-camera moment.

"Pick up any interesting information from Jorge?" Frank asked as I took my seat on the full bus.

"Nothing in particular," I said.

Since Frank had already drunk the Agua Fresca (or whatever the south-of-the-border equivalent of Kool-Aid was called), there was no point in explaining that nothing had happened beyond Jorge parroting the lines I'd already heard. Clearly he was in on whatever was going on.

Frank was actually right, though. It was far too twisted to think that Geo, Anastasia, or anyone else would not only have Alejandro killed, but then have the brazen nerve to have us conduct an investigation into their crime.

Which, as far as I could tell, was exactly why they figured they could get away with it.

I had to admit the whole thing was sort of brilliant—except for the part where they might actually have killed someone. And that they might then encourage us to implicate an innocent man or woman in a crime he or she hadn't committed...

But, other than the boys' chance run-in with a waiter who'd tipped them off to Alejandro's aquatic prowess and seeming sobriety, what hard evidence was there for us to zero in on a real, live suspect? Ominous words from the mysterious Sombrero Woman? Zelda's impassioned *ten cuidado* (be careful)? The smoothie guy's warning about sharks? (He was just messing with Trent, right?) There was no reason to believe anything I heard from the rest of my force-fed list of suspects/confidantes, each of whom had a unique spin on Alejandro's death and even more tenuous thoughts on who could possibly be involved:

There was Antonio, the heir apparent to the timeshare sales office, whose pointed on-camera mention of the Enrique-Elena-Alejandro love triangle only served to make him look that much more suspicious.

Chef Benito, who'd admitted he felt Alejandro was too strong a swimmer to drown, but who was called into question the next day by one of his staff saying he had a temper.

Enrique, who *couldn't think of any one particular person* who might want Alejandro dead.

Jorge, who I stupidly assumed might be willing to answer a candid question.

And finally Elena, who, despite her own issues with her husband, couldn't imagine *who would want to kill Alejandro, of all people.*

As we headed toward the water park, Frank made a *we're even happy off-camera* show of slipping his arm around my shoulder.

"I like that bathing suit and cover-up on you," he said.

As if on cue, my head began to throb.

While our driver, who didn't seem to speak much English, whistled along to Spanish pop music, I closed my eyes and willed myself not to think about the how, why, and what-was-in-store of it all. I focused instead on the low hum of the engine, the balmy mid-morning in coastal Mexico, and the snippets of mundane conversation from the kids, seated in front of me:

"Do you want to try the zip line or the cliff diving first?"

"Ivan says—"

"Does every one of your sentences have to start with *Ivan says*?"

"If you're going to be like that, I'm not going to tell you what he said was the most fun …"

To my left, I heard giggles followed by a conspicuous silence I assumed had to be from Body and Dave the groomsman.

"She's all over him," one of her sisters confirmed from behind me. "Totally."

"This time it's your job to pick up the pieces when it all falls apart."

"I say it's Stasia's turn."

"She'll still be honeymooning when he stops returning her texts, or whatever it is he does when his vacation fling is over."

"Ladies," said a decidedly louder, distinctly East Coast voice from behind them. "You're the sisters of the TV bride, right?"

"We are," one of them said.

I turned slightly, opened an eye, and glanced behind me as the older redheaded woman I'd seen various times around the resort peered between their headrests.

"I'm just curious," she said. "Did you get your water park tickets for sitting through that timeshare nonsense too?"

"My sister gave them to us as bridesmaids gifts."

"Good for you," she said. "I was promised two tickets for going to the presentation, but once I said no thanks to a timeshare, they tried to pull a bait-and-switch by giving me miniature golf coupons instead."

"Really?"

"I mean, it's a shame what happened to the manager, but I have to say, I felt like tossing him in the pool myself," she said. "All due respect, of course."

"Of course."

"If you don't mind my asking, how much did they want you girls to put down for a place?"

"My husband hashed out the numbers with our salesman while I was in the restroom," Hair said, "so I don't know."

"I told my salesman that I'm a single mom in the midst of a divorce and I couldn't begin to think about a down payment on a timeshare until things are finalized," Face said.

"And he took no for an answer?"

"After a while," Face said with a nervous laugh.

"They have quite a reputation where hard-selling is concerned," the redhead went on.

"Really?" one of the sisters said with disinterest.

"My salesman asked me what I could afford for a down payment. I gave him such a low number, I figured he'd laugh. Instead, he started crunching numbers to make it work. That's when I began saying no until he took me seriously."

"Glad it worked out for you in the end," Face said.

"Listen to this warning from one of the travel sites," the red-headed woman said, not getting the hint the sisters wanted to be done chatting:

My husband and I went on vacation to Hacienda de la Fortuna last year. The moment we arrived, we were seated with a private concierge who talked to us about golf, lobster dinners on the beach, and a fantastic water park. When we expressed interest, this concierge told us we could enjoy these excursions and opportunities once we completed the timeshare tour. I explained we had no desire to spend any portion of our vacation listening to timeshare information. She continued to pressure us, became extremely rude, and would not answer many of our questions. Unfortunately, we had to go through her to book any activities we wanted to participate in for the rest of the weekend. Each time, she was rude and had trouble booking the tours we wanted to take. DON'T go to this place if you want a timeshare-free vacation.

"That's terrible," Face said.

"I mean, our salesperson was kind of out-of-sorts yesterday, but we assumed it was because of the accident," Hair said.

"You shouldn't assume," the woman said. "Listen to this…"

I almost felt sorry for the sisters as the woman assaulted them with additional comments from whatever conversation thread she'd Googled.

There was major pressure to buy right then…

When we said no, the salesman, our former best buddy, became a bully. He actually said, "So you're telling me you never plan to travel again?"

As the woman rambled on and on, the annoyance, stress, and lack of sleep must have gotten to me because I started to feel particularly sleepy. The last thing I heard was, *I asked the salesman for his card so my wife and I could think about it and call him back. His response: Visa, Mastercard, or American Express are the only cards I'm interested in.*

I opened my eyes a half-hour later to the screech of hydraulic brakes. Momentarily unsure who or where I was, I reentered reality from the midst of one of those jumbled nap dreams in which Geo was urging me to jump into bubbling, churning water.

¡Agua caliente! he yelled. *¡Viva la agua caliente!*

SIXTEEN

DESPITE WAKING UP TO real live Geo standing outside the bus waiting to escort us through the VIP entrance (and wearing green and white tiger-striped swim briefs with a coordinating *Family Frugalicious* tank top) the water park, quite literally, blew me away.

Even with the description we'd been given, I still pictured miles of hot concrete and towering pale blue water slides that promised a cheap thrill and an epic water wedgie. Instead of a man-made, kitschy theme park, however, I found myself marveling at majestic beauty that could only be the work of Mother Nature. The lagoon, as Jorge called it, was an enormous inlet of impossibly blue water surrounded by lush jungle. The shark-protection fence on the ocean side (which featured a view that went on for miles) was capped by an expansive floating footbridge connecting the commercial segment of the resort to the activities on the other side.

"And you can't even see the walking paths, the animal sanctuary, or all of the smaller inlets," Geo said, handing out *Family Frugali-*

cious tank tops to all of us as well as the various wedding guests who'd come along.

"Clever," Frank said, examining the capital Fs that morphed into dollar signs.

"Think of them as a thank-you gift for the extended duty."

Meaning he'd brought them along in anticipation of giving them out to us this morning?

"We saw a place in town that made up T-shirts and thought they would add a little something special to today's shoot," Geo said, seemingly reading my mind. "So put them on. It's time to get cracking."

————

Wearing our entirely conspicuous tank tops and collecting a growing crowd of gawkers, we ticked off our first scenes and shots, all of which seemed to be geared more toward promoting the water park than looking for who might have information about Alejandro's demise. Then we worked our way down the day's call sheet.

9:30: Orientation turned out to be an informative, if somewhat dry, overview of the habitats, conservation efforts, sustainability, and other related aspects of the park with the head naturalist.

At 9:50, a camera captured us applying our specially purchased natural sunscreen (a better deal for our family than the $5 per person fee, I explained to the camera,[24] plus we'd probably need more sunscreen than I'd packed if our vacation kept being extended by this go-nowhere investigation) and receiving our snorkels, face masks, flippers, and complimentary life jackets.

---

24. Vacationers can easily fall into price traps and high convenience charges while they are trying to relax, but those dollars add up! Be ready to crunch numbers even in paradise.

Eloise perked up when Ivan arrived, but she was slightly less enthused to discover he was only escorting us for certain unguided portions of the day, and that the *10:05: Group snorkeling adventure* included fish.

Despite Eloise's general distaste for nonhuman creatures, we proceeded to spend forty-five magical, unimaginably colorful minutes swimming among nearly ninety marine species, including angelfish, parrotfish, snappers, groupers, and puffer fish. With no sign of anything more lethal than Geo in neon swim trunks, Eloise grudgingly agreed with me that the fish were beautiful and I found I began to share Eloise's impatience about having some alone time with Ivan. After all, I needed her to ask him at least a few of the questions from the list I'd given her so I could figure how he fit into all of this. I wanted to know what Alejandro was really like, whether he drank or not, what was up with his wife and Enrique, and how everyone was reacting to his death when the camera crews weren't around.

Not to mention the most important question of all ...

"You know that note Alejandro had you deliver to me?" I managed to whisper on the fly as we headed en masse toward the manatee habitat for our next camera shot.

"Yup," Ivan said, shaking water out of his dreadlocks.

"Did he ask you to deliver notes like that often?"

"Like, other notes to prospective timeshare owners?"

"Exactly," I said, thankful he'd phrased the question so I could answer without blushing.

"Only once," he said looking suddenly pensive. "And it was kind of freaky."

"How so?"

"I gave it the woman when her husband was beside her. They read it together and he seemed to get super annoyed."

"How so?"

"Hey, Maddie," Geo said, sidling up beside us with his usual impeccable timing. "Frank is supposed to feed the manatees in this shot, but he suggested you do it together, which I think is a terrific idea."

A better idea would have been to let Ivan answer my question, but since Geo began to walk with us, it was clear that wasn't going to happen.

"And Ivan, I need you to head over to the bike rental area and make sure everything is set up for the cycling shoot."

"You got it," Ivan said.

And other than leaving behind a lingering trace of patchouli, he was off and running.

Twenty minutes later, Frank and I had been given a quick tutorial by the manatee handler and were busy meeting, feeding, and frolicking in the water alongside the manatee couple as though we were out on some sort of aquatic double date—a date where one couple was mated for life and the other just until their show got canceled ... or until someone in charge was arrested for murder.

There was no way of knowing whether the former or the latter was more likely.

————

The group bike tour had us pedaling across the floating footbridge and winding around various inlets through the jungle on a narrow mangrove-lined path. While the excursion was indescribably beautiful and ended with us parking our bikes and clipping in for a heart-pulsing zip line ride from a high cliff, over the water, and back toward the park's central plaza, the most notable thing that had happened since we'd arrived at the water park was that nothing had happened at all.

Not sleuthing-wise, anyway.

Frank had excused himself from the zip line (and his overwhelming fear of heights) by claiming he once again had an urgent need to use the men's room, but even he seemed somewhat wary about what wasn't going on as he met up with us at the main restaurant for lunch.

While I expected pizza, hot dogs, charred burgers, and, if I was lucky, a soggy pre-packaged salad or two, à la an American amusement park, I was delighted to discover yet another elaborate, multi-station, internationally themed buffet.

"No time or need to get in line," Geo said, leading us toward the camera crew who'd set up around a table that both overlooked the water and was set at the most advantageous lighting angle. "We just had plates made up for you."

"I was hoping for tacos today," Trent said. "I mean, when in Rome and all."

Eloise, pouty after being parted from Ivan again, rolled her eyes.

"No worries," Geo said. "If you don't have what you want at the table, we'll send someone to get it."

There were tacos, as well as taquitos, chile rellenos, and everything Mexican we could desire, along with pasta, gyros, fried rice, and cuisine from just about every other country I could think of. And there was way more than even the boys could possibly eat.

We were seated, the camera clicked on, and we were digging in, when a couple of Philip's law enforcement buddies just happened to chance by.

Frank gave me a pointed smug look as one of them lifted his glasses and looked over his shoulder as if to check that no one was within eavesdropping distance. (That was, aside from the camera and all the people watching from nearby tables.)

"We got up early and made a few inquiries with the *Federales*," he said, as though he'd been waiting his whole life to deliver such a line.

"And?" Frank asked.

"They certainly don't have the same procedures in place as we do." The other officer shook his head.

"Meaning what?" I asked.

"We tried to talk to someone about reconfirming the cause of Alejandro Espinoza's death. We asked about witnesses who could have seen or heard anything."

"And?"

"It was weird. No one seemed to want to say there was any possibility other than that he drowned."

"We even asked them straight out if a mistake could have been made."

"How did they answer?" FJ asked.

"And I quote: 'Too much tequila.'"

"She whispers sweet lies," I said to myself.

"Cut," Geo said, twisting his hair into a man bun. "Great job, but can we do another take without the facial expressions from Frank?"

I gave Frank a pointed smug look of my own. "Interesting that no one down at the police station will say anything."

"We were told not to expect much," Geo answered.

"And what about security cameras?" I asked.

"Not working around that particular pool area," one of the American officers said.

"Then we'll just have to try to confirm things another way, I guess," I said. "Do you suppose we'll have an opportunity to do a little more in the way of looking into things today while we're here?"

135

"Maddie, you know we gotta do things in the order that works best for our schedule, not necessarily how life happens," Geo said.

Frank nodded in agreement.

"But don't worry," Geo said with a wink. "The day is still young…"

———

"And action," Geo said as we stood in the front of the Dolphin Encounters line waiting for our *1:00: Meet, greet, and ride* on what I had to assume were not only one of the most intelligent but also the most patient creatures on the planet.

While the other camera crew shadowed Face, Hair, Body, Liam, Hair's husband Michael, and the parents of the bride and groom for their Dorsal Pull package (which promised *an exhilarating swim and spin around the aquarium holding onto the dorsal fin of a gentle, beautiful dolphin, and including a kiss good-bye with commemorative photo*), we were to have a "candid discussion" about our lunchtime revelations regarding the local police.

"What do you think it really means that no one down at the station would say anything?" I repeated, this time on camera and at Geo's instruction.

"Maybe they think Alejandro's death *was* accidental," Trent said.

"And they don't appreciate a bunch of gringo cops thinking they know better when maybe they don't," FJ added.

"Could be," Frank said. "But how can we not try to find out for sure before we leave town?"

Geo motioned for us all to nod in agreement and for me to pull out the updated version of the PEOPLE TO QUESTION spreadsheet Geo had written and stuffed into my pool bag.

"Your dad has a point," I said, modifying my line from *We're all in agreement, then*! I handed the spreadsheet to Frank to look at and pass around.

"I see that you want me to try and talk with Felipe and Enrique some more," Frank said, eyeing the names and which family member I (Geo) had assigned to question them. "But neither of them are here today."

"Nor are Benito, Jorge, or Elena, any one of whom could be key to figuring out what's going on," I said, rather pointedly.

FJ glanced at the list. "The only one who is around today that we could possibly talk to is—"

"Ivan," Eloise said. "And I already did."

"You did?" I asked. "When?"

"On the bike ride."

"Why didn't you say anything?"

She shrugged. "I guess there wasn't all that much to say."

"Did you ask him the questions I gave you?"

"I mean, I asked him what he thought about the whole Alejandro thing," she said fussing with the fringe on her bathing suit. "And everything."

"And …?"

"He said he just didn't know what to think."

"End of story?"

"We pulled up at the zip line and parked the bikes right after that."

"But that's all he said?" I persisted.

"That, and that we probably shouldn't talk about it anymore because the walls have ears," she said. "Which was kind of funny because we were in the jungle."

"Cut," Geo said. "That's great."

Eloise continued as though the camera was still rolling. "Isn't the person we really need to talk to that Sombrero Lady?"

"Exactly," Geo said. "Which is what I want all of you to focus on for the rest of the afternoon."

"Here?" Trent asked. "Why would she be here?"

"She wouldn't, but most people who work here live in town, and everyone seems to know everyone," Geo said. "If Eloise will ask Ivan a few more questions and the rest of you see what you can find out from everyone you run into, maybe we'll start to fill in a piece or two of this puzzle and locate the woman."

A nearby dolphin seemed to whistle in agreement.

Geo pointed us toward the aquarium. "Sounds to me like your next interviewee is ready to talk."

———

The dolphins definitely communicated, but I could only imagine they were saying something a lot more along the lines of *You take the heavy one this time* than *How much more evidence do you need before you accept that you're not going to find out what really happened to Alejandro?*

I certainly didn't need to speak dolphin to understand their series of disapproving clicks.

And their trainer, while friendly, pleasant, and informative, was from Florida, lived in some kind of hut outside of town with her boyfriend, and only spoke passable Spanish. In other words, she hadn't heard a word about Alejandro's death, suspicious or otherwise.

I wish I'd listened a little more closely as she explained the "foot push," however, because I soon found myself being raised to the water's surface by two dolphins, who lifted me up by the bottoms of my feet with their noses. Screaming first in terror and then in delight, I found my balance. The next thing I knew, they were propelling me across the surface of the dolphinarium.

The experience of riding upon such graceful agile creatures and entrusting them to whisk me safely around was pure joy.

That was, until I heard a rip and felt the lining of my priced-to-sell bathing suit begin to give way, right at the crochet detailing along the seams.

———

Luckily the tear was a lot smaller than it sounded and was at my waistline, as opposed to anywhere less strategic. Unluckily, since we were all in swimwear for the day, the wardrobe assistants were off enjoying the park and no one nearby seemed to have a safety pin.

On my way to the equipment van to locate someone else that might have one handy, I passed Anastasia's sisters seated on a bench in the midst of an on-camera confessional.[25]

"It completely blew my mind to be able to swim with the dolphins," Body said.

"I enjoyed it," Hair said, "but I'd really rather spend my day with a book on one of those hammocks."

"No surprises there," Face said.

"Dave and I plan to do everything," Body said with a giggle. "I mean, here at the park."

———

25. A commonly practiced type of reality TV interview segment where participants are captured away from the rest of the show's cast in a private booth or area where they are encouraged to speaking openly and honestly about other individuals and events taking place on the show.

"Just don't forget you've only known him for a few days, Sara," Hair said.

"We have the most amazing connection."

"Like the connection you felt with Mark?" Hair said.

"And Todd?" added Face.

"And what was that one guy's name before Todd?"

"Nico," Body said. "But—"

"We're really happy for you," Face said. "We really are."

"Stasia told me she picked him to be a groomsman specifically because she thought—"

"You two were perfect for each other?"

"Cut," the assistant director said.

"That's not what she told me," Face said, as though she hadn't heard the scene end.

"Oh? What did she tell you?" Body asked.

"She said she made Philip ask Dave to be in the wedding because he'd look good in the pictures."

"Well, he is really handsome, you have to admit."

"Yes, but he isn't even one of Philip's close friends," Hair said. "Stasia may have told you she was thinking about you, but we all know she was only thinking about how her wedding would look on TV."

"And she suggested you 'belonged together' because a hot weekend romance doesn't hurt the show's ratings," said Face.

"Maybe it will work out between us anyway," Body said, sounding more than a little deflated by her sisters.

"And maybe Stasia won't get pregnant and have her first baby during sweeps week while Mrs. Frugalicious *just happens* to be doing an episode on discount baby supplies."

"Here you go," a production assistant said, appearing beside me with two safety pins.

"Thanks," I said, as the sisters began to bicker about Anastasia, Dave, and the wedding in general. "So Dave isn't one of Philip's close friends?"

"Steve is Philip's best friend. But since he's not exactly telegenic, if you know what I mean, Anastasia had Philip ask Dave to stand up in the wedding and they had Steve get his online license so he could officiate."

"So he isn't really a reverend?"

She laughed. "He's a cop."

"Isn't that kind of sketchy?"

"No sketchier than half the things we do around here."

"Meaning what?" I asked, looking her straight in the eyes.

She looked down and shrugged. "Meaning that's just how things roll in reality TV."

———

"Where's Eloise?" I asked Frank, having visited the ladies' room to jerry-rig the lining of my bathing suit and then being sent to the aptly named Leap of Faith in time to watch my teenage sons jump off the highest cliff.

"She and Geo went to meet up with Ivan at the underwater caverns," said Frank, standing on the lowest ledge, white-knuckled and clutching a jagged piece of rock on the wall behind him. "Wish I were with them."

"Are you really going to jump?"

"Have to," he whispered, not daring to wipe the sweat dripping from his brow.

"Why didn't you tell Geo you're terrified of heights?" I asked, peering out at the sparkling blue water below.

"I tried," he said.

"Let me guess. That only made him more eager to have you jump?"

"It wasn't like that."

"Then how was it?" I asked as FJ came flying by us and landed in the inlet, emitting a delighted *whoop* as he emerged from beneath the water.

"I probably should have been more forceful about it," he said.

"Along with our desire to stay out of this crazy investigation and get out of Mexico ASAP?"

"Maddie, I believe you do what you have to for the show. I also believe we're doing the right thing by looking into things."

"For Alejandro or the ratings?"

"Why can't it be both?"

"Did you know Anastasia thought Philip's best friend Steve wasn't good looking enough to be part of a televised wedding party, so she basically recruited Dave and had Steve, who isn't even a reverend, officiate instead?"

"Can't say that it matters much to me right now," Frank said grasping the rocks even tighter.

"I suppose it doesn't matter to you that every single thing that's happened today has been completely scripted."

"You have to stop being so suspicious, Maddie."

Liam did a double flip from the highest cliff.

"Pretty sporty, I'd say," I commented as he barely made a splash entering the water.

"Sports-*minded*," he said. "But that was pretty good."

"Maybe you need to stop being so suspicious too."

"I can't think about anything else right now but what I need to do," he said squeezing his eyes closed. "What matters is that our show is a success …"

"Even if it means that an innocent person had to die?"

"The only person who's going to die is me."

"Hardly," I said. "And you're anything but innocent."

"Ready for your Leap of Faith, Frank?" the assistant director announced.

"I don't know if I can do this," Frank said, now visibly trembling.

"Me either," I said.

"See those people floating peacefully on inner tubes down there?" the assistant director said.

"Yes," Frank said, not looking.

"That's where we're headed next, so no worries."

"I'm so worried," Frank whispered.

"As am I," I said. "But, as you say, what choice do we have?"

"And, action …"

Without waiting for Frank's nod, I began to count.

"One, two …"

In lieu of saying *three*, I grabbed my almost-ex-husband's hand and jumped.

We plummeted toward the water in brain-numbing delight (me) and mortal terror (Frank). We both emerged from the drink at the same time. Frank was panicky and gasping for breath, but otherwise none the worse for wear. I was ready to climb back up the steps carved into the side of the rock and go again from a higher cliff. And I surely would have, were it not for my bathing suit, which had torn at the site of the safety pins and was now ripped all the way from armpit to hip.

———

"You're Mrs. Frugalicious!" one of the salesgirls in the water park gift shop exclaimed. "Right?"

"That's what they tell me," I said, holding my suit together with my right hand and offering my left for a shake.

"Told you so," she said to the other salesgirl. They both giggled. "This is so exciting!" Numero Uno said, in heavily accented English.

"I didn't realize anyone down here knew about the show."

"We have satellite TV."

"That's terrific," I said, appreciative of the show's growing audience, but not entirely certain I wanted fans witnessing my swimwear trials and tribulations.

"We heard you were coming to the water park today," Numero Dos said.

"And we were hoping we'd get to see you," Uno said with a nervous giggle. "But we didn't think you'd come into the store."

"When did you say you heard I was coming?"

"Saturday," Uno said.

"Not yesterday?"

"I was not working yesterday," she said.

Meaning the water park staff knew I was coming before I did? Why was I surprised?

"Can we have your autograph?"

"Sure," I said. "But maybe after I've picked a new suit? I don't exactly have a free hand."

"The bathing suits are right over there," Dos said, pointing to the back corner of the gift shop.

"We have a whole rack on sale," Uno said, with a conspiratorial wink.

"Perfect," I said, knowing my selection had just been limited by her expectation that I would never buy anything at full price, even in an emergency.[26]

Despite what seemed to be a few cute choices among the full-priced offerings, I went straight for the 20%-off rack and grabbed three bathing suits in slightly different styles, all with a hideous multicolored tropical leaf pattern featuring the water park's kissing dolphin logo embroidered on the center of the chest.

"They're cuter when you put it on," Numero Dos said.

"But it's too bad your bathing suit ripped."

"I have another one in black back at the hotel," I said as I closed the curtain to the dressing room. "But I need to get through today."

"You're staying at the Hacienda de la Fortuna?"

"I am," I said, feeling another uptick in my pulse. "How did you know?"

"My cousin's friend works there," she said. "Everyone was very excited about having your show at the hotel."

"How is she doing after what happened on Friday night?" I asked.

"What happened?" one of the girls asked.

"You haven't heard?" As the second girl launched into what had happened in Spanish, I listened, unsuccessfully, for familiar words and tried on a one-piece that was too tight in the hips and too loose in the bust.

---

26. Let's face it, resort gift shops are one of the least likely spots to save money. In fact, the mark-up can easily be double what you'd normally pay, so try not to forget that toothbrush or nail clippers and splurge instead on keepsakes that will forever remind you of that special vacation.

"Please tell your cousin to tell her friend I'm sorry," I finally said when there was a lull in the rapid-fire Spanish. "It must have been quite a shock."

"No need," she said, as I pulled off the suit and stepped into the next one. "My cousin said she couldn't stand the guy."

I pulled the straps up and quickly tugged open the curtain. "What?"

"Most everyone who works there hated him."

My heart was now thumping. "I only met him a few times, but he seemed really charming."

"To special guests, yes. My cousin said he ordered all the employees around like he owned the place."

"But practically everyone from the resort went to his wake and funeral," I said. "They were all in tears."

"Of course," she said. "Tears of joy."

So:

I didn't entirely buy Enrique and Elena's claim that everyone loved Alejandro.

I agreed it was entirely odd for a man, who, on the whole, watched what he drank and was a champion swimmer, to drown so quickly and easily in a familiar pool.

The investigation by the local police could only be called suspiciously rudimentary.

And now the salesgirls not only knew I'd be at the water park before I did, but that *everyone* except for the people on my potential suspect list hated Alejandro?

My head was swimming as Uno wrung up my purchase, complete with an additional 10% VIP discount *just because.*

I figured I'd gotten away from my nonspontaneous day and chanced into the gift shop all on my own, but with her *blasé* revelation that an impossibly large number of people had a motive to kill

146

Alejandro, I felt sure my wardrobe malfunction was just as choreographed as a Super Bowl halftime show, just like everything since we'd arrived at the water park.

Make that, since we'd arrived in Mexico.

I mean, if Zelda could slip a note under my pillow, how hard could it be for someone else to sneak in and snip a seam on my bathing suit that would surely rip at the water park?

Wouldn't I have to go into the resort store for a new bathing suit and a chance conversation where I would pick up exactly the information we needed to substantiate the mysterious Sombrero Lady's claims?

Just like Geo had urged us to do with our afternoon ...

As I signed two autographs and said good-bye to the friendly, overinformative salesgirls in my new suit (ugly but functional), I had to give Geo credit. He'd organized a glorious day filled with primo promotional footage, orchestrated a perfectly timed absence for my Leap of Faith, and in one brilliant off-camera shot (assuming there weren't hidden cameras placed in the gift shop), introduced the largest pool of potential suspects yet.

I had little doubt about the "reality" of the situation, but I took some comfort in that fact that with so many possibilities, there was no way anyone could make me narrow down the killer to some poor innocent for the sake of the show. Not in a few days, or weeks, or however long they intended to keep us there fake investigating, anyway.

Since my best course of action—really, my only course of action—for the remainder of the day was to follow directions according to the schedule, I headed toward Frank and the boys, who were floating on inner tubes in the gentle current of the freshwater river that fed the inlet. Seeing as the call sheet had us on an *afternoon snack break* and then slated for a shot in which we were to *relax and*

147

confer in the hammock area after our float, I didn't expect much more in the way of the unexpected.

I was halfway to the inner tube stand when the boys and Liam came running in my direction.

"Hurry," FJ said, grabbing my hand.

"I thought we were supposed to be floating on the river," I said as he pulled me in the opposite direction.

"We were," Trent said.

"Where are we going?" I asked, already out of breath despite the treadmill wind sprints I'd been doing to make sure I looked as bathing suit–worthy as a middle-aged mom of teenage boys could possibly look on camera.

"To the underwater caves," Liam said.

"Isn't that where Eloise is?

"That's why we're hurrying over there," FJ said.

"What's going on?"

"We're not sure," Frank said, catching up to us and then sprinting ahead.

"Did you hear from her?" I asked the boys.

"No way for her to contact us from in there," Trent said.

"Have we heard from anyone on the crew over there?"

"No, but—" FJ began.

"Someone drowned," our cameraman said as he passed by. "Or nearly so."

———

"Do you know what happened?" I asked one of the onlookers crowded onto the dock beside the entrance to the underwater caves.

He pointed to a nearby boat. "They just sent a bunch of divers and equipment down to help bring the people up."

"People?" I asked, my stomach now churning.

"How many people?" Frank asked, looking equally alarmed.

"We should know shortly," the man said.

Shortly was an endless eternity as we stood staring at the water, jumping at the slightest rustle or fleck of color from a passing fish.

A million seconds later, bubbles floated up from beneath the water and two people emerged. One was a water park employee in scuba equipment. The second wore some sort of weird breathing apparatus.

My heart stopped when I spotted a blue-fringed bikini.

Frank pushed through the crowd and dove into the water.

He reached Eloise just as her rescuer removed what looked like an astronaut's helmet from her head and handed it to someone on the boat.

"I'm okay," I saw her say to Frank as they helped her over to the dock.

FJ, Trent, and I rushed over to meet them. Liam kept a respectful distance.

"I'm okay," she repeated to us as we helped to lift her out of the water. "That breathing thing was just to help get me out of there."

"Are you sure?" I asked, grabbing a nearby towel and wrapping it around her shoulders.

"I wasn't hurt," she said, despite the tears filling her eyes.

"We were *so* worried," FJ said.

Trent nodded in agreement. "What happened?"

"I'm still not sure," she said in a shaky voice. "We were going through this tunnel to an underground cavern. I went in first, came up from underwater, and waited. Neither of them turned up behind me."

"Neither of them?" I asked.

"Ivan ..." She dug her head into her brother's shoulder.

"And ...?" I prompted.

"Geo," she whispered.

"Geo was with you?" I asked.

"He was wearing the GoPro or whatever it's called to get underwater footage."

"Not the cameraman?" Frank asked.

"Geo really wanted to check out the caves, so he went instead."

Frank and I exchanged meaningful glances. "This isn't good," I said.

"No." Eloise began to cry in earnest. "I'm afraid ..."

"I'm afraid too," I whispered to Frank. "If Geo was down there with them, and now Ivan is ..."

More commotion sounded as bubbles began breaking the water's surface. Everyone stopped speaking and stared at the water, waiting. A diver and what appeared to be Ivan wearing a breathing apparatus identical to Eloise's emerged from beneath the surface.

"He certainly doesn't look dead," Frank said.

"He's definitely alive," Trent said, as Ivan removed his oxygen helmet.

"Thank God!" Eloise said.

"Doesn't look so great though," FJ said.

Ivan was, as FJ noted, shaky and pale as his rescuer helped him over to the dock and directed him toward a waiting medic.

"You okay?" he asked, stopping to hug Eloise first.

She nodded. "What about you?"

"A little shaken up, but I'll be fine."

"I was waiting and waiting and neither of you showed up," she sobbed. "The next thing I knew, there were people in diving equipment and I had no idea what happened to you or Geo."

"This is all my fault," Ivan said. "I wanted Eloise to see this one really amazing cave, but you have to hold your breath to get there, so I sent her in first to keep an eye on her. Geo was supposed to go next, but he insisted he go last so he could get some video." Ivan's voice grew more raspy. "I don't know how, but he went into the wrong tunnel."

The water began to began to bubble a third time.

"He was down there a while before I found him…"

"Geo!" we all said in unison as he emerged from the water flanked by two divers.

He managed the weakest of waves before they helped him toward us, not removing his breathing gear until he'd been taken out of the water.

The moment he was on the dock, everyone began firing off questions.

How long were you under water?

Were you really stuck in there?

You had to be terrified.

Did you get any footage?

"No questions right now," said a *paramédico*. "Everyone that's not family needs to disperse."

"Something pulling on my leg…" Geo finally whispered after everyone other than us was guided off the dock. He patted his head as if questioning his memory and checking for the underwater camera that was no longer there. "So twisted around…"

"We checked him out for bite marks," one of the divers said to the medic.

"Anything?"

The diver shook his head in a way that told me encounters with unfriendly wildlife weren't as unheard of as Jorge had insisted.

"Thank you," Geo gasped, grabbing Ivan's hand. "You saved my life…"

SEVENTEEN

Geo was loaded onto a stretcher and rolled away to an awaiting ambulance.[27] Eloise and Ivan were taken to the water park infirmary to be checked out more extensively, just to be sure they didn't need any further medical assistance. Frank, the boys, and I were escorted to a shady grove outside the first-aid building to "relax" until they were released.

Despite the lush scenery, comfy hammocks, and abundant shade trees, I could honestly say relaxing wasn't even a remote possibility.

"I was sure I had this all worked out," I said, anxious for Eloise to rejoin us and get back to the relative safety of our hotel suite. "Now I have no idea what to think."

"I don't want to say I told you so," Frank said, "but—"

"But you didn't think there was anything to this whole situation at all?"

---

27. Illnesses and accidents can happen, and the resulting medical bills can be overwhelming. Before you travel abroad, be sure to check your coverage; if it's not adequate, consider taking out a short-term travel health insurance policy.

"I never said that," Frank said. "I said there was a logical solution."

I didn't have to look at him like he was an idiot because both boys and the two assistants assigned to get us safely back to the hotel did it for me.

"Any word on the missing GoPro camera yet?" FJ asked.

"They're looking for it now," one of the assistants said.

"And I'm sure they're talking more to Ivan about what he saw," Trent said.

Everyone nodded in agreement.

"I can't believe someone tried to take out Geo," one of the assistants said.

"What are we going to do?" the other assistant said.

"Drink heavily?" I said as waiter appeared pushing a mobile frozen margarita machine. "At least for the moment."

"Sounds like a plan," Trent said.

"Trent!" we all said in unison.

"Kidding," he said, but not convincingly enough for my taste.

The strawberry margaritas, however, were as tasty as could be. And given the events of the afternoon, they were necessary medicine for the of-age crowd. This included Eloise, who exited the infirmary just as the waiter filled cups for the boys from the nonalcoholic side of machine.

Frank hugged her tightly. "How are you doing, sweetie?"

"I was annoyed that they insisted on checking me out," she said, accepting hugs from the rest of us, as well as a full-strength marg. "But it's a good thing they did."

"Why?" I asked, my alarm growing. "Are you hurt, after all?"

"I told you, I'm fine," she said. "But you told me to find things out, so find things out I did."

"Meaning what?"

153

"Meaning everyone in there was talking about what happened."

"In English?" FJ asked.

"Mostly Spanish, but Ivan translated a few things I couldn't understand," she said smugly, as though he'd only filled in a word or sentence or two.

"What did they say?" I asked.

"A bunch of stuff about how crazy it was, and how nothing like this has ever happened here before." She waited for the waiter to roll the cart out of earshot, and whispered, "And you know how everyone supposedly loved Alejandro at Hacienda de la Fortuna?"

Everyone nodded but me.

"Well," she said, taking a dramatic sip, "one of the nurses knows someone who works at Hacienda de la Fortuna and she said that no one's surprised he's dead."

"Because everyone actually hated him?" I said.

"You already knew?"

"The store clerks at the gift shop told me they'd heard he was a tyrant around the resort."

"Why didn't you tell us that, Mom?" Trent asked.

"I really didn't have the chance until now." I felt badly to have preempted Eloise, who seemed disappointed not to have the scoop, but it seemed high time to feel out the assistants around us, who had to have more information than us, the on-air talent. "The clerks also mentioned they knew we were coming to the park today."

"We gave advance notice to the park that we'd be here taping either yesterday or today," one assistant said, too quickly. "For weather reasons."

"Don't you find it curious that I happened to rip my bathing suit, happened into the gift shop, and two salesgirls not only happened to know where I was staying, but happened to tell me that basically anyone could be a suspect?"

"There was nothing on the call sheet or anywhere else about a setup in the gift shop," an assistant said. "Not that I know of, anyway."

"Me either," the other one added. "And Geo was determined to stay on schedule by having the investigation wrapped up by the end of the day tomorrow."

"And just how was he planning to do that?" I asked.

The assistant shrugged. "He just said he had things all figured out, somehow."

"I wonder if he still feels that way."

"We gotta figure out who did this to him," the assistant murmured as we all looked toward the entrance to the park where Geo had so recently been loaded into a waiting *ambulancia* and taken to the hospital.

"When they find the camera, I bet we'll be able to see something," FJ said.

"*If* they find the camera," Eloise said. "It was pitch black in that area and Ivan told me there are underwater currents that could have carried a device that small and deposited it just about anywhere."

"How is Ivan doing?" Trent asked.

"Physically, he's fine," she said.

"But otherwise?"

"He's super upset about Geo."

"He's a hero in my book," Frank said, looking pointedly at me. "He saved the man's life."

Eloise smiled. "That's what I kept telling him, but he kept insisting that he'd dropped the ball by letting Geo follow behind him."

"That's ridiculous."

"Does he remember seeing anything when he realized Geo wasn't behind him and turned back to check?" I asked.

"The security people were just starting to interview him about that when I left."

"And?"

"He said all he remembers is looking back, not seeing Geo, somehow finding him, and getting him to the surface before it was too late."

"Too bad," Trent said.

"He definitely thinks some*one*, and not some*thing*, grabbed Geo, though."

"Why's that?"

"He's sure now that Alejandro was murdered," she said in a whisper, checking again to make sure no other park guests were close enough to hear us. "He said he was suspicious before, but once this happened, he said he was sure the truth was being swept under the rug."

"Maybe because everyone hated Alejandro?" Trent asked.

"He had to have known that already though, right?" FJ said.

"Ivan said people grumbled, but that Alejandro was always cool to him."

"Did he say why everyone we talked to up until this afternoon claimed to love the man and couldn't imagine that everyone else didn't feel the same way?"

"Maybe because they're all managers and stuff?" FJ suggested.

"They either hated him or were related to him," Eloise said.

"What?" I said.

"Ivan told me that pretty much everyone in a position of respon-sibility at the resort is a brother, sister, or some sort of distant cousin."

EIGHTEEN

The first thing I did when we got back to our suite (after bolting the door, of course) was run into my room, open the bureau drawer, and check the other bathing suit I'd brought for loose seams, tiny rips, or any point of potential malfunction.

Nothing.

The second thing I did was open the leather-bound welcome binder from the Hacienda de la Fortuna and begin to scan for names, starting with the general welcome letter.

It was signed: *Enrique Espinoza Garcia.*

Meaning Enrique and Alejandro Espinoza were, in fact, related? I continued to leaf through the binder:

Assistant Manager of Resort Sales: Antonio Espinoza Lopez
Bell Captain: Jorge Lopez
Head Chef: Benito Flores Olveras
Wedding Planner: Elena Flores Espinoza

The various combinations of the last names Espinoza, Olveras, Garcia, Flores, and Lopez repeated on from *Head Groundskeeper: Ricardo Flores* to *CFO of De la Fortuna LLC: Esteban Garcia Cortez.*

I unlocked the safe, grabbed my laptop, booted it up, and Googled "Spanish last names."

The first website I clicked on seemed to explain the commonality between names: In Spanish, a last name is not called a last name but an *apellidos*, which translates into "surnames" because there are often two of them. The two surnames are referred to as the first *apellido* and the second *apellido*.

Take, for example, a man named Luis Valdez Molina. Valdez would be the first surname of his father. His second surname, Molina, would be the first surname of his mother (in US terms—his mother's maiden name).

His father: Jose Valdez Rivas

His mother: Josephina Molina Salas

Him: Luis Valdez Molina

When Luis gets married, he keeps his name as is. His wife (let's say Rosa) keeps her first surname (her father's first) and often takes husband's name as her second surname. Sometimes the word 'de' is added between the two surnames to show that the second surname is her husband's.

So, if her dad is Juan Barrera Rivera and her mom is Juanita Leon Pérez, Rosa's birth name would be Rosa Barrera Leon. After marriage, Rosa becomes Rosa Barrera de Valdez or Rosa Barrera Valdez.

As in, Luis Valdez Molina and his lovely wife Rosa Barrera Valdez.

Whether she changes her second surname to Valdez or retains Leon, Rosa becomes Mrs. Barrera. This is very different from the United States, where if the change occurs at marriage, the woman assumes the husband's last name. Luis is Mr. Valdez, while his wife Rosa is Mrs. Barrera.

Luis and Rosa's children's apellidos *will be Valdez Barrera.*

In the United States, the family as a group is usually addressed by the last name of the husband. In Hispanic circles, the family is addressed by the combination of the first surname of each of the partners in the marriage, which is the same as the surnames of the children of the marriage. So the family would be referred to as the Valdez Barreras. This makes it clear that it is the family formed by the union of a Valdez and a Barrera, and it also differentiates this family from their parents' households (the Valdez Molinas and the Barrera Leons).

I logged off the Internet, opened my spreadsheet, and attempted something of a family tree by cross-referencing the members of the various clans.

Espinoza = Enrique, Alejandro, Antonio, Elena (marriage)

Lopez = Antonio, Jorge, Alejandro, Esteban (CFO)

Flores= Benito, Elena

Garcia = Enrique, Esteban (CFO)

The director of pool safety was a Cortez and the manager of the salon was a Lopez. As I looked for, but couldn't find, any mention of our driver Felipe or his last name, I had to wonder why so many of the higher-level employees seemed to be close relatives. While the fact that they were related might explain why they were unaware of the pervasive hatred toward their sibling/cousin/uncle/whatever Alejandro was to them, how was it that no one seemed eager to question the unusual circumstances surrounding the drinking and drowning death of a family member?

I opened the SUSPICIOUS BEHAVIOR spreadsheet that I'd hidden under the heading SHOPPING TIPS 101 and glanced through all the entries, starting with Alejandro's sudden and prominent appearance at the beginning of the shoot on down to the shooting schedule extension and budget increase with a single phone call to execs about an "accidental" death. Seeing as almost every entry pointed to someone associated with *The Family Frugalicious*, I added an entirely new subsection below it entitled FAMILY CONNECTION. I managed to type in only one word (*Why*) before there was a knock on the bedroom door.

"Maddie," Frank said, popping his head in, "there's a police officer out here to talk to us."

"I see," I said, quickly closing the spreadsheet file.

I put the computer back in the safe, reset the combination, and ventured out in the living room to see the same police officer who'd first responded to the scene of the crime on Friday night. The very same officer who'd also been at Alejandro's funeral on Sunday.

While he questioned us about the incident at the water park, detailed the extra attention that would be given to the resort and all of its guests while they were getting to the bottom of what was going on, and gave us his assurance we could rest easy knowing that no stones would remain unturned where the incident with Geo was concerned, all I could see was his nametag, which I'd paid absolutely no attention to during either of our last meetings.

Garcia Lopez.

NINETEEN

DESPITE STARTING THE DAY thinking I had everything figured out and ending the day full of questions about everything but the fact that something was rotten in the state of *Dinamarca*, I was out cold the moment my head hit the pillow Monday night. I woke Tuesday morning from a dreamless, saturation-point sleep to the smell of coffee and stumbled out toward the kitchenette. Frank was standing in the living room.

"Good morning, Sleeping Beauty," he said, without any trace of a fairy tale lilt, and certainly not for my benefit given that Anastasia Chastain-Stone stood beside him.

"What are you doing here?" I blurted, not yet awake enough for proper decorum.

She pointed at plate filled with assorted baked goods. "Brought you breakfast."

"Aren't you're supposed to be honeymooning?"

She glanced at her sparkling engagement ring/wedding band combo for the briefest of seconds. "It looks like it's gonna be a bit more of a working honeymoon than I'd anticipated."

My blood pressure went into instant hyperdrive. "You're here because Geo—"

"Is going to be okay," she said quickly. "And sooner rather than
later. At least I hope."

"Meaning what?"

"They're moving him out of intensive care as soon as possible."

"He's in intensive care?"

"They put him on a respirator last night, but they've got him
stabilized now."

"Dear God," I said, beelining for the coffee, where I filled a mug
and helped myself to a big gulp without bothering with cream or
sugar. "Please tell me you've been called in to expedite the process of
getting us the hell out of here."

"In a manner of speaking," she said.

"Which means?"

"Well, we can't just pack up and leave without Geo."

"Not all of us, of course," I said, over the flush of a toilet in the
kids' bathroom. "But, seeing as he's on the road to recovery, and my
children's safety is of a certain amount of concern to me ..."

"Maddie, we're absolutely safe," Frank said. "You heard the police officer last night."

"By police officer, don't you mean Alejandro's cousin?" I said.
Anastasia nodded.

"Wait. So you already know they're all related?"

"The Hacienda de la Fortuna is a family-run corporation," she
said. "And this is apparently a small town, particularly where the
more prominent families are concerned."

"Then you don't find it suspicious and more than a little scary
how quickly Alejandro's death was swept under the rug?" I asked,

borrowing heavily from Ivan. "Particularly by his relative or relatives in the police department?"

"We seem to have a real mystery on our hands," she said. "And seeing as the first flight we could get anyone on isn't until Thursday morning—"

"You've got to be kidding," I said.

Anastasia flashed a smile fraught with possibility and that telltale reporter-on-the-trail-of-a-hot-story glow I knew only too well.

Frank's smile was no less luminous. "Great TV is not about shying away from danger."

"By pretending to investigate like we did all day yesterday?" I asked, almost as annoyed by Frank's devotion to the party line as I was worried about being in the thick of yet another murder.

"The setups and shots were planned in advance," Anastasia said, "not your investigation into what happened to Alejandro."

"Not according to what I heard," I said. "Geo planned to have things wrapped up, with a suspect in tow, by tonight."

"Wouldn't that be great," she said wistfully. "An episode in the can and back on my honeymoon by tomorrow…"

"Assuming no one else gets—"

"They won't," Anastasia said, cutting me off.

I looked into her calculating cobalt blue eyes. "And how can you make a promise like that?"

"Philip has agreed to head up our security detail," she said.

"And we'll have an officer and the camera crew watching the kids at all times," Frank added.

I looked from Stasia to Frank and back again. "Level with me," I said.

"Maddie!" said Frank, giving me the don't say-anything-that-might-compromise-our-career-come-hell-or-high-water glare.

"Shoot," she said.

"What did Geo know that he wasn't telling us?" I asked.

Frank looked immensely relieved that I'd refrained (for the moment, anyway) from voicing any of my more sinister suspicions where cast and crew were concerned.

Stasia shook her head. "I tried to find that out myself, but until he's off the ventilator, back in a regular room, and fully lucid, we're not going to know."

"Then what exactly is it you plan to have us do in the meantime?"

"Keep looking into everything and everyone who could possibly be involved."

"Which could be anyone, given that Alejandro wasn't exactly Mr. Popularity."

"Yes, that is a problem. So is the fact that the suspects Geo had originally listed all had alibis during the time of the water park incident."

"So those people are no longer suspects?"

She looked unsure for the first time. "They're worth requestioning before we spread out from there."

"Just like we did yesterday with Geo?"

"No cue cards this time," she said. "You ask whatever you need to ask."

"So the Espinoza/Lopez/Garcia clan has agreed to ad lib as necessary?"

"They want to find whoever is behind this as badly as we do," she said. "Which is why Philip himself is headed back to the police station to try and find out whatever else there is to know."

"His buddies didn't get much response the first time they tried to get involved," I said, doubtfully.

"Things have changed," she said.

"How so?"

"I'm back on set again," Anastasia said, reaching into her purse and handing us copies of the day's call sheet.

I looked over the schedule, which was admittedly much less regimented than Geo's, but still had us locating and interviewing the same people. After which, our investigation was to continue on as part of a Mayan ruins trip. Frank simply read the sheet, folded it, and tucked it into his pocket. Apparently he was a-okay with Stasia's plans.

"You really think we're going to come up with anything?" I said.

"Who knows? I'll settle for an Emmy," she said.

At least I knew she was being honest about one thing.

TWENTY

"MURDER IS DEADLY FOR business," Enrique admitted, looking nervous to even utter the words. "First it scares the guests away, then it gets around, and the next thing you know, we're running a loss-leader sale and praying we'll fill rooms."

"So you're admitting there was a cover-up?" I asked, uncued, just as Anastasia promised, but hardly impromptu. In fact, instead of seeking out various persons of interest and interviewing them on the fly, Frank had been sent to round everyone up and bring them to me where I was to *ask them anything* in the safety of a closed conference room.

"You must understand that nothing like this has ever happened here," Enrique said. "Given the circumstances and the fact there are TV cameras everywhere, we simply decided it was best for all concerned not to question the findings of the authorities."

"By *authorities*, don't you mean your cousin, Officer Garcia Lopez?"

"Third cousin."

"Close enough to suggest to me that he'd lie about a cause of death for the sake of the family enterprise."

"He didn't have to."

"Why's that?"

"The coroner made the final determination."

"Another cousin?"

Enrique looked down at his shoes. "Even more distant," he finally said. "The truth is, we really wanted to believe they were right. That was, until the incident at the water park."

"And now?"

He sighed. "Now, we can't ignore the facts."

———

"It certainly looks like someone finally had as much as they could take of Alejandro," Benito said, picking a dried piece of something off his otherwise immaculate chef's jacket.

"Which doesn't surprise you."

"No," he said.

"I understand a lot of people disliked the man."

Benito nodded. "Including me."

I was surprised to hear someone finally admit what I suspected just about all of them felt. "Because?"

"He was always up to something he shouldn't have been," Benito said. "You have no idea what he put my sister through."

Unfortunately, I had a bad feeling I just might. A piece clicked into place. "Elena is your sister."

———

"Ah, Benito," Elena said, looking somehow pale despite her beautiful, naturally bronze skin. "Such a good brother."

I nodded. "He seems to love you very much."

"And Alejandro was..." She paused. "Alejandro was many things."

"That's what I hear," I said, hoping to draw her out.

"He was just trying to fulfill expectations, make his family proud..." She put her head in her hands. "That's all either of us were ever trying to do."

———

"The truth about Alejandro?" Jorge said, as a sobbing Elena was escorted away by the ever-patient and understanding Enrique so she could collect herself enough for further conversation.

"Please," I said. "And I think we can all agree that *tragic accident* doesn't hold water at this point."

"Forgive me," he said. "I was simply doing my job as concierge to make sure your stay was as worry-free as possible."

"Of course," I said. "But you do think he was murdered?"

"I think he had some serious vices that made him susceptible to that sort of thing."

"Like?"

"He loved gambling and beautiful women," Jorge said with the hint of a knowing smile.

"And tequila," I said, fighting a flush in my cheeks.

"That's the thing," Jorge said. "He always kept his wits about him when he drank."

"But you implied..."

"Once again, I was trying not to alarm anyone—especially the esteemed Mrs. Frugalicious and her family."

"I'm more alarmed that so many people disliked him and no one would tell me."

Jorge's posture stiffened.

"Why exactly did people hate Alejandro?"

"I'll admit I've overheard a choice comment or three," he finally said. "Mostly it was because he was so ambitious—in all things."

"Perhaps you'd be so kind as to make a list for us of everyone you've heard complain about him and the various complaints you've heard?"

"Of course," he said, with practiced concierge agreement. "I'll get it to you ASAP."

"Thank you," I said. "And while you're at it, how about narrowing down a few key *sharks* that might also have been to the water park yesterday."

"I've already been thinking about that," Jorge said.

"And?"

"I always figured the most likely culprit would end up being a disgruntled guest. Like your husband, for example," he said, confirming that he was aware of the contents of the note he'd passed along.

And Frank would have been a good bet—were he were actually still my husband and as concerned about the sanctity of his marriage and the safety of his family as he was about his precious relationship with the TV network.

"That was, until whoever it was went after Geo," Jorge said before I could.

"And now?"

"Now I can only think there was an entirely different motive."

"Which is?"

"I know it's my job to have all the answers," he said, "but this time, we're all looking to you to solve this mystery."

169

———

"I said to be careful," Zelda, head of housekeeping, said through a translator. She shook her head. "No one listens to me."

"We're listening now," I said, waiting for the translator to repeat my words for her in Spanish. "Why did you think we needed to be careful?"

Fear filled the woman's face. "I can't say."

"Because?"

"Because it's bad luck to speak ill of the dead."

"Not if it keeps more people from ending up that way."

Zelda listened to the translator and seemed to consider my words for a moment.

"He no good," she finally said in English, crossing her arms across her chest. "He bad seed."

"How so?"

The translator took over once more. "Things always happened around him that shouldn't."

"Like?"

Zelda looked at me like I was exceptionally slow on the uptake. "One dead person. One almost dead person. Isn't that enough?"

"More than enough," I said. "But—"

She fired off something in rapid Spanish. "But bad news comes in threes," the translator provided. Zelda crossed herself. "Two down, one to go."

———

I wasn't superstitious. I also liked to think I wasn't stupid, but after the off-the-cuff soundbites I'd just gotten from the staff of Hacienda de la Fortuna, I had to wonder just how gullible everyone else thought I was.

Specifically, Anastasia.

While it was true that I'd been free to *ask whatever I was compelled to ask*, the answers all followed a similar theme. Everyone that was related, admitted they were related. Everyone knew Alejandro had enemies. They all finally agreed that despite the findings of their cousins in law enforcement, he'd been murdered. Most important, no one seemed to have any idea how or why Geo had been dragged, nearly fatally, into the fray.

Maybe I was a newbie in reality TV, but I'd been around long enough to know Geo would do almost anything for a shot—short of offing himself, that was. Which left me looking for the murderer of a less-than-wonderful man for a variety of vague reasons. Not to mention the attack on Geo for seemingly no reason at all. My suspect and ally list had suddenly merged into a conglomeration of relatives who seemed to have the means and motive, if not the opportunity, to want to kill Alejandro and have his death put to rest as quickly as possible:

Enrique wanted and now had Elena to himself.

Benito freely admitted that he hated Alejandro.

Elena could have wanted to be free of an unhappy and possibly arranged marriage.

And Jorge did what he was told; did his job description include killing the bad seed, Alejandro?

Or maybe it was all of them working together.

"That would explain why everyone was so eager to rule the death an accident," Frank added with the smirk that had been plastered on his face since it became clear that his theory about whatever was happening was more accurate than mine.

171

A conspiracy was consistent with the death being immediately classified an accident. What it didn't answer was something that had been bugging me since I first began questioning members of the Hacienda de la Fortuna staff:

Why would a bunch of people be so willing to be interviewed like potential suspects from the get-go if they were actually guilty?

As Frank and I approached the kids, who were chilling by the pool with one of Philip's officer buddies for safety and the camera crew that was setting up for an unscripted update during our poolside lunch, I realized that not one of the staff members I'd just interviewed was anywhere near the water park during Geo's attack.

Meaning there were even more family members involved?

"I mean, it's certainly possible," Trent said as we were placed in the most favorable ocean view positions, the food was arranged around us, and Anastasia gave us the go-ahead to eat and confer.

"Maybe someone in the family works at the water park," FJ said. "Or was there for the day."

"It doesn't explain why they all claim to be happy that we're down here helping them figure out who did it though," I said, eyeing the various wood-fired pizzas set out for our lunch, but not terribly interested in eating much of anything.

"True," Eloise added from a nearby deck chair where she'd been camped all morning sunning herself, and, I presumed, hoping Ivan might turn up even though he'd been given the day off. "And why would they send someone to go after Geo if they wanted to keep the murder looking like an accident?"

"Especially if the resort is all worried about bad press," FJ said.

"I mean, why would anyone go after Geo at all?" Trent added, grabbing a slice of pizza.

"I think that's the big question," I said.

With Anastasia's approving smile and signal to cut, I knew I was between a rock and a hard place. Given what we knew, it made little sense that Alejandro's family had done him in. And while I could believe someone in the upper ranks of *The Family Frugalicious* might be willing to sacrifice a seemingly innocent bystander for the sake of TV verité, why would they double their own jeopardy by arranging to do in the show's director while they were at it?

As the next camera shot focused in on the boys eating and discussing the results of their informal survey as to *who might have hated Alejandro* (potentially every rank and file staff member) and why (he was demanding and difficult, for starters), I found myself zoning out of the "official" conversation and eavesdropping on the exhausted-looking couple who'd just settled into a nearby pair of partially submerged cement lounge chairs.

"No strings attached?" the woman said. "I didn't think we were ever going to get out of the timeshare offices."

"I'm sorry, honey, but I really wanted those free golf passes."

"The ninety-minute presentation was almost four hours long! You could have golfed and been back by now if you'd just paid for the tee time."

"I'll admit it was kind of intense."

"Kind of? Three sales people, all that personal information they kept demanding from us, and that one guy who kept saying, *What's your price? What's your price? What's your—*"

"At least we got a week in paradise every year from now on," the husband said.

"Are you sure about that?" The wife turned to her tote at the side of the pool and pulled out some paperwork. "I mean, what exactly is this Sampler Package you agreed to? That manager guy was talking so fast, I have no idea what we even bought…"

With the word *manager*, I glanced over at the vacation sales office. Two things seemed suddenly clear: First, I had experienced a very different version of the timeshare presentation than they had; and second, Frank had tracked down every single person on my persons of interest list, save Felipe, who was scheduled for a chat while he drove us to the ruins that afternoon.

All except Antonio, the newest manager of the vacation sales department.

———

"May I help you?" Beti the receptionist asked without looking up from her computer.

"I'd like to speak to Antonio, please," I said, glancing out the window behind her desk. While the boys were doing a retake, I'd excused myself to the bathrooms, veered off as soon as I was out of sight of the two officers assigned to keep an eye on us, and slipped into the vacation sales office for what I hoped would be an actual impromptu conversation with Antonio. "Quickly, if that's possible."

"Write down your name and what you want to see him for," she said, still not looking up, nor batting so much as a fake eyelash in my direction as she pointed to a clipboard labeled MANAGER RE-QUEST LIST.

"Okay…" I said as I wrote down *Maddie Michaels* in the box for my name and *Alejandro* as my reason for meeting.

I left the clipboard on the counter and took a seat on a couch that faced the sales floor. In the back corner of the room, I spotted Antonio in the glass-walled manager's office. He seemed to be staring at his desk.

"I see he's in," I said. And he certainly didn't look otherwise occupied.

"Yes," Beti said, finally reaching for the clipboard.

Her put-upon expression completely changed the moment she deigned to read my name.

"Oh!" Beti looked up. "I'm so sorry! I didn't realize … If I'd known it was you, I'd never have …" Her cheeks, which already sported a liberal swath of blush, burned crimson. "I'm supposed to discourage … I mean, they generally don't like for people to come in and talk to the manager or any of our salespeople without an appointment. I'll call Mr. Espinoza right away," she said, picking up the phone.

"Did you say Mr. *Espinoza*?"

She nodded.

"Hang on," I said before she started dialing. "So Alejandro and Antonio were—"

"Brothers."

"Brothers," I repeated, wondering why I hadn't made the connection before, given how similar they looked.

"And Antonio's taking it really hard," she said. "Other than coming out to do paperwork with you, he's pretty much been sitting in his office staring into space since it happened."

Hardly the reaction one would expect from a man who'd killed his own brother to get his job. "That's awful."

"For him, yes." Beti glanced over her shoulder to make sure no one was coming. "But, between us, this whole situation has made things a bit easier for the rest of us."

"Because Antonio hasn't left his office?"

"Because Alejandro is gone," she said.

The fact that Beti was admitting she was glad he was gone told me she probably wasn't a relative, but another member of his ever-growing legion of haters. "I've heard he was a bit difficult."

"Well..." She lowered her voice. "We haven't had a single guest demanding to see the manager since Antonio took over, if you know what I mean."

"I think I might," I said. "It certainly explains why you were instructed to discourage unscheduled meetings."

"In part, anyway."

Before I had a chance to ask her another question, the front door banged open and the woman who had been sitting near me at the pool came barreling in.

"I need to see the manager," she said, waving her contract.

"Please sign in," Beti said with a *there went that* sigh.

"Immediately," the woman insisted. "We purchased a vacation package that our salesman assured us had a forty-eight-hour cancelation policy,[28] but I was just reading the fine print and it seems to say that The Sampler, which is what we bought, is nonrefundable and I—"

"Sign in and take a seat," Beti repeated, giving me a *see what I mean* look. "There's a guest ahead of you."

"I don't know how they do it, but I swear they somehow hypnotize you into signing on the dotted line," the woman said to me. "Did you sign up for this Sampler, whatever it is, too?"

---

28. Most timeshare contracts contain a clause for cancellation within a specified period of time. Other than that, the only legal ways to end timeshare contracts involve transferring ownership by selling, donating, or giving it away. Ending the contract any other way can be considered a breach that comes with legal ramifications.

"No," I said looking out the window toward the pool and noticing that Philip had joined Anastasia and they were conferring with my family and the crew. "I'm dealing with an entirely different situation."

The situation became more complicated when one of Philip's officer buddies headed in the direction of the bathrooms looking, I could only presume, for me.

"In fact, I'm afraid I'm going to need to reschedule my meeting with the manager for later," I said. "Hopefully, that will shorten your wait a bit."

———

"Here's what we now know," Philip said, looking at us but clearly aware he was on camera. "Murder is bad for the resort."

Duh, I wanted to say, but kept my mouth shut.

Luckily so did the kids, who I feared, judging by both FJ's and Eloise's expressions, might blurt the same thing.

"And seeing as tourism makes this whole area tick, it makes a certain amount of sense, financially and psychologically, that everyone needed Alejandro's death to be an accident."

"So you agree there was a cover-up?"

"I think it's fair to say there's been a widespread *don't ask, don't tell* policy in effect," Philip said. "But, now, the facts can no longer be ignored."

"And what are the facts?" I asked.

"We have confirmed that Alejandro died sometime between 8:05 p.m. when he was last seen and 8:45 p.m. when he was discovered floating in the pool. We've also confirmed that while he did have alcohol in his body, the police detected the presence of something else as well."

"Which was?"

"Rohypnol."

"He was roofied?" Trent blurted.

"Seriously?" FJ asked.

I was simultaneously bothered and glad my kids were so well aware of what was commonly known as the date rape drug.

Philip nodded. "The new theory is that someone slipped a roofie into his cocktail of the day."

"Wouldn't he have immediately passed out or something, though?" Trent asked.

"Not right away. Rohypnol commonly causes disinhibition and slurred speech, followed by respiratory distress and paralyzing effects," Philip said. "And, unfortunately, it's odorless, tasteless, and dissolves quickly—Alejandro wouldn't have noticed until he was feeling the effects.

"Not good," Trent added.

"As soon as his memory got fuzzy and his inhibitions left him, the killer likely encouraged him to drink more alcohol and somehow coaxed him into the pool."

"And no one saw any of this going on?" I asked.

"The video surveillance in that pool area was not working that evening."

"What a coincidence," I said.

"They've interviewed all the bartenders, servers, and staff who were working when it happened—most of them immediately after the incident. We know he was in the bar, possibly waiting for someone. Then he got a call, headed toward the other side of the property, and never returned."

I felt my cheeks flush. Seeing as we were on camera and surrounded by Anastasia and the crew, I couldn't quite get myself to admit that Alejandro might well have been in the bar waiting for me.

Or that if I had met him, he might still be alive.

"Are they checking his cell phone records?" I asked.

"The call came from one of the courtesy phones at the resort, so there's no way to know which one," Philip said. "A cabana boy says he saw Alejandro heading for the pool around eight thirty, and wondered if he was a little tipsy but didn't think much of it because he swam regularly for exercise."

"Alone?"

"Apparently."

"Or is that just another cover-up?" I asked.

"Maddie believes there was a conspiracy to get rid of him," Frank said, somewhat dismissively.

"Given how many people disliked the man for one reason or another, it's a definite possibility," Philip said. "And the local authorities agree."

"Do you believe them?" I asked.

"They are competent, and we've been assured that the various relatives within the department have been reassigned to other cases, so yes."

"They've certainly changed their tune down at the station," I said.

"They claim it was the blood work," Philip said.

"What about the incident at the water park?"

"That too."

"Did they find the camera yet?" Frank interrupted.

"Not yet. There are weird tides, and lot of surface area to cover," Philip said. "As for the Geo incident…"

"Let me guess," Eloise said. "Another accident?"

179

"No," Philip said. "The new working theory is that whoever came after Geo wasn't actually after Geo at all."

"What?" I asked.

"They don't believe Geo was the intended target."

"What?" the rest of my family exclaimed.

"Who do they think the killer was after?"

Philip looked directly into the camera. "Ivan."

"Ivan?" Eloise repeated, reaching for her phone.

Philip saw her move. "You won't be able to get a hold of him, he's down at the station now."

"OMG!" Eloise said. "Why would someone go after Ivan?"

"That's what we still need to find out," he said, looking meaningfully at me. "All of us."

"Cut," Anastasia said, looking as gleeful as Eloise did stricken. "Perfect."

TWENTY-ONE

"MAKES NO SENSE AT all," Felipe said, shaking his head as he chauffeured us to our afternoon shoot/tour of the local Mayan ruins in a black SUV without so much as a license plate rim or a parking sticker to mark it as belonging to the Hacienda de la Fortuna fleet.

For added safety, we were told, after being reassured that no one from the cast or crew was in danger because the killer wasn't after Geo or any of the rest of us. Seeing as everyone around from *The Family Frugalicious* let out a collective sigh of relief, I decided not to point out that Geo, who was still hospitalized, had been in someone's crosshairs, accidentally or not.

"You said, 'What's done is done,' after Alejandro died," I said to Felipe. "What exactly did you mean by that?"

"Alejandro had his enemies," Felipe said as the cameraman assigned to capture our various reactions to the latest news zoomed in on him. "But everyone loves Ivan. Who would come after him?"

"Great," said the assistant director, who rode in the back row of the SUV. "Since we're almost at Tulum, we need to move onto Felipe filling everyone in on the history of the place."

With that, any additional insight we might have gleaned from Felipe was immediately preempted by his informative, if much less illuminating, monologue on the Mayans:

Cancun as we know it didn't exist prior to the 1970s, but Tulum, the Mayan word for fence *or* wall, *was built in the thirteenth century during the Mayan Postclassic period...*

Everyone had finally admitted they knew that Alejandro hadn't simply drowned. While I could understand why the Powers That Be around the hotel wanted to keep the word *murder* out of the conversation, something still felt orchestrated.

Not to mention secretive.

We have just enough information about the Tulum ruins for the history to become a giant puzzle for us to piece together...

The potential suspects were too numerous to count and included practically everyone—family, friends, coworkers, and hotel guests.

Soon after Tulum was constructed, the Spanish arrived. The Europeans attempted to conquer the Mayans, as well as the Inca and Aztec peoples. The Mayans, however, proved difficult to overpower...

What was the connection between the widely disliked Alejandro and affable hippie Ivan? And how had Geo gotten caught in the middle?

The Mayans and Spanish lived alongside each other for two hundred years before Spain finally took control of Mayan lands. Still, the people, culture, and language thrived. Many people living in the Yucatan today are of Mayan and Spanish descent...

How did the not-entirely-forthright members of Alejandro's extended family fit into the picture?

Tulum was a very advanced society. The Mayans had their own system of writing, were advanced in math and architecture, and invented the zero...

All of my working theories had been and continued to be blown out of the water. If whoever had gone after Geo actually meant to attack Ivan, then it was once again somewhat believable that the crew could be behind it for some extremely far-fetched ratings ploy—except not really, and particularly not on camera. Maybe there was a conspiracy to kill Alejandro but, if so, why try and kill Geo/Ivan afterward, for no particular reason, and risk being caught as a result?

In order to figure out who could actually be a suspect, I needed to find out:

1. What happened in the hour before Alejandro's death—what he was drinking, with whom, and why he left the bar area.

2. Why Ivan was also targeted and how the killer had confused him with Geo.

3. Who hated both men enough to try and kill them, particularly with so many cameras around.

We pulled up to the entrance to Tulum and I allowed everyone to pile out of the SUV ahead of me.

"Thank you for the ride," I said to Felipe as soon as I was the last one in the car.

"*De nada*," he said.

"Can I ask you a question?"

"Anything for Señora Frugalicious," he said, looking into the rearview mirror, but somehow not at me.

"You're one of the few people who didn't deny that Alejandro could have been murdered from the very start."

"I'm not surprised no one wanted to say so," he said. "The family—they are all very protective of each other."

"Then you aren't part of the family?"

"Only by marriage," he said, as though that made him an outsider.

"They definitely seem to hire from within at Hacienda de la Fortuna," I said.

"That's just how it's done."

"Is there anyone who isn't related?"

"Ivan," Felipe said. "Which is what worries me most."

"Why?"

"Because if he is in danger …" Felipe glanced out the passenger side windows and then over his left shoulder. "Then every single person who works at the hotel could be in danger too."

———

"That's all he said?" Frank asked.

"He saw someone walk behind the car, got all nervous, and completely clammed up after that except to add that he would see us at pick-up time."

"That certainly doesn't give us much to go on," Frank said, sounding dismissive of my sleuthing abilities, "now does it?"

"Something's still being covered up. I'm sure of it."

"That, or maybe the man is skittish," Frank said. "I mean, how would you feel if someone tried to kill two people in your life in as many days?"

"Seriously, Frank?" I said, looking at the kids, who were just ahead of us on the path that led to the ancient walls surrounding the ruins. "I swear, if anything happens to—"

"Nothing will happen to us or the kids."

"How can you be sure?"

Two of Phil's officer buddies joined the kids, flanking them on either side.

Frank flashed a self-righteous smile that made me want to clock him.

As promised, we toured the ruins trailed by a camera crew, taking in the cliffside temple of El Castillo where we learned about the Secret of Tulum—small windows in the shrine that were lined up perfectly with a gap in the offshore barrier reef and reflected during daylight hours to help incoming canoes navigate safely into shore.

"Smart," FJ said, as prompted.

"There are different windows for night guiding too," Trent added. "Like a lighthouse, but without a light."

As our designated tour guide detailed the Mayan obsession with the movements of the heavens, their uncanny ability to mathematically predict almost every astronomical event, and their eerily accurate calendar thousands of years ago, we all agreed the Mayans were a brilliant bunch. We also marveled not only at the architectural achievement of the Temple of the Descending God, but that this and all of the structures were built without the help of machinery or modern technology.

The only real surprises of the afternoon were Eloise's lack of distress about the geckos darting about (Ivan had warned her about them and assured her they were friendly) and the notable break from stress. Despite the minor headaches inherent in TV production, the tour itself was enjoyably sunny, scenic, and predictable. My admiration of the Mayan aesthetic grew as we hiked down and around the sheer cliffs for our *11:00: Family beach frolic* on one of the most beautiful stretches of beach I'd ever seen. We took in the view of Cozumel off in the distance, took off our various cover-ups, and were basking in the sun and, in fact, frolicking in the stunning turquoise Caribbean surf as though we truly were on vacation.

That was, until I was reminded that the feeling of too-good-to-be-true was as potent a warning (at least for me) as the blood-curdling cry that echoed suddenly from atop the cliff.

———

"What's going on?" I asked a fellow tourist after counting to make sure everyone in my family was safe, present, and accounted for.

"I don't know, but we were supposed to meet for our tour right where the screams are coming from," she said as we scrambled along with the crowd in the direction of the high-pitched shriek. "Thank goodness they'd already changed the location."

Eloise, who'd rushed ahead along with the boys, looked up and stopped dead in her tracks. "OMG!"

"Frank," I said breathlessly. "I'm afraid there may be a—"

"You've got to be kidding me," FJ said, as we reached the kids before I could utter the words *serial* and/or *killer*, much less add anything along the lines of *on the loose*.

The scene unfolding before us was almost as shocking. And, judging from the strategically placed camera, crew, and assorted equipment, it was a highly choreographed scene at that.

At the top of the steep, crumbling stairs of El Castillo, in front of the shrine, a body lay on a makeshift altar.

Body—as in Anastasia's shapely sister Sara—covered from head to toe in blue paint.

Face, AKA Sally, stood over her, along with her son Liam, Hair's husband Michael, and Dave, Body's weekend squeeze. All were dressed as Mayan priests.

Face held a sacrificial knife.

"That was good for a rehearsal," Anastasia, announced through a megaphone from the bottom of the stairs. "But remember, Sara, it's an honor to be sacrificed, so I need a scream that's feels as much like pride as it does fear."

I didn't quite know whether to laugh, cry, or simply give in to what seconds before had felt like an imminent heart attack.

"This time, we're running through the whole scene," Anastasia announced. "And remember folks, we've only got one take."

As Dave helped Body up off the slab of stone and everyone headed back down the steps, an assistant rushed over from behind the shrine to re-prep the area. The *actors* reached the bottom of the stairway and disappeared around a corner. Hair, AKA Susan, remained in front of a second camera positioned at the bottom of the steps.

"I just can't believe this," I said to no one in particular as we watched the reenactment from about twenty feet away, along with the rest of the vacationing crowd.

"Believe it," muttered one of the assistants assigned to accompany us. "Anastasia's sisters wanted more lines so they could get their Screen Actors Guild cards."[29]

"They want to be actresses?"

"Ready, Susan?" Anastasia asked.

The assistant sniffed. "You'd have thought the scenes she already wrote them into would have been enough."

"To qualify for a SAG card?"

"As if any of them have what it takes to act. They make perfect Hollywood siblings, I suppose."

"And action!" Anastasia said.

Hair tossed her luscious locks and gave it her all:

"Sacrificial scenes have been depicted in many ancient Mayan ceramics, sculptures, and murals," she said in a stiff documentary voice. "Typically, animals—including crocodiles, iguanas, dogs, peccaries, jaguars, and turkeys—were sacrificed to appease the Mayan gods. While it may seem shocking to us, ancient peoples did not view sacrifice as a devaluing of life, but believed that life was being given up for a greater purpose. The supreme sacrifice being the human life." She paused meaningfully. "Truly, it isn't all that different than our modern-day willingness to give up our loved ones for the cause of war. In fact, the ancient Mayans actually battled it out through games to compete for the opportunity and honor of being sacrificed."

---

29. Becoming a member of the Screen Actors Guild is often a conundrum for aspiring actors because you can't get a SAG card until you are hired by a SAG production, and you can't get hired by a SAG production unless you have a SAG card!

The camera panned to Body attempting to look equal parts honored and horrified while being dragged around the corner and up the steep steps by Face, Michael, Dave, and her nephew Liam.

"I can't believe Liam never mentioned a thing about this," FJ said as they forced her onto the slab and held her down.

"Probably sworn to silence," Trent whispered.

Hair spoke once more. "After being painted blue, the sacrificial victim was led to the summit of the pyramid and laid over a stone altar. Then, with his or her arms and legs firmly held by assistants, to the high priest, known as the nacon—"

"OMG!" Eloise said as Hair recited something in what had to be a badly mispronounced Mayan dialect. As she brandished the obsidian knife, Body let out a shriek that sounded more like a cat in heat than a terrified maiden about to be sacrificed for the greater good.

"This is horrifying," I said.

"It's not too accurate either," a voice said from behind us. "In Tulum, they celebrated the God of Life, so only animals were ever sacrificed."

A hint of patchouli wafted in the breeze.

Eloise turned and hugged Ivan, who had maneuvered his way through the crowd and was standing behind us.

"I heard you guys were coming here while I was down at the police station," he said. "I thought I would make sure everyone is doing okay."

"That's so sweet!" Eloise said, all but batting her lashes.

"I also didn't want to miss how they were going to try and reenact this whole business," he said before the boys had time to roll their eyes at their sister. "Particularly the cutting out of the heart."

"They're not really going to …?"

189

Michael plunged the knife in the general direction of Body's heart and blood (fake, I could only pray) spurted high into the air.

"Whoa!" FJ said over the gasps of the crowd.

We all gasped again as Face reached down and grabbed a bloody, dripping rubber heart from wherever the blood had come from. She held it over her head.

"Cut," Anastasia announced.

"Wow!" Trent said, looking almost as wide-eyed as I'd ever seen him despite the various incidents we'd already witnessed. "I don't see how they can top that."

"Which has me wondering why you're out and about?" I asked Ivan. "It can't be safe."

Frank made a show of nodding in agreement. "My thoughts exactly."

"I figure there's safety in numbers," Ivan said, lowering his voice and confirming his concern about *the walls having ears*. "At least I hope so."

"Let's move on to the second half of the scene," Anastasia announced into her megaphone.

Face, Dave, Liam, and Michael stepped back. Body sat up, got off the slab, and disappeared into the shrine area. A moment later, an assistant emerged with a bloodied, blue-painted dummy with a gaping hole in the chest and set it in Body's place.

"Places everyone," Anastasia said to the remaining members of the cast.

Everyone rearranged themselves accordingly around a latex corpse that I hoped satisfied Zelda's *bad news comes in threes* body count.

"And action," Anastasia announced.

Over the sound of seabirds, the group proceeded to do a ceremonial chant of dubious historical accuracy.

The crowd, aware of their role and/or caught up in the pageantry of it all (not unlike the ancient Mayans and every other culture who engaged in public displays of punishment, torture, and sacrifice), buzzed with energy.

"Ivan, I really am worried about your safety," I said, using the commotion as cover.

"Thanks Mrs. F.," he said, but with fear in his eyes. Particularly as the priest and her assistants lifted the stunt maiden and carried her above their heads. "But I hope they're done coming after me."

A hush descended on the audience of tourists, employees of the ruins, and onlookers as the body was heaved over the edge of the temple steps.

It tumbled with a sickening series of thumps and stopped at the foot of the stairs in a tangled bloody blue heap.

"And scene!" Anastasia announced.

I pulled Ivan just far enough away so we could talk without anyone overhearing.

"They?" I asked. "What do you mean by *they*?"

"Alejandro's murder had to be an organized effort," he said, confirming my suspicions. "It's the only scenario that makes sense."

"By the Espinoza Garcia clan?"

"They'd never kill one of their own."

"Are you sure?" I asked, finally getting a few straightforward answers to my ever-growing list of questions.

"Especially not him. A lot of money funnels through that timeshare department and out to other interests in the family."

"But his brother took over."

"Antonio isn't even close to what Alejandro was capable of—financially or otherwise."

Which went a long way toward explaining why the family seemed to be so forgiving of Alejandro's less than stellar qualities. "What about a group of Hacienda de la Fortuna employees, then?"

"No one from the resort is crazy enough to kill him."

"You don't think that someone, or a group of someones, could easily have had enough of his bullying and just snapped?"

"Definitely," he said. "But everyone around here knows that if you even cross someone from *La Familia de la Fortuna,* you're out of a job. Get involved in a murder of one of them and no one in your extended family will ever work again. And that would just be the start of your troubles."

"They have that much power?"

"Look around you." Ivan glanced at the crew assigned to hose the fake blood off the steps of El Castillo. "It doesn't just happen that a producer from your TV show decides she wants to reenact a sacrifice scene at a sacred Mexican landmark, much less drip fake blood all over it, and she just gets to. Not without power, connections, and some money changing hands."

"But someone killed Alejandro, not to mention tried to kill you."

"The police think whatever happened to Geo was supposed to be more of a warning," he said, grimly.

"A warning?"

"To keep me quiet."

"How do they know?"

"Someone called the police tip line and left a message for me to keep my mouth shut *or next time we'll get the job done.*"

"Were the police able to trace where the call came from?"

"They're working on it." He shook his head. "I just wish I knew what it was I'm supposed to shut up about."

"You have no idea?"

"The only thing I can think of is that I recently took a group of VIPs sailing. I didn't see anything out of the ordinary beyond a little drinking and some flirting with the pretty girls they always have on the Hacienda de la Fortuna sailboat, but I must have heard something—or someone thought I did."

"And you have no idea what?"

"I mean, at one point, I went to use the bathroom and heard chatting outside the door. When I came out, Alejandro, one of the high-roller guests, and our mayor were standing there. They did look at me like I'd full-on interrupted them."

"Did you hear any of the conversation?"

"Only jumbled random words," he said.

"Like?"

"*Deal, money, development*—you know, typical businessman speak."

"And you didn't hear anything else?"

"Not really, but they sure eyeballed me like I had."

"Did you tell the police?"

"I made it very clear to the police that I didn't hear or know anything." Ivan lowered his voice. "Whoever killed Alejandro is … big."

"Big?"

"So powerful they aren't afraid to scare the extended Hacienda de la Fortuna family enough to try and pass off a murder of one of their own as an accident."

"Are you saying you think they're—"

He shook his head so I wouldn't utter the word *mafia*, or whatever the Mexican term for it was.

"Ivan," I said. "You need to fly back to the States with us when we leave on Thursday."

"No can-do," he said. "That would definitely make it look like I know something I don't. I figure it's better to stay in Mexico and keep my head down. When I don't say anything, they'll think I'm following their directions and leave me alone."

"I can't believe this," I said, shaking my head. "We come down here for what was supposed to be a sunny, fun, bargain wedding shoot and now were in the middle of a ..." With Ivan's panicked expression, I stopped myself from saying *gangland retribution* or anything remotely similar. "I can't even say I'm taking any comfort in the fact that Geo might really have been attacked by accident, or that I don't have to worry about there being any involvement by the TV network or anyone involved with *The Family Frugalicious* like I originally thought could be the case."

Ivan narrowed his eyes. "You sure about that?"

My heart, still very much inside my chest began to thump. "What do you mean?"

"I'd say it's a pretty big deal to have a reality TV show filming around here," he said. "I know we all thought so when we heard you were coming down."

"Are you saying you think the show could be connected to Alejandro's murder after all?"

We both watched as a suit-clad man and an official from the ruins approached Anastasia. As they began to confer, I realized the man looked vaguely familiar. While I'd never met him, I'd seen his picture in the leather-bound welcome binder back in our hotel suite.

"Isn't that—?"

"The CFO of Hacienda de la Fortuna," Ivan said.

"Great news, folks," Anastasia announced into the megaphone a few minutes later. "We've been authorized to do one more take, so I'll need everyone and everything ready ASAP."

"Like I said," Ivan said, "nothing happens around here by coincidence."

TWENTY-TWO

ONE BLOOD-SOAKED, SCREAM-LADEN TAKE later, we—cast, crew, and our homegrown police escorts—regrouped in the small tourist village just outside the archeological site.

"Quite a scene," I commented to Anastasia, my eyes on the traditional dancers, acrobats, and various barkers hawking everything from made-in-China commemorative shot glasses to the much more authentic leather sandals. "Of course, it's hard to follow up the last one at the ruins."

"I really should have had the crew set up here too, but the sacrifice went longer than I expected," Anastasia said, watching Body and Dave transfer stray smears of blue paint as they flirted, kissed, and fed each other tacos from the hole-in-the-wall stand where half of us had been served and the other half awaited our order. "Plus, everyone was starved and needed a breather."

Out of concern for Ivan's well-being, I didn't tell anyone what he had told me, other than to share what we all knew: that he'd been to the police station, confirmed the threat had been meant for him, and that he had no idea why. My bigger concern, at least for the moment, was an answer to the question he'd asked about how my family had gotten tangled up in these increasingly sinister south-of-the-border dealings in the first place.

Did Anastasia contact the Hacienda de la Fortuna and offer them the chance to host her televised wedding, or was it the other way around? he'd asked.

"I had no idea you were planning something so involved today," I said to Anastasia as Frank grabbed a tray filled with tacos. "I didn't see anything about it on the call sheet."

"I didn't want to get anyone's hopes up, mainly my own, until I was sure we'd be able to pull it off," Anastasia said.

"I'd say you killed it with that second take," Frank said as we neared the picnic bench where Face and Hair were already seated. "You've gotta get the sacrifice in the promos—it'll make a perfect teaser for the real murders."

"Don't you mean *murder*, singular?" I asked.

"Murder," Frank said, putting the tray on the table. "Of course."

"The sacrifice scene is only going to end up as a promo?" Body said from the next table, not breaking eye contact with Dave.

"Stasia ..." Face, sitting at our table, was suddenly the face of consternation. "I thought you said this scene was going to be key to the overall story line?"

The sacrifice scene, which no one had mentioned but everyone but me seemed prepared for, was *key* to the overarching story line?

"No worries," Anastasia said.

Hair looked almost as worried as I felt. "When was this story line devel—"

"We're done eating," FJ said, appearing at our table with Trent, Eloise, and Liam. "We're going to check out the shops."

"But you'll stick together?" I asked. "Right?"

"They'll be fine," Frank said, reaching for a bottle of hot sauce from the center of the table.

"That stuff is *muy caliente*, Mr. Michaels," Liam said. "I almost couldn't take it."

"Just how I like it," Frank said, unscrewing the cap and dousing his taco.

"Check out the souvenir shop down the way and off to the right," Anastasia suggested, pointing to the intersection of the two streets that made up the town. "They've extended *locals* pricing to all of us for today."

"Cool, because I'm totally getting a bunch of those Mexican masks," Trent said.

"How in the world did you get a discount arranged in the midst of everything else going on today?" I asked her as the kids headed off.

Anastasia winked. "Connections."

"Connections?" I managed before Frank emitted a sound that could only be described as a hyena choking on a chicken bone. He grabbed the nearest beverage, which happened to be a beer one of the cameramen was bringing to his seat at a nearby table. He took a huge, dramatic gulp and chased it down with a handful of chips.

"If Liam says something is spicy, you'd better beware," Face said.

"Holy mother of . . ." Frank dabbed his eyes and then his tongue with a napkin. "I didn't expect that kind of heat."

"Unexpected seems to be the theme of this whole shoot, I'd say." While I needed to be more than a little subtle, I also needed answers to have any hope of figuring out what was going on, and what, if anything, I could do about it. "What are you planning to call this episode? 'Marriage, Murder, and the Mayans'?"

"Not bad," Anastasia said. "Not bad at all."

"Seriously," I said. "How are you planning to feature a simulated sacrifice as part of a bargain-shopping show?"

"The way I see it, local color and custom is part and parcel of getting married out of the country," Anastasia said. "Right?"

Two out of the three sisters nodded in agreement. The third, Body, was mid-smooch.

"Plus, it adds a kind of bridge between what we originally came to do in terms of the bargain destination wedding and the turn of events that have kept us here," she said with that unsettling, telltale gleam. "Don't you think?"

"Stasia," I asked, emboldened by her zeal for capitalizing on the unexpected. "How *did* we end up here in the first place?"

"The ruins tour was part of the overall package."

"I'm not talking about the ruins," I said. "I'm mean the package overall."

She looked at me as though I was asking the most obvious question ever. "We brought the show down to the Hacienda de la Fortuna in return for an all-inclusive wedding, lodging for the crew and select guests, and complimentary attendance to any and all attractions we deemed necessary for the shoot."

"Not to mention the timeshare incentives," Frank said.

This time, all three sisters managed an enthusiastic nod.

"Add a bonus murder to investigate as part of the deal and I suppose it was a can't-lose proposition," I said.

"Maddie!" Frank said sternly.

"I'm just trying to figure out the connection, if there is one, between Alejandro's murder, whatever it was that happened to Geo in the cave, and why we happen to be here in the middle of it all."

"Makes sense," Anastasia said, but wrinkled her pert little nose.

"So whose idea was it to come down to Mexico in the first place?" I asked.

"We wanted to have a destination wedding and it just happened to be a perfect concept for an episode of the show."

"We?"

"Me," she said with none of the hemming and hawing I might have expected. "And Philip, of course."

"So you researched resorts in Mexico and settled on Hacienda de la Fortuna?"

"I knew almost right away this was the place where I'd be able to have my cake and eat it too." As she flashed a smile I couldn't quite call entirely genuine, yet another scream pierced the air.

An authentic and too-familiar scream.

"Eloise!" Frank and I shouted in unison, both of us already up from the picnic table and running in the direction where the kids had gone off to shop.

The screamer was Eloise, and her distress was definitely real.

Theoretically, anyway.

We rushed over to the kids, all four of whom were standing in front of the mask display outside the store. Eloise, horror-stricken, pointed at the shoulder of an older man standing far too close to her for comfort. More specifically, the enormous creature perched on the man's shoulder. "It's—"

"Just an iguana," Trent said.

"Jeez, El," FJ added. "You didn't even flinch over any of the geckos we saw around the ruins today."

"Ivan was there, and they weren't so …" she faltered. "Huge."

The reptile in question was admittedly quadruple the size of anything I'd ever seen. It was also staring directly at my stepdaughter.

"It lunged at me."

"*Lo siento*," the owner of the iguana said with a smile. "Arturo is very friendly, and he does have a weakness for the ladies."

Arturo leered.

Eloise shuddered.

"Arturo," Liam said, tickling the wobbly skin under Arturo's chin. "What a cutie."

"You want to hold him?" the man asked.

"Ugh…" Eloise mumbled, backing away.

"I'd love to!" Liam said.

"Fifteen pesos," the man said.

"I don't have any more money," he said.

"I've got it," FJ said.

As he was reaching into his pocket to pay for Liam, Frank rolled his eyes. "This is more than I can take. I'm heading back to the table to finish my food."

I quickly paid for all three boys to hold Arturo, warned them to wash their hands after, and caught up with Frank.

"Ridiculous," he said, under his breath.

Unsure whether he was referring to Eloise's overreaction, Liam's effusiveness, the man's shameless hustling, FJ's attempt to pay for his friend, or some combination of the above, I simply said, "No more ridiculous than anything else that's going on around here."

"I suppose," he said, looking over his shoulder at FJ and Liam huddled together and fawning over Arturo the iguana.

"Liam really is a nice kid."

Frank shrugged. "I guess."

"He's a lot more clean cut than, say, Ivan."

"Ivan's a hero."

"Yes," I said. "A hero with a nose ring, dreadlocks, and a tattoo, not to mention a penchant for patchouli and your daughter."

"Whatever," he said.

"You're not usually so cavalier about suitors with less-than-corporate career paths."

"This is different," he said.

"Why's that?" I asked.

"We're on vacation," he finally said.

"It's definitely different than any vacation I've ever been on," I said. "You know, Frank. You really need to accept that FJ—"

"Holy moly, that really scared me," Anastasia said, catching up to us.

"I don't even want to think about it," Frank said, definitively.

I shook my head at Frank's level of denial. "Thank goodness it was nothing to get frightened over."

"I'm headed back to finish my lunch," Frank mumbled.

"You know," Anastasia said with a sigh as we followed behind him. "I have to admit I'm all but ready to head out of Mexico."

Hell, yes, I almost said, but then thought about the implications of what she was saying for her personally. "You're ready to leave your own honeymoon?"

"Not from a director/producer standpoint. But from a newlywed standpoint, and given that Geo's in a hospital bed, this whole business has been something of a win, lose, and draw." She blew an uncharacteristically stray hair from her eyes. "Not necessarily in that order."

With her candor, I almost started to tell her that the bad guys, whoever they were, weren't after her or Philip, and that they would be perfectly safe to resume their honeymoon as soon as we were gone. I wanted to recount my conversation with Ivan so she was assured that everything could still become a peaceful and bliss-filled memory for the two of them. I wanted to let her know that despite

Ivan's warning otherwise, the fact that she'd contacted the hotel and not vice versa meant that our shoot really did just happen to coincide with a lot of wheeling and dealing of a different variety.

I almost did.

That was, until I noticed a cameraman slink out a back door that corresponded to the shop where Anastasia had directed the kids. Where he'd apparently been taping the whole "spontaneous" iguana incident in secret.

Instead of saying anything, I returned to the picnic table, slid into my spot, stared at my half-eaten taco, and listened to Frank chew.

Not only was my appetite gone, so was my ability to believe anything—at least where my current reality was concerned.

TWENTY-THREE

"WELCOME BACK," JORGE SAID upon our return to the hotel. "How did everyone enjoy the ruins?"

"Cool," Eloise said, with less enthusiasm than she might have had she not endured a car-ride long *reminder* from Frank about not crying wolf.

"Very cool," added FJ with inflection, having managed to avoid any of Frank's potentially more controversial opinions.

Trent flashed the three masks he bought after the *chance* meet-and-greet with Arturo the iguana. "*Super* cool."

"Good," Jorge said, "because it's going to be hot around here all evening." He pointed to a white board filled with evening activities. "Pool volleyball starts in five minutes."

"Already wearing my swim trunks," FJ said.

"Me too," added Trent.

"I'm supposed to meet Ivan at the swim-up bar," Eloise said.

"They're serving margaritas poolside," Jorge said to Frank and me.

"Sounds like a plan," Frank said.

"I can't believe how much is going on," I said, scanning the board, which looked like a summer camp schedule for adults:

Pool Volleyball—la grande piscina

Fajita Fiesta—la terraza

Salsa Dancing—estudio de baile

Karaoke—bar junto a la piscina

Dessert Bar—la terraza

Moonlight Swim—la grande piscina

"Ready to put on your dancing shoes?" Jorge said.

"I don't know the first thing about salsa dancing," Frank said.

"No experience necessary," Jorge said.

"I'm exhausted just thinking about it," I said, feeling exhausted by the prospect of all the thinking I needed to do. "I'm going to have a little rest."

"Let's roll," Trent said.

"Enjoy! And you enjoy your siesta, Señora Frugalicious," Jorge said. "But one thing before you all scatter off…"

He walked back toward the bell stand and produced a familiar peach-colored envelope.

My stomach lurched as Frank reached for the note. "Apparently, we're all going to be doing some dancing tonight," he said, scanning the note.

"Seriously?" FJ said.

"I don't dance," Trent added.

"Ivan said he's a great dancer," Eloise said.

The boys rolled their eyes.

"Anastasia wants us showered, dressed, and down in the lobby at seven thirty."

"I thought we were free for the evening," FJ said.

"We basically are, but the hotel wants us to get a few promotional shots of everyone relaxing and enjoying the dancing, karaoke, and the moonlight swim," he said. "You know—business as usual…"

———

Tired as I was, a nap was entirely out of the question. Instead, I pulled my computer out of the safe, powered it on, and proceeded to review, revise, and revamp the information I'd collected since I'd first written it all down a few short days earlier. Aware that I would likely be asked to pull up my spreadsheets, possibly on camera, I began by deleting what was wrong, updating, and adding to what I knew:

WHAT REALLY HAPPENED TO ALEJANDRO?

Murdered
Why?
    He was a bad guy?
    Other?
By whom?
    Angry Hotel Employee?
    Disgruntled Guest?
    Other?
How?
    Drugged and drowned

I went into the POTENTIAL SUSPECTS and grouped all the suspects that had been already paraded by us into a master category entitled *Family,* and then crossed them all off.

Seeing as I couldn't add a second category called *Mexican Mafia* any more than I could add a third entitled *The Family Frugalicious* and list Geo, Anastasia, Frank, and everyone in the crew, I closed the file, opened EVIDENCE FOR MURDER, and put a line through everything but Sombrero Lady.

I narrowed PEOPLE TO QUESTION to two potential categories:

Sombrero Lady
Other

Unable to specify that by *other*, I meant the mob and/or someone(s) on the cast or crew of *The Family Frugalicious*, I went into to my stealth investigation sheet, SHOPPING TIPS 101, where I reread, crossed out the answered questions, added notes, and jotted down everything I needed to add to my spreadsheet:

Alejandro's sudden and prominent appearance at the beginning of the shoot. Coincidence, or by design?
Alejandro's unexpected flirtation and notes. Why?
Suspicious behavior:
    Anastasia
    Geo
    Crew

I added Frank to the list. Below the names, I listed all the suspicious incidents I could think of, including the crew proclaiming they'd gotten their *money shot* as fireworks reflected against Alejandro's sheet-covered body, Frank's overzealous protestations of innocence, and Anastasia's recent hijinks at the ruins.

The convenient timing of Alejandro's death—moments before he'd requested we meet, and at the very spot where the final group wedding photos were to be shot.

The killer knew the security cameras were down in that area. Did he/she/they also know the wedding photos would be shot there?

Investigation resolved very quickly and determined to be an accident by police despite suspicious circumstances. Why?

Fear of an organized group more powerful than the Hacienda de la Fortuna family?

Sombrero Lady. Key to finding killer?

Funeral scheduled even more quickly. Why?

The sudden parade of naysayers and people with potential motive.

I folded the final two spreadsheet items into the SUSPICIOUS BEHAVIOR BY CAST AND CREW category:

Shooting schedule extended and budget increased with a single phone call to execs about an "accidental" death?

Geo's initial persons of interest/questions list matching mine.

As I looked things over, it was clear I needed to simplify. Instead of adding items to the current spreadsheet, I created a new list entitled WHAT I KNOW and jotted down the facts:

Someone drugged and drowned Alejandro.

Someone injured Geo.

Alejandro was a tyrant.

I created a second list and called it WHAT I THINK I KNOW:

The killer was part of an organized group?

The Family Frugalicious *is somehow connected to this group?*

Whoever killed Alejandro was trying to either kill/warn Ivan and hurt Geo in the process?

After adding everything else I knew or thought I did, from my theories on why the family was so forgiving of Alejandro's various personality deficits, their reticence to question the suspicious nature of his death, and the fact that no one seemed to have any idea how or why Ivan was a target and Geo had been dragged into the fray, I had to believe that Ivan was on to something.

In order to figure out exactly what that was, I created the most important list of all, WHAT I NEED TO FIND OUT:

What was it that Alejandro did that resulted in his murder and a threat to everyone in the extended clan?

Why exactly did he/she/they send a warning/attempt to kill Ivan?

Why was The Family Frugalicious *in the midst of the fray?*

I was about to start figuring out exactly how I was going to go about answering those questions when I heard the door to the suite creak open. With the sound of voices in the living room, I closed the computer, ran to the closet, and placed it back inside the safe. While I made up a new code that wasn't some combination of our children's birthdates to keep Frank out, I had to wonder if it would even matter. What if my (ex) husband, as part of the staff of *The Family Frugalicious*, was already in bed with the hotel management?

And, perhaps, the mob?

Frank popped his head into the room. "Anastasia just called an emergency meeting."

"About?"

"Philip showed up with some new development he needs to share with us," he said, motioning me to stand. "We need to get downstairs ASAP."

TWENTY-FOUR

"I'm sorry to cut into your free time," Philip said. "But we've uncovered some important information."

"That's why we're here," Frank pronounced, as though Alejandro's murder was the sole reason we were down in Mexico in the first place.

For all I knew, it had been all along.

"Whadda ya got?" I asked, sounding like a bad noir detective.

Seeing as our interchange was already cheesy, and, of course, taking place in front of the cameras, I was sure Anastasia would yell *cut*.

Instead, she gave us the thumbs up.

So did our part-time reverend, full-time police officer, not-quite-attractive-enough-to-be-on-camera, newly minted technical consultant Steve.

"We've spent all day with the local authorities," Philip said. "And we have a number of new leads."

"Fantastic," Frank said, a bit too enthusiastically.

Philip reached for some papers Steve had just placed right outside of the camera shot. "Here is a credible list of people who might have had a grudge against Alejandro and/or Ivan."

"Ivan?" Eloise asked plaintively.

"Someone came after him for a reason," Philip said. "We need to find out what it is."

"But—"

"But whoever it is had to also be aware that the security camera wasn't working by the pool where Alejandro was found."

"So everyone on the list fits all three criteria?" FJ asked.

Philip nodded. "We believe one of the people on it is either the murderer, or is someone with a direct link to whoever's behind what's going on."

"Sweet," Trent said as Philip began to hand out copies, starting with me.

As I expected, the list was full of mostly unfamiliar names and long enough to keep all of us busy until we finally got to go home:

Cesar Y. / Recreational Equipment Manager

Luis T. / Bartender

Tito O. / Pool Maintenance

Pablo G. / Lifeguard Staff

Rosa R. / Front Desk

Ana S. / Spa Employee

Octavio B. / Groundskeeper

Victor C. / Food Services

Jesus M. / Food Services

Carmen L. / Hair Salon

Raul R. / Grounds Staff

Fernando P. / Maintenance

Marisol M. / Yoga Instructor

Unsurprisingly, I didn't recognize almost any of them. I was surprised, however, by two more familiar names on the list:

Zelda R. / Housekeeping

Beti B. / Vacation Ownership Staff

"How did you come up with this list?" I asked.

"Actually, you initiated it by asking Jorge about potentially suspicious folks. He sent the request up the food chain and these are the names they compiled."

"Nice work, Mom," Trent said.

"We want you to find out anything and everything you possibly can and report what you hear back to us," Philip said. "Then, we'll take it from there."

"Cut," Anastasia said and ran over to give Philip a smooch. "You're a natural, darling."

"Thank you," he said.

"Okay," she said to the rest of us. "Here's what we're going to do..."

I wondered how much more surreal things could possibly get as Anastasia began to outline her insta-plan: we would participate in the activities we were already scheduled to enjoy on camera and take turns tracking down information about various people on the list throughout the evening. That was, under the assumption that people who feared for their job security and the livelihood of their families might actually divulge why they hated Alejandro or disliked Ivan, and then admit that they knew the security system was down by the pool so they could commit a murder there.

"I'll mainly need Maddie and Frank for the salsa dancing shots, I'll want everyone for karaoke, and primarily the kids for the moonlight swim. Well, maybe one or two romantic moments with Frank and Maddie under the stars."

All three kids scrunched their noses.

"Since we'll have our cameras set up in the tango studio, karaoke bar, and the pool area, try to be seen talking to the suspects and other employees in those areas, if you can."

"What about audio?" Frank asked.

"You'll be miked, but we can't count on anything," she said. "So I'll set up a confessional for everyone to report what they've heard."

"So, I'm supposed to say to people, 'Hey, I'm kinda seeing Ivan. Do you hate him, or what?'" Eloise asked.

"That's not bad, actually," Anastasia said. "Use the fact that you're interested in him as an entrée to talk about him."

"I guess I could do that if I'm, like, not with him at the time."

"We'll figure out the details as we go along," Anastasia said as if she already hadn't.

"So basically we're on a resort-wide scavenger hunt to find out who hated Alejandro the most?" Trent asked.

"And why," FJ added.

"Exactly." Anastasia smiled as broadly as I'd seen her smile since she'd said *I do*. "See you in the dance studio at eight fifteen to salsa, sing, swim, and sleuth!"

———

I managed to shower, change, and get ready with enough time to run downstairs, locate Ivan by the swim-up snack bar, and show him the names before I had to meet up with cast and crew in the dance studio.

"Every person on here had a legit grievance of some kind with Alejandro," Ivan said.

"Grievances worthy of murder?"

"He insisted that Carmen give him free haircuts. He never, ever tipped Luis the bartender. And Ana Suarez…" He sighed. "But, to be honest, I'm just as bugged that this many people might not like me than I am worried about any of them hating Alejandro enough to kill him."

"All I've heard is how much everyone loves you around here."

"I mean, I thought I was tight with Jesus," he said, tucking a dreadlock behind his ear. "And Victor said he wanted to introduce me to one of nieces—you know, before I met Eloise and everything…"

"No need to explain," I said. "This list feels just as off as the last one, somehow."

"To me, it reads more like a secret probation list than anything else," he said. "I guess Tito qualifies because he'd have known the security cameras weren't working around the pool where they found Alejandro, but still… Where did you say the police got this?"

"I asked Jorge for some names. This list somehow made its way into the hands of the police and on to me."

"No surprises there," he said.

"No," I said.

We scanned the names again together.

"What's your take on Zelda?" I asked.

"Wacky, superstitious, and harmless," Ivan said. "Although Alejandro was constantly having her break housekeeping rules."

"Like having her deliver notes?" I dared to ask.

"Did he have her deliver a note to you too?"

I nodded.

He sighed. "That man was quite the operator."

"Poor Elena."

"Nothing poor about her," Ivan said. "Except that she really had no choice but to marry Alejandro."

"Why?" I asked.

"Family status, tradition, and a little fear." He pointed to a small infinity sign tattooed on his upper arm. "Speaking of which, Zelda claims this is bad luck and is always warning me to get rid of it."

"I certainly hope she's wrong."

"So far, she's been zero for zero with her doomsday predictions," he said. "But judging by this list, the *Familia de la Fortuna* is definitely running scared."

"Do you think there's anyone on here who could possibly be of note?"

"Only one person gives me any pause at all."

"And that is?"

"Beti."

"The receptionist in the timeshare office?

"She's no killer …" He waited until a busboy wiped down a nearby table and moved away. "But she might be able to clarify a bit more about what I heard that day on the boat."

"I thought you only heard a few jumbled words."

"Which I've gone over and over." He paused. "What I didn't think about was who was saying those words."

"Meaning what?" I asked.

"I realized the man they were talking to spoke Spanish with an American accent, which is why I didn't notice anything unusual."

"Why does that matter?"

"That's what I want to find out," he answered. "You start working your way down the list and I'll track down Beti for you. I know she'll feel safe talking to me."

"But is it safe for you to—"

"I trust her. Plus, they organized tonight's events to keep the guests relaxed and entertained, but mostly to keep the staff here and under close surveillance." He motioned with his head at the camera situated right behind us. "Couldn't be safer around here for any of us, or a better opportunity to try and speak to pretty much everyone. Like shooting fish in a barrel."

"Okay, but—"

"I'll get back to you ASAP," he said, not elaborating on exactly what it was he was looking for. "You ought to hear some interesting stuff in the meantime."

"I hope so."

He smiled a wry smile. "Some of it may even be true."

"What's the point of going through the motions again if it isn't?"

"For one thing, when the *Familia de la Fortuna* needs and expects something from you, you do it."

"And for another?"

"To be honest?" he said, a hint of color reddening his cheeks. "I'm curious to know why they think all these people don't like me."

"I'm quite sure this whole interrogation charade will put a rest to that issue," I said, "if nothing else."

"Starting with Rosa from the front desk," he said.

"Why's that?"

He pointed toward an attractive brunette. "Because she just got off her shift and she's heading toward the bar."

———

"Ivan's a little bit too hippie-ish for this resort if you ask me," Rosa said. "But everyone likes him and he's good at his job."

"And what about Alejandro?" I asked.

"Alejandro was a wonderful man," Rosa said over the bar noise, and clearly for the record. "Everyone misses him terribly around here."

"That's not what I'm told," I whispered.

An odd look crossed her face. "What do you mean?"

"It's no secret that he could be difficult."

"And flirtatious," she finally admitted. "On occasion."

"How many occasions?"

She looked around quickly. "Really, any occasion where Elena wasn't nearby…"

————

My head had already started to spin before I entered the dance studio and met up with an abundance of employees, all of whom were clustered together around the resort security cameras like bugs around a light bulb.

Or, as Ivan had described them, fish in a barrel.

"What we're going for here is the Frugalicious Family making the most of their vacation," Anastasia said as we collected in front of the camera. "And a show of sleuthing."

Despite the show, and the fact we were once again questioning predetermined "suspects," the encounter with Rosa had more than piqued my curiosity about what else we were going to hear.

"Here's the plan," Anastasia continued. "Instead of pairing off, we're going to have the men change partners at the end of each song.

That way, you'll each have the opportunity to speak with as many people as possible."

"And make idiots of ourselves with as many chicks as possible," Trent said.

FJ shook his head. "So not into this."

"Do I at least get to start the evening with my bride?" Frank said, his palms sweaty as he reached for my hand.

"Of course." Anastasia raised her bullhorn. "Everyone else take a partner."

Eloise, who was less than enthusiastic after getting the news that Ivan had to deal with something and would miss the dancing segment, surveyed her prospects.

"Maybe she should start off with one of the boys," I said, thinking a warm-up dance might help ease her into a friendlier, more inquisitive state of mind.

"That's what's worrying me," Frank said, glancing over at Trent, FJ, and Liam. More specifically, at FJ and Liam, who appeared as if they'd prefer to pair off with each other.

Eloise stepped over and pulled Liam onto the dance floor.

Trent sidled over to a pretty employee of about eighteen, who seemed pleased by the prospect of dancing with him.

The instructor, a certain Marisol who'd taught the yoga class and was now a member of the suspect list, took a surprised but somewhat bemused FJ by the hand and stepped up to the microphone.

Salsa music began to filter through the room on low and the cameras began to roll.

"Gentlemen, take your partner's right hand in your left and place your right hand on her left shoulder blade," Marisol said with a far-too-broad-for-yoga smile. "Ladies, keep your left hand on his right shoulder, with your arm over his."

Guiding FJ, Marisol did a demonstration for the crowd.

"When dancing, always keep your spine straight and your shoulders back. Keep your head held up or tilted to look directly at your partner. Never look at your feet, nor your partner's."

Marisol looked deeply into FJ's eyes.

He blushed, then went crimson when she added, "Most important, move those hips!"

The music grew louder.

"Now, let's find that salsa beat!"[30]

Despite any disinterest, distaste, or lack of desire to dance, the next thing I knew, we were all keeping 4/4 time in eight counts, switching partners, and shimmying our way across the dance floor and into some intriguing information ...

———

"Everyone in Pool Maintenance knew the cameras were down that night," Tito said as he dipped me. "Not to mention some of Food Services."

"Why's that?"

"We closed down the snack bar there because there was no way to monitor the cash register, or the pool, or anything else."

"I see," I said.

"I was on duty and with the technician the whole time he was trying to get everything back online. I'll give you his name and number if you need to confirm we were together when Alejandro died."

"What about Ivan's incident?"

---

30. If all else fails, have a drink before you get out on the dance floor. Don't drink? Try some herbal tea, or anything that relaxes you. The more calm and confident you are, the better you'll be at salsa.

"I was working that day too," he said. "I'm thankful he wasn't hurt, but between us, I'm sort of glad that guy was under water for a while."

"Why's that?"

Tito smiled. "I figure he can always use a bath."

———

My next dance partner was supposed to be Dave the groomsman, but since Body was unwilling to separate from him, I moved on to Cesar, the recreational equipment manager.

"Sure, I was mad when Ivan got the activities director job instead of me," he said. "I don't have anything against him personally, though."

"And Alejandro?"

"I can't say I'll miss him taking equipment without signing it out and just leaving it anywhere and everywhere."

"That had to be annoying."

"Not to mention a threat to me and my job," he said. "The police questioned me because there were weights near the pool where he died that hadn't been checked out by anyone."

"Why would Alejandro—"

"Who knows, but they sure wanted an answer from me."

"And what did you tell them?"

"That he annoyed me, but they should talk to the people that hated him the most if they wanted to find his killer."

"And who hated him the most?"

Before he passed me along to the gentleman next to me, he whispered, "I'd put my money on someone from Food Services."

———

"We'd have never paid one cent for that condo if we hadn't had so many margaritas before the presentation."

My next dance partner was the husband of the woman who'd come into the timeshare office complaining.

And now he was also complaining.

And also drinking.

"I continued to demand a refund," he said, with a slur. "But unlike their timeshares, which supposedly have a twenty-four-hour refund period, this Sampler nonsense we signed up for is completely nonrefundable."

"So what are you doing about it?"

"What can we do?" he asked in whiny voice. "Can't say I'm surprised or sorry someone bumped off the manager over there, though."

———

"Alejandro never missed a napkin with a spot, food on a utensil, or anything to do with the meal itself," Carlos, the head waiter said. "Sometimes, it seemed like there was nothing we could do right."

"It sounds like he was a real stickler," I said.

"I was okay with it because I figured he was just trying to make us an even better resort than we already are."

"It had to bother you sometimes, though."

"Not as much as it bothered the kitchen staff," he said. "They kept a dartboard with a photo of him in the breakroom."

———

After admitting that salsa dancing was *kinda fun, in a way,* Trent reported that Aracelli, who was friends with Jesus the sous chef, always knew when Alejandro was in the restaurant because plates started coming back to be remade.

Eloise managed to set aside her disappointment about Ivan's absence and find out that Pablo the lifeguard dreaded Alejandro's morning swims because he made the pool staff check the temperature before he got in, and they had to raise or lower it to his liking. The snack bar staff paid him back on behalf of the pool staff by "boosting" his morning smoothie with regular grass instead of wheatgrass. More important, Pablo thought Eloise was pretty. Too pretty for a hippie like Ivan, apparently.

FJ filled us in on Marisol, who, as it turned out, had a whirlwind love affair with a young, handsome, and not nearly so tyrannical Alejandro as soon as she moved to the area and began to work at the resort. While she still hadn't entirely forgiven him for neglecting to tell her he was duty-bound to marry someone else by year's end, she'd gotten over the old heartbreak through yoga, higher spirituality, and staying ten pounds thinner than Elena.

Frank's information seemed to top all. He whispered it only to me, directly from Ana Suarez, who worked in the spa as a masseuse: "The spa staff feel they all got the happy ending Alejandro *jokingly* asked for at the end of each and every one of his massages."

———

"She can't be serious," Eloise said as we read over the karaoke song choices provided us by a production assistant.

"Frank Sinatra?" Trent said.

"No can-do on the Neil Diamond," FJ said.

"There are plenty of options," Anastasia said, "We're trying to appeal to viewers of all ages."

"I guess so," FJ said as Frank ran up to the stage and began to belt out the first bars of "Margaritaville." Hopefully, the accompanying pitchers of margaritas adequately numbed the crowd in time for my off-key version of "I Love Rock and Roll," the boys' spirited interpretation of Journey's "Don't Stop Believin'," and Eloise's grudging "Holiday."

As we took turns singing, a steady stream of employees chanced by our table with increasingly interesting bits and pieces of information:

"Seeing as Alejandro had me pour vodka into a water glass on more than once occasion, it wouldn't have killed him to be appreciative," Tito the bartender said.

"You should talk to Raul," Octavio the groundskeeper said. "He thinks he might have seen something interesting near the pool area the night of the murder."

"Benito was fighting with his girlfriend, Carmen, by the bridge," Raul said. "She was begging him not to do something, but he said he had no choice."

"One of the other ladies from the salon told me Benito and Carmen are madly in love and never argue," Eloise said as Anastasia collected us for a quick note-comparing shot. "So they certainly weren't breaking up."

"According to Victor in food services, Benito was obsessed with how Alejandro constantly got away with bad behavior toward the employees in general, the food service workers in particular, and most of all, his sister Elena."

"Could it be that Benito …?"

We all looked at each other meaningfully.

"Has anyone spoken with Carmen?" I asked.

"We heard she's not here tonight," FJ said.

"She went home just before the dance lessons with a headache," Trent added.

We all looked at each other meaningfully again.

"Did Benito have a grudge against Ivan, though?" I asked. "I mean, wouldn't he have to hate Ivan too for us to consider him a suspect?"

"Victor said that Benito considered Ivan's dreadlocks a health violation," Frank said.

"But that doesn't seem like a motive for murder," I said. "Besides, almost everyone mentioned Ivan's appearance in some way or another."

"Seriously?" Ivan said, appearing from behind a scrim.

"They obviously just don't get style down here," Eloise said with a sweet smile as he joined us on camera. "But they all like you. A lot."

"Cut!" Anastasia said. "That was great."

She handed Ivan her personal copy of the suspect list we'd all been working from. "This is what everyone is talking about."

"Wow!" he said looking at the list as though it were for the first time. "This is heavy."

"No one say another word until we're rolling, then I want all of you to fill Ivan in on what you've found out this evening."

The moment she yelled *action* we did our part by recounting the various details, from Alejandro's misdeeds and flirtations to the mounting evidence that the killer hailed from Food Services and might well be Benito.

"Whoa," Ivan said when we were all finished. "I guess I'm not entirely surprised to find out that Alejandro didn't limit himself to one drink."

"What do you think about this Benito business?" Frank asked.

"Benito is a great guy," Ivan said. "Although he does have a temper."

"And more than one motive, according to Victor and pretty much everyone else."

"I know Benito was protective of Elena, but I never would have thought he could be capable of murder," Ivan said, clearly still processing everything. "I can't deny that he seems like a strong suspect, though." He shook his head. "Really strong…"

———

"Let me guess," I said to Ivan the moment Eloise ran into the pool house to change into her bathing suit for the moonlight swim. "Beti thinks Benito did it too."

"It's like everything's getting wrapped up in a nice bow."

"I don't believe this could really be happening."

"It's scary stuff."

"Do *you* think Benito had something to do with Alejandro's death?"

"I'm sure he resented him for all the reasons you've heard, but Benito got his job as head chef because of Alejandro in the first place."

"So you don't think Benito did it?"

"I think he's got a problem on his hands." Ivan looked as distraught as I felt. "But there could be bigger problems for all of us if everyone else doesn't go along with what's going on."

"Did Beti tell you all of this?"

"She didn't have to." He took a deep breath. "She did tell me something surprising though."

"Which is?"

He took a deep breath. "So, the thing is, it's no secret that Alejandro had been trying to annex some adjacent land that would have made the Hacienda de la Fortuna the only resort with a full-service marina and waterfront shopping complex."

"That sounds pretty amazing."

"And that much more attractive to potential timeshare owners. The problem is, it's theoretically impossible because the land is public and can only be purchased and owned by a Mexican business."

"Doesn't the Hacienda de la Fortuna qualify?"

"Yes, but they don't have enough capital to make it happen."

"So what you overheard was part of a financial transaction with a potential American investor or something?"

"I figured it had to be. I mean, it wouldn't be the first time an international company funneled money into this area through an established local business. Especially if the right people are paid off."

"Like the mayor?"

"Exactly," he said. "I also figured someone wanted that deal to be dead and buried badly enough to kill Alejandro over it."

"But now you don't?"

"The situation might be a little more complicated than that."

"Do you think the mayor's in danger?"

"As long as the deal is over, any risk has passed for him—at least, I hope."

"What about the American?"

"I asked Beti to try and find out who he is." Ivan sighed. "In the meantime, she told me that when Alejandro got back from sailing that day, he was in a really good mood and bragged to her that he was about to be a big star. 'In more ways than one.'"

"This boat trip—was it right before we arrived?"

"The weekend before anyone showed up from your crew."

"Then that's not entirely surprising," I said. "I know from Frank that they decided to fold in the whole timeshare element as part of the show in exchange for promotional consideration."

"Apparently, the plan was a bit more involved," Ivan said.

I felt my blood pressure tick upwards. "How much more involved?"

"He confided in Beti that he'd all but inked a deal for his own reality show about the resort and the world of timeshare sales—starring him, of course."

"That's the first I've heard of it," I said.

But was it?

Thank you for bringing your show down here to our resort, he'd said to me. *If everything continues to go this well, the payoff will be even better than I imagined…*

"So you think the conversation you weren't supposed to over-hear was related to that instead?" I asked, more queasy than I wanted to admit.

"It certainly seems to put an interesting wrinkle into things."

———

Anastasia had called me a total pro, but I hadn't come close to flex-ing my acting muscles until I had to do three takes of kissy-face with Frank in the moonlit water and then transition directly into poker face while Philip debriefed us:

"We've had someone positively ID Benito as being in the area where Alejandro was found at approximately the time of the inci-dent, and we've discovered that he may not have been in the kitchen overseeing prep work as scheduled during the time Geo was at-tacked at the water park."

It took all my strength not to say, *Of course you have.*

Or, more appropriately *Oh, what kind of tangled web did you weave?*

"Sure sounds like a slam dunk to me," Frank said.

"Nothing's a slam dunk if you don't cross your t's and dot your i's," Philip said, already sounding so much like a TV detective, I had to wonder if he'd been promised a show of his own too. "Which means we have legwork to do before we can bring him in."

"What kind of legwork?" FJ asked.

"The local authorities are going to locate Benito and keep tabs on him so he doesn't venture too far from here. While he's under surveillance, we want Frank and you boys to spend tomorrow morning continuing to question anyone and everyone you can about possible motives for killing Alejandro and for the water park incident."

"Isn't that going to seem even more obvious than what we've been doing tonight?" FJ asked.

"Not if you're playing golf while doing it."

"And tennis?" Trent suggested.

"Or any other resort-based activity you guys are interested in taking on."

"What about me?" Eloise asked.

"We've set you up for a hair appointment in the hotel salon tomorrow morning," Philip said. "You can have a nice, casual chat with Carmen."

"She's not touching my hair after what I saw come out of there the other day," she said, looking nearly as traumatized as Hair had been at the mere thought. "I think you need to send Maddie."

"Thanks a lot," I said.

"I'm afraid it has to be you, Eloise," Philip said. "Maddie's got a bigger job to do."

"Which is?" I asked.

"It's time for you to locate and talk to the Sombrero Lady," he said.

TWENTY-FIVE

DESPITE FEELING EQUAL PARTS manipulated, scared, and sure the only people I could trust had the last name Michaels (but not the first name Frank), it was time to figure out exactly who had really killed Alejandro, injured Geo, and sent Ivan a threatening note before Benito was arrested. As soon as I did that, I planned to cancel my TV contract on the grounds of false pretenses. No way was I continuing on as the star of a reality show where the true premise was *murder on the cheap* or whatever it was that had been negotiated with heaven knew whom.

I spent all of Tuesday night awake trying to figure out exactly how I was going to go about that. By Wednesday morning, I found myself in town with a bare-bones crew consisting of a cameraman, an assistant director, and a local police officer to translate and play bodyguard.

Unfortunately, I still had no idea what I planned to do.

We began with a street-by-street search starting outside the jewelry store where I'd first noticed the lady in red and her sombrero cart. Needless to say, there seemed to be as many vendors selling sombreros as there were sombreros for sale.

And everyone seemed to know the particular woman I was looking for:

Ah yes, Conchita...

Sí, Yolanda...

You mean Silvia?

And everyone seemed to know her schedule:

I was just talking to her last night...

She only works weekends...

Mañana...

But no one knew exactly where she was.

Lured by the smell of vanilla, cinnamon, and the promise of a badly needed café Mexicano, I suggested we continue our so far fruitless search at a nearby coffee shop. We grabbed our drinks and were about to continue on when the assistant director's cell phone rang.

Our police officer/bodyguard/translator's also rang at the same time.

I understood the only two words of his rapid-fire Spanish I needed to know: *Señor Geo.*

Combined with the translation provided by the assistant director via his own phone call, I got a pretty good idea what was going on:

"When did they move him into a regular room?"

"Una gran noticia!"

As they each listened to what seemed to be the dual language details of Geo's upgraded condition, I looked up at the prominent red cross atop the five-story building looming in the distance.

"Qué hora están visitando horas?"

"So Anastasia and Philip are leaving their hotel for the hospital in fifteen?"

I knew immediately what I had to do. I needed answers, and I needed them now, before anyone else filled Geo in on everything that had happened since he was attacked at the water park and taken away in an ambulance.

"We can be there in thirty to set up and get some arrival footage. No problem."

And I needed to be there a lot sooner than that if I was going to have a chance to talk to him alone.

"Geo's doing better?" I asked as the assistant director hung up.

"He's doing so well, he's been moved into a regular room."

"Thank goodness."

"Tell me about it," he said. "But it only gives us a half hour to try and find the Sombrero Lady and get to the hospital before we need to get some footage of the three of you greeting Geo."

A woman from a nearby group of tourists asked a passing local, "*Donde está el baño?*" in an overloud, too slow voice.

As the man pointed to a freestanding public restroom very much like the one where I'd actually met Sombrero Lady, my wholly unoriginal, downright plagiarized, and already misused plan came together.

"We better get a move on," the director said, taking a big sip of my coffee.

As everyone agreed, I slid my hand to my stomach and made the same face Frank had made to facilitate my initial meet-and-greet with Alejandro.

"Are you okay?" the cameraman asked.

"Fine," I said, adding a heaping dose of impending-GI-distress to my voice. "I think."

"Are you sure?"

"Actually"—I forced, then stifled a belch—"I'm not sure at all."

"You don't look so well," the cameraman said.

"I don't feel so well all of the sudden," I said.

"Ah," the police officer/translator/bodyguard said. "They come out of nowhere."

"I need to use the restroom," I said with urgency. "Now!"

Without waiting for a response, I took off in the direction of the bathrooms, rushed around the building toward the door to the ladies' room, and ran inside. I looked around for anyone resembling Sombrero Lady, just in case, then took off down an alley concealed from view by the building.

———

"Maddie," Geo rasped, his voice rough from the breathing apparatus that had been removed from his throat. He reached for my hand and squeezed it weakly. "I'm glad you're still here."

"We've all been here, waiting for you to get better," I said, trying to ignore the assorted tubes and wires attached to him and hanging beside him.

"Thanks," he said groggily. "I'm starting to feel better."

"How much do you remember about what happened?"

"Not much," he said sounding choky and as though he was reliving the panic. "I remember being trapped, out of air . . ."

"You do know that whoever grabbed you was really after Ivan?"

He looked as if he was trying to shake off whatever sedating drugs he'd been given by the hospital. "Ivan?"

"No one told you?"

Geo looked thoroughly confused. "No."

"The police believe it was the same person, or people, behind Alejandro's murder."

"Murder?"

"He drowned because someone slipped a roofie into his drink and lured him into the pool."

Geo looked more confused than ever.

"You don't remember that we were investigating his death?"

"I do, but that wasn't…"

"Wasn't what?"

"You're saying he was really murdered?"

"Definitely."

Geo now looked as pale as his sheets. "I don't understand."

"Neither do I, which is why I need you to tell me everything you know, starting with how we ended up in Mexico at Hacienda de la Fortuna."

"Anastasia," he finally said.

"She did the research, found the name of Hacienda de la Fortuna, and called them?" I asked. "Or someone contacted her and proposed the idea?"

"She contacted the hotel, then they got right back to us with a fantastic proposal," he said.

"Who got back to us? Alejandro?"

"I know he was involved, but Anastasia handled most of the arrangements and logistics."

"Which were?"

"The wedding with all the bells, whistles, and extras in exchange for showcasing the resort."

"And the timeshare department?"

"Especially the timeshare department," he said. "The whole vacation-property angle fit with the overall bargain-hunting theme of the show."

"What about a reality show for Alejandro?"

"We were in talks. Until he ..."

"Died?"

Geo nodded.

"As in, another murder for Mrs. Frugalicious to solve?"

"That didn't happen," he said.

"But it did."

We were both silent for a moment.

"I'll admit we had Frank at the ready for when you objected to signing a contract without doing all the proper research," Geo said. "The hair, makeup, and romance stuff with Anastasia's sisters was all planned in advance. And a few other details."

"Like?"

"Like after Alejandro died, we were told to rework the story line to make what we all believed was an accidental death worthy of investigation."

"Did reworking the story line include you wrapping things up by having me come up with a bad guy by the end of the episode?"

"Just someone we could hand over to the local authorities for them to quietly let go after we were gone."

"Which is exactly what's happening, except someone's going to be arrested for a bona fide murder."

"Holy—"

"Exactly."

"Who?"

"Benito, the head chef," I said.

"But he was on that initial list of suspects that were ..."

"Family members?" I offered.

He nodded. "And not legitimately suspicious."

"But now, suddenly, he's the prime suspect because he openly hated his brother-in-law, Alejandro."

"Is it possible he did it?" Geo asked.

"I suppose, except he had no reason whatsoever to come after Ivan," I said. "Or you."

"What are you getting at?"

Geo listened carefully as I laid out everything that had happened since he'd been hospitalized.

"Whoa," he simply said when I'd finished.

"Everyone around here is terrified…" I lowered my voice to a whisper. "They believe the actual killer acted on behalf of a cartel who wanted Alejandro dead and Ivan silenced in order to halt a land-development deal that may have been tied into Alejandro's TV show."

"Who did you say the American was?" Geo asked.

"I didn't," I said, dread fluttering across my belly.

Geo glanced down at the IV taped to the top of his hand.

"What is it?" I asked.

"When we were in the planning stages of all this, I walked in on the tail end of a conversation Stasia was having with one of the execs." He took a raspy breath. "He was complaining that the wedding alone wasn't going to be interesting enough or cost-effective enough to justify the expense for all of us to come down there. Even with the perks."

"And how did she respond?"

He looked up at me. "She guaranteed him the show would be a hit."

"As in, everything is playing out exactly as it was supposed to?"

"I can't rule out that Anastasia got us involved in something heavier than she ever imagined."

The phone beside Geo's bed rang.

"That's got to be her," I said. "She and Philip are on their way up to see you. In fact, I'm supposed to be meeting them up here with the film crew."

"You need to find out who the American was in that meeting," Geo said.

"Yes, but I should check in with the crew before I do. I kind of ditched them in the midst of looking for Sombrero Lady."

"They'll be fine without you," he said and picked up the phone.

I looked at him quizzically as he greeted Anastasia and confirmed they were in front of the hospital and would be up in five minutes. Geo hung up the phone.

"Why will they be fine without me?"

"There is no Sombrero Lady."

"What?"

"The woman you met was a local actress," he said. "We thought it was a pretty clever way to get you to buy into the investigation."

"We?"

"Actually, the Sombrero Lady was Frank's idea."

"Frank's idea?" I could barely get out the words.

"When we let him know about the reworked story line, he said you'd balk about investigating, just like you'd balked about signing up for a free timeshare. He said Sombrero Lady would give the investigation the legitimacy you'd need to stay and look into things." At my horrified expression he added, "Because you're way too smart for the usual reality TV rigmarole."

Clearly I needed to be a lot smarter. "Frank said all that?" I managed.

"Yeah. And I say you better get a move on fast before Stasia and the crew get up here."

———

I rushed out of Geo's room, raced down the hallway opposite the elevators, and exited the building via the stairwell.

Once outside, I ducked into a nearby T-shirt shop.

"*Teléfono*?" I asked, offering the clerk everything in my pocket, which came out to be the peso equivalent of approximately three dollars and fifty cents.

In exchange, he led me to the phone and helped me to dial the main number for the Hacienda de la Fortuna.

"May I speak to Ivan, *por favor*?" I asked after being forwarded to the Activities office. I wanted to question him further about the identity of the American he saw meeting with Alejandro on the boat.

"He's at the dock," the young lady who answered the phone said. "I think."

"Can you transfer me there?" I said. "It's important."

"You probably won't be able to reach him," she said. "But I'll try."

"Not sure where he is," said whoever answered down at the dock.

"This is Maddie Michaels and I really need to speak to him. Can you please have him contact me if you see him?"

With his lackluster *no problemo*, I was certain the dock attendant hadn't bothered to put pencil to whatever scrap of soggy paper might have been laying around the equipment shack.

Clearly I wasn't going to be able to connect with Ivan quickly, so the only logical Plan B was to get back to the resort and see what, if anything, I could find out, starting with Beti in the timeshare office.

Seeing as my money and credit cards were in my purse, which was locked in the crew van, how I was going to get there was another problem.

I quickly decided my best chance was to plead my case to a nearby cluster of taxis, the drivers leaning against their cars, waiting for fares.

I was halfway there when I heard a familiar pitch.

"*Hola, Señora!* How would you like to treat yourself to a spa day or treat your entire family to free water park tickets?"

From my research on timeshares, I recognized the smiling man as an OPC.[31]

While other people avoided direct eye contact with him as they hurried by, I stopped.

"There's a water park nearby?" I asked.

"Only the finest, most breathtaking eco water park you will ever experience," he said, with a decided gleam in his eye.

"How would I go about getting those tickets?" I asked.

"It's quite simple ..."

I nodded along with interest as he launched into his spiel about the gourmet lunch and ninety-minute no-obligation tour of one of my choice of resorts that would qualify me for my free passes.

"Does that include the Hacienda de la Fortuna?" I asked.

"No reason to bother with that place."

"Why?" I asked.

"*Mucho problemos,*" he said, shaking his head.

"What kind of problems?" I asked.

"We don't talk about that around here," he said, looking around. "The resort you really want to tour is Cielo en la Tierra—Heaven On Earth."

"Sounds great, but my friend said I really needed to see Hacienda de la Fortuna."

---

31. Many potential timeshare clients are approached off-site by a person offering a free gift or discounted attraction. These are known as an OPC (off-premise contact). Located at high-traffic tourist areas, their job is to direct as many potential buyers to the timeshare sales center as possible.

"How about—"

"My friend owns a timeshare there and she loves it."

"You won't."

"The pictures looked spectacular," I said.

"Pictures lie," he said, offering photos of his own. "I will show you Heaven."

"But you can't take me to Hacienda de la Fortuna?"

"How about I give you the spa day and the water park tickets?"

"I bet they'll make the same deal for me at Hacienda de la Fortuna," I said.

"You can try," he said, looking disgusted. "But I doubt it."

After another few minutes of haggling, he finally relented, pointing to a similarly dressed man standing across the way with a nearly identical setup of brochures and information. "Go talk to Raul if you really think you have to go to that place, but tell him he owes me for this one."

I stepped across the plaza.

"Hi Raul," I said with a smile. "I'm Maddie and I'm interested in a timeshare."

Five minutes later, I was in a prepaid cab on my way back to the resort.

TWENTY-SIX

THE FRONT LINE SALESMAN[32] was waiting to greet the car, looking like a pet snake gazing at a baby mouse dangling above his cage. His enthusiasm gave way to surprise and then quickly disappointment as he opened the door for me.

"Aren't you—"

"Mrs. Frugalicious," I said. "And I'm sorry to have misled your representative in town and now you, but I need to talk to someone in your office ASAP and I had no other way of getting back here."

"What can I do for you?" he asked, less than enthusiastically.

"Actually, I need to talk to Beti."

"Beti, our receptionist?"

I nodded.

---

32. After being approached by an OPC, you will typically be greeted by a front line salesperson. He or she will treat you to breakfast or lunch, present the benefits and features of the property, answer questions, address all your concerns and reservations, and hopefully convince you to sign a contract, all within a couple hours.

"Whatever," he said, looking more than a little annoyed and motioning me to follow him to the timeshare office.

Our silent walk together was even more uncomfortable than my interchange with the OPC, who'd thought he'd chanced upon a sure-fire sale, only to have to pass me along to his frenemy, Raul. When we finally reached the office, the front line salesman opened the door just long enough for me to pass through.

"Must be on break," he said.

I looked at the empty desk receptionist's desk.

"And everyone else is in the middle of a sales conference, so . . ."

"I'll wait."

———

I'd assumed Beti's break would likely last fifteen minutes—as in a standard, OSHA-mandated, American-style morning coffee break. Why it took me until well past the twenty-four-minute mark to remember I wasn't even in my home country, I wasn't sure, but it likely had something to do with the sales presentation by the *master closer* filtering into the lobby from the sales floor:

"A chain is only as strong as its weakest link, so every step in the timeshare sales presentation is equally and critically important. Yes, folks, everything—the meet and greet, the warm-up, touring the resort, the discovery, and closing the deal.

"There's one even more important, more crucial, element if you want have any chance of making it in this business.

"Listen," he said in a near whisper, and then shouted, "LISTEN!

"What I'm saying here is don't just give an ear. You have to LISTEN to prospective owners. That means monitoring facial expressions and body language and then adjusting your conversation accordingly and constantly, from the very moment you shake hands until the ink is on the contract.

"Fail to listen and you won't hear what they like, don't like, would use, not use, and most importantly, what you know they need!"

I couldn't help but think I hadn't been listening from the moment I signed on for this whole *Family Frugalicious* TV odyssey.

"Despite what you may or may not have heard, you must not only listen, you must PRE-JUDGE as well in order to understand your prospects and adapt the presentation to fit the prospects' wants, desires, vacation lifestyle, finances, and so on."

I thought I could pretend to play happily married and no one would be anything but bargain wiser. Why hadn't it occurred to me that I might just as easily be played too?

Before I could ponder that particular question, a door creaked open from the private hall on the other side of the sales floor. I looked up hoping to see Beti emerge from the kitchen/break area. Instead, Antonio appeared from inside a conference room with a familiar-looking older gentleman. I assumed he was an executive I'd met briefly or passed on one of the pathways over the last few days, until two men in suits emerged from behind him, took positions on either side of the man, and attempted to look nonchalant.

As if the reek of aftershave and steroids didn't give them away as bodyguards.

"The pros can, like a winning sports team, modify their tactics at any time during the presentation in order to achieve maximum results and victory…"

My heart began to thump as Antonio and the man shook hands like they'd just completed a business deal.

Followed by an emotional hug.

Then I realized that I'd seen him at the funeral, seated beside Elena.

The mayor.

"One of the greatest mistakes I see is the salesperson who finally starts to listen but must make adjustments in the presentation during the close, Hail Mary–style."

"Mr. Mayor?" I blurted as he started past me.

His goons closed in around him.

"I'm Maddie Michaels," I said, before either of them decided they needed to strong-arm me into leaving him alone. "Mrs. Frugalicious."

He stopped, dropped the haughty VIP veneer, and flashed the smooth polished smile of a consummate politician. "Mrs. Frugalicious—of course." He smiled that much more broadly as he stepped over and offered me a kiss on each cheek. "I understand you and your crew are doing an excellent job of bringing peace and safety back to our community."

"I hope so," I said. "I was also hoping you might have a moment to talk to me about a few things."

"I'd love to," he said in accented but impeccable English. He looked at his watch. "But I'm afraid I'm already running late for another appointment."

"I'll only need a second."

One of his goons gave me the *back off or else* eye.

"Please?"

"Very well," he finally said, motioning his bodyguards outside and Antonio away.

"Thank you," I said, as Antonio disappeared into the sales conference.

"Whatever I can do," he said, somehow not entirely convincingly.

"Sir, it has come to my attention that you were in the midst of some negotiations with Alejandro and a third party," I said as soon as we were alone. "An investor of some sort?"

"How do you know about that?"

"Police intelligence," I said, to avoid any mention of Ivan.

"The deal was totally on the up and up," he offered so quickly that I could only doubt that was true. "All by the book."

"Was the third party an investor?"

"More of an interested party, I would say."

"But foreign?"

"American born with Mexican citizenship," he said. "So, as I said, completely legitimate."

"Of course," I agreed. "There's been some speculation that Alejandro might have been killed to keep the deal from happening."

"That simply doesn't make sense," he said definitively.

"Maybe his murder could be related to the investor?"

"I don't see how," the mayor said, glancing nervously out the window at his bodyguards.

"What about the connection with the TV show deal?"

"TV show deal?" he asked, looking genuinely surprised.

"Surely you're aware of the reality show Alejandro was in the midst of pitching my producers?"

"He'd certainly been bragging about something along those lines," he said with a nod. "And while there's no denying the possible notoriety such a show would bring to the resort specifically, and our community in general, it had nothing to do with any negotiations in which I've been involved."

"So the events were unconnected?"

"Completely," he said. "Just as I'm completely sure the facts will prove to be different than whatever it is that may have been speculated regarding what did or didn't happen."

Now that was politician-speak if ever I heard it. "You're sure about that?" I asked.

"Positive," he said.

———

I was downright confused about where to go or what do to next as I left the timeshare office, headed down the path, and almost walked head-on into Beti, her nose in a Spanish romance novel.

"Just the person I thought I was looking for," I said.

"I'm just getting off break," she said. "But I'll be back at my desk in five minutes to help you any way I can."

"How about we talk now?" I asked.

Without waiting for her response, I led her over and into a nearby ladies' room, where I was reasonably sure we wouldn't be observed by any security cameras. As soon as I was certain we were alone I said, "Ivan told me he trusts you and that he spoke with you yesterday."

She nodded.

"I just talked with the mayor."

"In our office?"

"Yes," I said. "And when I asked him about Alejandro and his plans for a reality show, he claimed he knew about it, but it had nothing to do with any negotiations he was conducting with the American investor."

Beti considered. "Alejandro told me he just needed to jump through a few hoops and the Hacienda de la Fortuna empire was going to explode because he'd all but inked his own reality show about the resort and the world of timeshare sales."

"That's pretty much what Ivan told me," I said. "But did Alejandro specifically say he'd been discussing the terms of the deal that day on the boat?"

"Not specifically," she said. "But Alejandro did say you were key to making it happen."

"Me?"

"He definitely mentioned you."

"I wonder why? I don't have any ability to get him a show beyond suggesting it might be an interesting idea."

"I don't know," she said. "But he said the producers told him his best chance of getting it green-lighted was to somehow convince you."

"Convince me?" I heard myself repeat.

"He also said he planned to do whatever it took."

As I stood there trying, unsuccessfully, to digest what had to be the unsavory truth of the whole Alejandro-romance subplot, Beti asked, "Is the mayor still there meeting with Antonio?"

"You already knew he was meeting with Antonio?"

"It makes sense that he would," she said.

"Because he's the new manager?"

"Because I'm sure the mayor is helping Elena to settle estate matters."

"Why would he help Elena?"

"Well, he is her father."

I felt like the wind had just been knocked out of me. "Did you just say the mayor is Elena's father?"

"Most important marriage around here in years," she said. "When Elena and Alejandro got married, there was a ceasefire in the decades-long feud between the two richest, most competitive families in the region."

"But if Elena is the mayor's daughter," I said, doing the math, "then Benito is—"

"His son."

———

Alejandro had been set up to seduce me in exchange for a TV show. The mayor knew about Alejandro's plan for stardom, but claimed it had nothing to do with the "totally on the up and up" land deal they were transacting. In addition, the mayor was "completely sure the facts will prove to be different than whatever it is that may have been speculated regarding what did or didn't happen," where the murder of his son-in-law was concerned. The son-in-law he hadn't thought to inform me was the husband of his grieving daughter.

Did that include the speculation about his own son, who everyone, including him, would have me believe killed Alejandro, almost killed Geo, and sent Ivan that threatening message to keep quiet?

My head felt like it was going to burst as I rushed back toward our suite. The feeling intensified when I rounded the corner and spotted a piece of peach-colored stationary dangling from a piece of tape on the door to our suite.

My hands trembled as I ripped the tape from the wood and read the block-letter message:

STICK WITH THE SCRIPT OR THE FAMILY FRUGALICIOUS WILL BE CANCELED FOREVER.

TWENTY-SEVEN

"Did you find her?" FJ asked, looking up from the Xbox that was part of our in-suite entertainment center.

"Find who?" I managed, hoping the boys wouldn't notice I was shaking so hard I could barely get the key card in the door, much less walk into the room.

"The Sombrero Lady," Trent said through a mouthful of tortilla chips and looking at me like I was mentally challenged.

"Not exactly," I said.

"Is everything okay?" FJ asked.

"Just a few complications," I said, not wanting to alarm them. "I'm sure we'll find her soon."

"Too bad," Trent said. "I was hoping you'd have figured this whole mess out by now."

"That makes two of us," I said. "Hey, did you guys hear or see anything unusual since you've been up here?"

"Like what?"

"Noise or people out in the hallway. Anything like that."

The boys shook their heads.

"We've been playing," FJ said, pointing to the screen.

"For how long?" I asked, but without the punitive tone I normally reserved for that particular sentence in relation to my boys' gaming habits.

"Not that long," Trent said. "Maybe half an hour or so."

Seeing as I'd only been back at the resort for forty-five minutes, someone had to have been watching my every move.

"Where's your dad?" I asked.

"In there," Trent said, pointing to the bedroom door. "Taking a little *siesta*."

"Is Eloise still at the salon?"

Trent laughed. "Nope. She came back with the dumbest-looking braids all over her head."

"Where is she now?"

"She and Ivan took off a little while ago."

"Where did they go?"

"Jet skiing."

"Eloise said they were headed to some island that has an amazing beach and underwater caves and stuff," FJ said.

"And you guys didn't want to go with?"

"Of course we did." Trent made kissing noises. "But we weren't invited."

———

"Frank," I said, shaking him awake.

"Wha …?" he said groggily.

"I need you to get up, now!"

"Did you find the Som—"

249

"There is no Sombrero Lady and you know it."

"I—"

"I know she was your idea, so don't bother. In fact, I know about most everything you've been part of to trick me into this whole investigation disaster."

"Maddie." He sat up. "I swear it was for the sake of the sh—"

"There'll be time for swearing later, Frank. At the moment, we have a bigger problem on our hands."

I proceeded to recount everything I'd learned from Ivan, Geo, the mayor, and Beti, including the overwhelming likelihood that a ruthless cartel was behind Alejandro's murder.

"So you're saying that Alejandro may have been killed to halt a land development deal, which may have been dependent on his TV show deal and an infusion of funds from some foreign investor, who may or may not be legit, and that Benito agreed to play guilty because he's Elena's brother and the mayor's son?"

"I'm saying everyone around here is so afraid of this powerful cartel or whatever they are that they set Benito up so we can wrap up our investigation with a killer and go home having restored 'peace' in vacation land."

"And Anastasia somehow got all of us entangled into the middle of it all?"

"Clearly she has."

"I hear you. I really do," he said. "But I don't quite understand a few things. For one thing, how does killing off Alejandro necessarily kill off this land deal, whatever it is? Couldn't someone else from Hacienda de la Fortuna step in and negotiate in his place?"

"I agree there are missing pieces to the puzzle, but I'm afraid I've made a terrible mistake by trying to find out what they are."

I handed him the note.

His eyes widened in horror as he read the message. "Where did this come from?"

"It was taped to the door," I said.

"Our door?"

"Someone had to have been watching my every move to know when I came back to the resort," I said. "Someone who knew when to kill Alejandro, how to scare Ivan, when the security would be down by the pool, and how to time it so *The Family Frugalicious* was on the resort taping."

"Oh God," he said, rereading the note. "We're in trouble."

"I'm afraid Ivan is in even more imminent trouble for having spoken to me about it at all."

"Are the boys still here?" he asked, alarm now punctuating his voice.

"In the living room. Playing Xbox."

"And Eloise is…"

"With Ivan," I said, finishing his sentence.

"We've got to get to them," he said, already halfway across the room and headed for the bathroom where his swim trunks were hanging on a hook. "Now."

TWENTY-EIGHT

"BOLT THE DOOR BEHIND us and don't open it for anyone or go anywhere," Frank barked at the boys as we raced into the living area.

FJ paused the Xbox. "What's going on?"

"I think our investigation is causing a problem and we need to warn Ivan," I said.

"What if we get hungry?" Trent asked.

"Eat what's in the mini bar," Frank said.

"Seriously?" FJ asked. Mini bars were notoriously expensive.

I nooded. "Don't leave the room," I said. "For any reason."

"Liam is going to come up here, and we were going to—"

"No!" Frank said, far too insistently. "You are not to open the door, answer the phone, or go anywhere. You hear us?"

"Okay," FJ said, looking both angry and glum. "But I want to know where you're going and what it is you're so worried about all of the sudden."

"We're going to find Eloise and Ivan," Frank said.

"Once we're back and have them safely here with us, we'll tell you everything," I said. "We promise."

———

"I think I saw him leave on a jet ski," the man working at the dock said in heavily accented English.

"Was my daughter with him?" Frank said.

"*Muy bonita*, curly hair and blue eyes?"

"That's her," Frank said impatiently.

He nodded. "She with Ivan."

"We need to find them," I said waving a prescription bottle I'd grabbed on the way out of the door to explain our urgency to anyone who might be watching. "She has to take these."

"My sons said they were headed to an island," Frank said. "Where would that be?"

"Which island?" the man asked.

"How many are there?"

"A few." He pointed off into the horizon. "They all out that way."

———

Fifteen minutes, $200 American dollars (half of which went toward silencing the man as to our whereabouts), a series of safety instructions in heavily accented English, and one questionably worded release form[33] later, and we were off to try and find Eloise and Ivan.

We flew across the impossibly blue, if slightly choppy, water with the sun on our shoulders, sea birds chirping us on from above, and the wind in our hair.

Living the dream-turned-nightmare, you could say.

As we headed *that way* at full speed, I prayed we were going the right direction for whatever island Ivan and Eloise had gone to before anyone else reached them. My postcard handsome hubby, who couldn't drive because he hadn't thought to wear his motion sickness bands, clutched my waist hard enough to leave marks.

Over the sound of the motor, I could hear him praying not to throw up.

Worse, as we neared what did indeed appear to be land in the distance, I realized the rental guy's definition of *a few* meant a long string of islands.

"What are we going to do?" Frank said.

"I don't know," I said, not wanting to make him toss his cookies just by telling him I'd already decided the best way to look was to figure eight my way in and around the seemingly endless locations for the ideal secluded beach.

What I couldn't decide was what I was going to say to Ivan, assuming we found them in time.

---

33. Jet skiing can be great fun but be careful of scams, especially abroad. People often don't pay attention to what they're signing, or to the damages already on the equipment, and then get charged for misusing the equipment upon return. Jet skis can be tricky to operate and easily damaged. By not showing people how to properly work them, operators know things will go wrong. They can and will collect for damages. They even have their own claims adjusters.

I'm so sorry I've put your life in jeopardy . . .

I tried to find you before I went to the timeshare office to track down Beti . . .

I should have known that if the mayor himself was so scared that he'd offer up his own son, things had to be more perilous than I could manage . . .

Oh God, why hadn't I just stuck to the script?

And then something I hadn't thought of occurred to me:

Why hadn't Ivan ever mentioned that Elena was the mayor's daughter, and that Benito and Elena and were brother and sister in the first place?

As we sped past the beach of one tiny scenic island and around toward the other side of the next, I had another troubling thought:

Why would Ivan even mention, much less consider, exploring another underwater cave given his and Eloise's recent experience at the water park?

While I had to assume he thought the best way to deal with trauma was to get right back on the horse, I couldn't help but feel increasingly traumatized myself. Whoever killed Alejandro had to have been aware that the security camera was down by the pool where Alejandro was found, had to have been at the water park at the time Geo was injured, and had to have known how to time the whole scenario around *The Family Frugalicious* taping schedule. Other than the fact that he was a victim, and an almost fatal one at that, wasn't Ivan the only person I knew of who actually fit that bill?

The thought was entirely too ridiculous to consider.

That was until we'd whizzed past islands number two and three and were approaching a mostly nondescript (where stunning Caribbean islands were concerned, anyway) but larger land mass that appeared to be primarily rock outcroppings. It seemed to lack the rolling jungle appearance of anything else we'd passed thus far.

"Go faster," Frank shouted over the engine. "The fuel smell makes me extra queasy when you slow down."

"The odor is the same unless I'm idling, and I have to slow down," I yelled back, pointing to something that appeared incongruously red and blue beside a rock jutting out from the shore.

"A jet ski!" Frank exclaimed.

I headed toward what appeared to be the same make and model as ours.

And Ivan appeared atop a nearby rock.

Waving.

We waved back and he motioned us around, over to a makeshift natural dock, and directed us to park our jet ski beside his.

As we neared him, I swore I could smell patchouli. With one look at what he was doing, however, I definitely smelled fuel, and it wasn't coming from our jet ski.

TWENTY-NINE

"WHAT ARE YOU DOING?" Frank asked as we got off our jet ski.

"He's siphoning the gas," I said, my heart was growing heavier by the moment.

"Why do you need to—"

"I hope it wasn't too hard to find the island," Ivan said by way of answer, inserting a hose into the gas tank of his jet ski. "Sorry I couldn't give more specific instructions, but I'm sure you understand."

"Instructions?" Frank asked.

"I figured I'd left enough of a hint with the boys that you'd figure out how to come find me."

"What's going on?" Frank asked.

"I made an even bigger mistake than I thought," I said. "We fell right into his trap."

Frank looked thoroughly confused. "What?"

I took a deep, centering breath before stating what was quickly becoming clear. "The *someone* who killed Alejandro, attacked Geo, and timed everything to happen while we were on the resort taping our show is Ivan."

"Yes," Ivan agreed. "And I'm afraid I'll need to take the keys to your jet ski off your hands."

I clutched them firmly and tried to gauge whether I could hop on and race away for help.

"Don't even think about it," he said. "Not if you want to see your daughter again."

"Eloise!" Frank shouted, then coughed from the noxious gas fumes. "Eloise!"

"Don't bother. She can't possibly hear you from here."

"What have you done with her?"

"She's perfectly safe," Ivan assured us. "In fact, she's waiting for me to come back with the surprise I promised her."

"You mean me and Frank?"

"Plus a picnic lunch," he said, reaching for the keys.

Frank responded by throwing up in the sand.

"Why?" I asked, as Frank puked his guts out.

"I didn't want to," Ivan said, "But I couldn't let Alejandro get away with ruining even one more life."

"Like you almost ruined Geo's, you mean?" I asked. "Ivan, he nearly died!"

"I wouldn't have let that happen."

"You were ahead of Geo in the tunnel, weren't you?" Frank managed. "How could you have—" Then he spun around to vomit up more of his last meal.

"That was one of the trickiest parts of all this," Ivan said. "But I had to get suspicion off myself."

"It worked to mislead everyone," I said. "I assume the anonymous threat via the police department and the note on my door were both from you?"

"I called the police right before I walked in the door, and I made sure the note was taped to your door by a worker who didn't speak any English just after I took off for this island." He smiled. "Isn't it amazing what people see or don't see when they're led in a certain direction?"

"So there's no cartel or mafia?" I asked.

"Cartels are a very real problem down here—so real that no one doubted that Alejandro had gotten himself into something he couldn't slither his way out of. The Hacienda de la Fortuna isn't so squeaky clean where mob ties are involved either, so no one really wanted to question what happened. If you and your family hadn't started to investigate, I could have easily gotten rid of the scourge that was Alejandro Espinoza."

"Never mind that Benito would rot in prison for a crime you committed?"

"That would never happen," he said. "A little money changes hands and problems resolve themselves, especially when you're the mayor's son."

"Which you conveniently didn't mention."

"And you inconveniently sniffed out. Believe me, I never wanted it to come to this," Ivan said, turning to siphon fuel from his jet ski into ours, then proceeding to pry open the hull of his machine and pull out its inner workings.

As he prepared to upend his jet ski into the water, Frank stopped throwing up long enough to jump him from behind.

I screamed.

They tussled.

But it was over as quickly as it started. Frank, who spent far too much time toning and strengthening at the gym, was in a chokehold in less than thirty seconds, courtesy of the younger, stronger, and more naturally fit Ivan.

"I didn't want to kill Alejandro, or harm Geo, and I don't want to hurt any of you," Ivan said, twisting Frank's arm behind his back. "So how about not making this any harder than it has to be?"

"Give me a break," Frank said.

"Don't make me," Ivan said, holding him tighter and guiding him around some bushes. "Both of you be quiet, and Maddie, you stay beside me where I can see you."

I did as I was told, staying in his view while he led us out of the cove, over a hill, and through some dense brush.

"We're here," Ivan finally said, stopping by a stand of trees.

"Where's Eloise?" Frank looked around frantically. "Eloise!"

"You'll see her very soon," Ivan said. "But I need you to promise me there'll be no more funny business from either of you."

We both nodded.

"Don't move," he said, letting go of Frank.

Ivan disappeared around a nearby boulder and returned a second later with two full backpacks. He put one on and gave the other to Frank. Without another word, he led us toward a stunning white sand beach and stopped about twenty-five feet from the shore beside a clear cenote the size of a large Koi pond.

As we looked at the water-filled cavern at the edge of the pond, Ivan pulled a rope from the tall grass beside the water.

"What are you going to do to us?" Frank asked.

"If you'd just gone down the investigation path I laid out for you, I wouldn't have had to any of this," Ivan said, not answering the question.

"Meaning what?" I asked.

"I promise I'll explain everything," he said, making a slipknot of some kind at the end of the rope.

"But first you're going to tie us up?"

"I'm tying us together," he said. "So I don't lose one of you underwater."

Horror filled Frank's face and my soul. "Underwater?"

"Eloise is waiting for you in the coolest underwater cave you'll ever see."

"Holy sh—"

Ivan slipped the rope over my head and around my waist. He cinched me up, measured out some slack, and moved on to Frank. "The key here is to keep calm."

"Right," Frank said. "Like that's possible in this situation. We're literally tied to a killer."

Ivan tied the other end of the rope around his own waist and leveled his gaze at me. "I'm dead serious."

Of that, I had no doubt.

"Maddie, you'll dive down by the wall of the cavern first. Once you are a full body length below the surface you'll see a tunnel. Enter it. Then feel your way left, right, right, left, straight, and you'll be there."

"And what if I make a mistake?"

"Don't," he said.

"Left, right, right, left, straight?"

"You got it," he said.

"Ready?"

I wasn't, but I nodded anyway.

"Frank?"

"Left, right, right, left, straight."

"We're ready," Ivan said. "Let's go."

The next thing I knew, he'd counted to three and we jumped as a group into surprisingly warm, clear water that would have felt heavenly under different circumstances.

"Everyone take a breath," Ivan instructed.

Both Frank and I took a breath.

"Deeper," he said. "Maddie, take the deepest breath you can, hold it, and go."

Without allowing myself to think about just how unbelievably panicked I was, how much I hated confined spaces (particularly pitch black ones underwater), or where I was really going, I did exactly what I'd been told, hoping left, right, right, left, straight was, in fact, right.

And not left.

I dove down into darkness, found the tunnel, and burrowed my way toward I didn't know what, using my arms to alterately breast-stroke and feel the walls of the tunnels. Just when I was sure my lungs would burst, the tunnel seemed to fall away and I saw light from behind my eyelids. I feared it was the proverbial light at the end of the tunnel, but then I broke the water's surface into what was, indeed, one of the most stalactite-and stalagmite-filled crystalline cavern I'd ever been inside, willingly or otherwise.

And I was looking straight at Eloise, who, despite a head full of Bo Derek–style braids, was as unharmed as promised.

She was, however, as shocked as I was in shock.

"You're the surprise?" she asked, looking more than a little disappointed.

"Eloise, thank God you're okay."

"Why wouldn't I be?" she asked. "I mean, I was a little weirded out about the whole diving straight into a cenote to get to a cave thing, after what happened to Geo and Ivan and everything, but if he can keep me from being afraid of reptiles and stuff, I totally had to trust him. And isn't this just the coolest place? Can you believe how there's all this natural light from above?"

"It's beautiful, but—"

I felt a tug around my waist, and Frank popped up out of the water.

"Daddy?"

He coughed up some water. "Eloise!"

"Why are you here?" she asked, finally voicing just how unusual our presence really was.

"Honey, sometimes, when you're particularly charmed by a man"— I pointedly didn't look at Frank—"you can get distracted and miss a few key signs."

On cue, Ivan appeared from below the water.

"Ivan?" Eloise asked. "What's is going on?"

"A picnic," he said.

"That, and Ivan killed Alejandro," Frank blurted.

"*What?*"

As Eloise's incredulous voice echoed through the cave, Ivan swam over to the ledge where she'd been awaiting his return, got out of the water beside her, untied himself, and began to tow us over. "As I said to your parents, I'm sorry to have to do this, but I can't have you ganging up on me. I really hope you understand."

"I don't understand at all," Eloise said.

"Ivan killed Alejandro and almost killed Geo," Frank repeated.

"That's impossible," she said. "He was almost killed himself in that—"

"Cave?" I asked, noting a stalactite formation that looked like a church organ. "I'm afraid it's true, honey."

She turned to him. "Ivan?"

263

"Sit there and don't move," he said, directing her to a flat spot between two rock spires while he relieved Frank of what was an apparently waterproof backpack and tied the two of us near each other but just out of arm's reach.

"I thought you really liked me," Eloise said.

"I do," he said, securing Frank and me to nearby rock spires. "That's one of the main reasons this is happening." He finished tying us up, then secured Eloise. "I'm not hurting you, am I?" he asked.

She looked at him like he was as insane as he truly had to be.

We all watched as he quietly unpacked sandwiches, fruit, and chips from Frank's bag.

"Lunch?"

"No thanks," we all said, basically in unison.

"Suit yourselves," Ivan took a bite of a peanut butter and jelly sandwich. "But I suggest you eat the perishable stuff first."

Frank looked like he was about to vomit again as Ivan chewed, swallowed, and sat down on a rock. "First of all, I never intended to kill Alejandro," he said.

Whether or not we believed him, we all nodded in agreement.

"I came down here to Mexico on my honeymoon..."

"You're married?" Eloise and I both asked, she looking more horrified than she had been to hear he was a murderer.

"Not anymore."

"Wait," Eloise said. "You said you were only twenty-three."

"I'm twenty-nine," he said, "but the dreadlocks shave off a few years."

"Does it even matter?" Frank said.

"We landed in Mexico," Ivan continued, "and we were guided toward a man sitting in a booth near the airport exit who we assumed was with our resort. So we listened as he explained all the sights and attractions. He told us if we signed up for a hour-and-a-half presentation at the Hacienda de la Fortuna and paid twenty dollars each, we would receive free tickets Chichen Itza, which was a three-hundred-dollar value."

"Were you staying at Hacienda de la Fortuna?"

"No, but he promised us the presentation would get refunded through our hotel if we changed our minds, so we signed up. Later that night, we decided we didn't want to waste time at a timeshare presentation, so we spoke to someone at our hotel and showed them our receipt."

"Let me guess—they knew nothing about it?" I offered.

"Exactly. And since we wanted to go to the ruins, we decided to just go on the tour. So we went, had the gourmet breakfast, and took a tour of the property. No big deal. That was, until they started the whole hard sell business on us. Six hours and a lot of free drinks later, we finally stopped saying no, signed a contract, and handed over a credit card that we couldn't afford to max out."

"Sounds brutal," Frank said, twisting his hand back and forth. "But that's hardly worthy of murder."

"Twisting will only make the rope tighter around your wrists."

Frank stopped working his wrist.

"At the time, I had two years of law school under my belt."

"You're a lawyer?" Eloise asked.

"At that point I was sure I was going to be, so I asked about everything during the contract signing. There was one Spanish document I asked about in particular, and I was told that it pertained to our forty-eight-hour right to cancel. My wife, who was also a law student, asked how we went about canceling if we needed to, and our salesperson provided her an email address.

"By the next day, we'd sobered up from all the alcohol they'd given us to make us sign and decided we'd made a bad decision. We scanned our contract looking for a phone number, but all we could find was the booking line so we wrote up a signed letter, attached it to an email, and sent it off to the address the salesperson had given us."

"Did you also dispute the deposit with your credit card company?" I advised, forgetting about our circumstances long enough to put on my Mrs. Frugalicious cap.[34]

"Absolutely. But when we got home, we got a call almost immediately, welcoming us to the Hacienda de la Fortuna. I informed the agent that we had canceled our contract. Later that day, I was called by none other than Alejandro Espinoza, who claimed we'd signed away our right to cancel because we got a special deal and that the document in Spanish was a waiver to the usual forty-eight-hour cancelation."

"I heard a story like this in the timeshare office," I said.

"There are a lot of them," he said. "Alejandro insisted our only option was to downgrade our package, but we wouldn't get the deposit back. I said we wanted our contract canceled and our deposit refunded. He threatened that our contract was headed straight to the legal department and that I should be prepared to play hardball. Frustrated and worried, I started doing some research and found various complaints and articles from other people who had been in our exact situation. I started emailing every address I could find,

---

34. While spending money you don't have is a bad idea, using a credit card can allow you to use the credit card company's considerable influence when disputing fraudulent charges. Not to mention the points and bonuses you can accumulate—just make sure before you sign up that you will actually be able to use those point and miles.

filed complaints with the Federal Consumer Board, and sent a certified letter to the Hacienda de la Fortuna.

"That's when the dogfight really began.

"For months, Alejandro and the legal department kept calling and threatening us, everything from collections to sending thugs after me. Instead of giving in and keeping the timeshare like I probably should have, I became obsessed with fighting back."

"I'd have done the same thing," Frank said, sounding way more cavalier than I'd ever seen him act.

Ivan sighed and hung his head for a moment. "Well, by that time, my wife had decided I was far too compulsive for her. She left me for one of our law professors."

"That's awful," Eloise said.

"At that point, I had nothing to lose."

Frank looked like he was ringside at the fights. "So you came down here to kill Alejandro?"

"My plan was to come down and fight him in court and/or the court of public opinion. I mean, why are these outfits allowed to lie and manipulate people? Why hasn't anyone stepped up to stop this kind of unethical behavior?"

"That is a good point," Eloise said. "It really is."

Ivan smiled at her. "So I came down here, got a job at the resort, and started collecting information that would expose the operation for what it is."

"Didn't Alejandro recognize you?" Eloise asked.

"Not with the dreadlocks I'd grown to disguise myself. Plus, I quickly discovered I was one in a sea of strong-armed timeshare owners, so he probably wouldn't have known who I was anyway. I managed to collect enough information to get some traction, then—"

"*The Family Frugalicious* showed up," I said. "And messed with your timetable."

Ivan nodded. "Something like that."

"How did we mess things up?" Eloise asked, looking more than a little hurt.

"For one thing, you made me feel things I didn't think I could feel after my wife left." He smiled sweetly at her. "But when Alejandro started bragging about how he was bringing the TV show down here and was about to be both rich and famous no matter what it took, I knew I had to act right away. No way could I let him destroy your family or any other family that came down here as a result of watching your show."

"So you roofied and drowned him?" Frank asked.

"I slipped a little something into his cocktail and called him on a house phone to meet me near the Estanque Reflectante, where I knew the security cameras were down. I'd planned to get him to admit to his timeshare tactics, and insist he make amends. That, or I was going to expose the web of Hacienda de la Fortuna corruption and cartel ties I'd also uncovered.

"What I didn't know was that he was drinking vodka instead of water half the time and that the combination with the Rohypnol would make him erratic. He met me at the pool. I let him know who I really was and what I expected from him. Then, instead of some slightly out of it conversation where he admitted what I needed to know, he called me a bunch of awful names in Spanish, picked up a hand weight, and chucked at it my face."

Ivan lowered his head.

"I'm afraid that's when I lost it and pushed him into the pool." He paused. "I couldn't exactly say how it happened, but the next thing I knew, he was ... sinking."

None of us said anything.

"At first, I panicked," Ivan continued, his voice shaky. "Then I realized that no one would be surprised, nor would they want to really investigate the untimely drowning of a tyrant with known mob connections."

"So that romantic beach walk we took during the reception was really just an alibi for you?" Eloise asked.

"No," he said emphatically. "It was only after you guys decided to start investigating that I realized I'd need one. That, and I needed to get creative if I wanted to stay off your radar."

"So you nearly drowned Geo?" I asked.

"I was trying to scare you into halting your investigation."

"Which had the opposite effect," Frank said. "After all, we are investigative journalists."

I sighed.

"My only choice was to stay one step ahead of you."

"By trying to convince me the murder was connected to Alejandro's land deal?" I asked.

"I wanted you to know who the people your show is doing business with really are. I mean, along with the timeshare hard selling, that whole public-land-for-private-use sweetheart deal was all about kickbacks, payoffs, and sketchy connections."

"The mayor insisted the deal was completely on the up and up," I said.

"Of course he did," Ivan said.

"He admitted that the investor you saw was American, but said he was also a Mexican citizen."

"Did he tell you who the man actually was?"

I shook my head.

"His name is Godofredo 'Jeff' Kortajarena."

"Sounds authentic to me," Frank said.

"He made a fortune in the US selling clothing made in south-of-the-border sweatshops." Ivan shook his head. "They don't come much dirtier than him, making it an easy leap for everyone, including the mayor, to think Alejandro was killed by a rival bent on stopping the deal."

"And you get away with murder," I concluded.

"I stopped one man," Ivan said sadly. "I just wish there weren't so many Alejandros out there, eager to bully people out of their money and happiness for the illusion of paradise."

The word *paradise* echoed through the cave.

"At least Alejandro's death had nothing to do with Anastasia or the show," Frank finally said.

Ivan snickered. "Considering he'd all but inked a deal for his own reality show about the resort and the world of timeshares, I'd say his *life* certainly had everything to do with your show coming here."

"And Geo told me that when they were in the planning stages of this shoot, he walked in on a conversation between Stasia and one of the execs. He was concerned that the wedding alone wasn't going to be interesting or cost-effective enough to justify the expense for all of us to come down there."

"What did she say?" Frank asked.

"That she'd make sure it would be."

"I'd say the same thing if I were her," Frank said. "It's all about making things happen in this business."

I looked down at the rope tied around my hands. "And look what happened as a result."

Frank was uncharacteristically silent.

"On that note," Ivan said, reaching for one of the backpacks, "I believe my work here is finished."

"You're not really going to leave us here to die," Eloise wailed, "are you?"

"I'll let someone know how to find you as soon as I get where I need to go," he said. "In the meantime, you have provisions and Eloise's survival expertise to rely on."

"*Eloise's expertise?*" Both Frank and I asked simultaneously and incredulously.

"From everything she's told me, she's picked up quite a few handy outdoor survival techniques from watching reality TV."

"I should never have told you that," she said. "Or anything else."

"What exactly were you telling him?" Frank asked.

"Ivan, is that how you kept one step ahead of Maddie?" Eloise asked. "By asking me all of those questions about my family?"

"I was truly interested," he said, looking straight at her. "And not just because I needed the information."

"I thought we had something—"

"Special," Ivan said, lopping off a handful of his dreadlocked hair. "We did. I'm truly sorry it has to end like this."

"You don't have to do this, Ivan," she pleaded.

"But I do," he said, big chunks of hair falling into the water. "Ugh. I hate these damn dreadlocks even more than that nauseating patchouli."

"I think she meant you don't have to leave us here," I said.

He swung his gaze over to me. "Sorry. This is how it has to be."

"But it doesn't," I said, hoping my prior history of talking my way out of danger with murderers (albeit not entirely successfully) might serve me. "No one knows you killed Alejandro except us."

"I would have done the same thing," Frank said.

"Alejandro deserved what he got," Eloise added.

"I agree," I said. "We'll never say a word to anyone. You'll still get away with your plan."

"We swear," Eloise said. "Never, ever."

"We'll take you back to the US with us. We're supposed to leave tomorrow night."

"Sorry, folks," he said. "But you should know that I have to get a lot farther away than that to be free of the reach of the *Familia de la Fortuna*."

"But we're the only ones who know what happened," I protested.

"It's just a matter of time before people start talking and figures it all out too."

"If they do, we'll vouch for you …" I reasoned.

"It's completely unfair what happened. Anyone could have snapped," Eloise said.

"Really, you're a hero …" Frank added.

"Have any of you ever been to Mexican prison?" he asked.

Eloise began to cry. "But—"

"I'm sorry," he said, wiping a tear from her cheek. "I really am."

We watched in impotent silence as he reached into the bag again, pulled out a battery-operated shaver, and transformed before our eyes from a lovable, bushy-haired hippie into a buzz-haired, cold-eyed killer on the lam.

"Much better," he said, rubbing his shorn pate.

"I really liked the dreadlocks," Eloise muttered.

"Maddie and Frank, I wish you all the best," he said and then smiled at Eloise. "And Eloise, you're beautiful and fantastic. I'm sorry it couldn't have worked out differently between us."

"Me too," she said.

As a final act of misplaced benevolence, he placed the scissors on the ledge where she could reach them with her outstretched feet.

He slipped into the water.

And then he was gone.

THIRTY

IN A YEAR'S TIME, I'd been tied up and nearly killed, locked away and nearly died, and now, both tied up and locked away. The mere thought that I might actually die like this, once again, was way more than I could bear.

At least I wasn't alone this time.

"I was just trying to make him think I knew things about the outdoors when I told him I watched survival shows," Eloise wailed. "I ... like ... hardly ... ever ... watch ... those ... shows."

"Zelda said bad luck comes in threes," Frank fairly wailed himself in a panicked voice that could make anyone cry. "I'm too young to die."

On second thought, alone had its advantages.

"We're all too young to die," I said. "And we all need to calm down, just like Ivan said."

"He also said he liked me so much he was going to save up to come visit me at school because he couldn't wait until the next time we came down here to see me."

"People often make promises they can't keep when they're caught up in the euphoria of a new relationship," I said. "Even under the best circumstances, it's a particularly tough lesson."

"Is this a nightmare or is this really happening?" Frank moaned.

Alone was sounding more and more preferable … except for the scissors and battery-operated clippers our captor had been merciful enough to place within stretching distance of Eloise's feet.

"Eloise, can you reach either of them?"

"I'm trying," she said, tears streaming down her face as she attempted to hook a toe through the scissor handle. "I hope it doesn't take Ivan long to send someone to rescue us."

"I wouldn't hold your breath waiting," Frank said caustically.

"Really, Frank?"

"Sorry, bad choice of words. But Ivan did have a point about the whole timeshare business, and I admire his resolve in coming down here and trying to do something about it. Seeing how things turned out, I don't exactly have faith that he'll actually send someone for us, though."

"If we got in here, we can get out," I said. "It was left, right, right, left, straight, so we just turn it around."

"Wasn't it right, left, left, right, straight?"

"I'm sure it wasn't."

"I'm sure it was," Frank insisted.

"I wasn't paying attention one way or the other," Eloise said, pulling the scissor handle toward her with her big toe. "But if Ivan really wanted us to die, he wouldn't have bothered to leave these provisions, right?"

"El, honey, it's clear that he cared about you, but he had bigger problems on his hands," Frank said.

"I can't believe I was falling for a lying—"

"Don't even say it," I said, not saying what I was thinking: *Like father like daughter.*

"All I know is that if we do survive, I'm picking out who you date from here on out," Frank said.

"Does this mean you're finally admitting that Ivan is a less suitable match for Eloise than Liam is for—"

"Do you think the boys are in any danger?" he asked, clearly trying to change the subject.

"Ivan's probably halfway to Central America by now."

"How long before they start worrying about where we are?"

"Who knows how long it will be before they even leave the room?" I said. "We warned them to stay put at all costs and not to speak to anyone."

"Okay, now I'm worrying," Frank said.

"You already were," I said. "But you didn't answer my question."

"About Liam?" Eloise asked, carefully lifting the scissors with her toes to where her right hand was tied to a spire. "First of all, he's way too young for me because he's like seventeen. Secondly, he's —"

"Don't." Frank shook his head. "Just don't go there."

"Why not?" I said.

"Shush!" Frank said.

"Don't shush me," I said.

"Stop bickering," Eloise said, somehow maneuvering the scissors onto her thumb and forefinger and setting to work on the piece of rope restraining her left hand.

"We're not bickering," Frank said.

"We've just been wondering if—" I said.

"*You've* been wondering," Frank said to me with a *shut up* glare. "Not me."

"It's about FJ," I said to Eloise. "And Liam."

Eloise looked up with an expression of surprise that made her look like a female version of Frank. "Are you thinking Liam has a crush on FJ or something?"

"And maybe vice versa."

"No way," Frank said.

"They do seem to be spending a lot of time together," I said. "And since he lives in Denver too …"

"Interesting," Eloise said, returning to her cutting. "I hadn't really thought about it."

Consternation filled Frank's face.

"Has FJ ever brought up the subject of dating with you?" I asked.

"I do know he's definitely shy and very picky," she continued. "Although I'm pretty sure he likes girls."

Frank looked equal parts relieved and *I told you so.*

"At least, I think so," she qualified.

"But you're not positive?" I asked.

"Either way, you know he'll make better choices than I have." She sniffled. "Or Trent …"

I didn't bother to even raise an eyebrow in Frank's direction. "What about Trent?"

"If I were worried about anyone, I'd worry about him."

"Because?"

"His taste in girls can be summed up in one word: trampy."

I cringed.

Frank chuckled.

"That's okay with you, Frank?"

"It's a perfectly normal phase in a young man's life."

"Not in my opinion."

"He'll grow out of it."

"And what if he doesn't?"

"I thought I said to stop bickering," Eloise said.

"All families have issues they need to work through," I said.

"Especially ours," Eloise sighed.

"Starting with honesty," I said. "Which leads me to another issue I believe needs clearing up."

"Which is?" Frank finally chimed in, but with more than a touch of hesitation.

"We now know who killed Alejandro and why, but I still don't think I quite understand what Anastasia meant by *having her cake and eating it too* where the show and the Hacienda de la Fortuna are concerned."

"It seems obvious," Frank said. "She was negotiating a deal with Alejandro on top of doing our show down here."

"Did you know that Alejandro was told by the producers that the best chance of getting his show green-lighted was to somehow convince me?"

"You? But you don't have any ability to ..." His voice trailed off as he seemed to realize the implications.

"Then why was he led to believe such a thing?"

"Maddie, I already told you I had nothing to do with any of that."

"And I told you I knew you were part of the plan to make Alejandro's death investigation-worthy. Why on earth should I believe you weren't part of the plot to stir up some potentially serious marital drama? I mean, we all know it's great for ratings, and ratings are the bottom line, aren't they?"

"I would never—"

"Only because it would make you look bad," I said. "But it's weird. You don't know anything, Geo doesn't know anything, but somehow, I was being pursued by a man who happened to be in the midst of negotiating a TV deal."

"Yes, but—"

"I know you told Anastasia I was too smart for the typical reality TV nonsense, but what else did you tell her? Something must have led her to believe it was okay to try and pull off a stunt like that."

"Umm," Eloise suddenly looked as sheepish as I'd ever seen her.

"Umm, what?"

"Since we're being honest and all ..."

We both turned to her, best as we could while still restrained.

"I'm afraid I maybe might have said something that, like ... I don't know ..."

"You don't know what?" Frank asked.

"Maybe I might have tipped her off that things weren't so perfect between you guys."

"What are you talking about?" Frank said. "We—"

"It's not like you've been the best role models, relationshipwise."

"We've worked out our differences."

"Seriously, Dad?"

"We have. Haven't we, Maddie?"

"What did you tell Anastasia?" I asked, not answering Frank.

"It just kind of slipped out," Eloise said.

"*What* slipped out?"

"It was before we came down here, when we were prepping for this episode, Stasia was showing us the website for the resort and made some comment about you two renewing your vows down here." She paused. "I accidentally said 'yeah, right.'"

"And that's all?"

"I might have also said you barely speak when you're not on camera."

"Oh my God!" Frank attempted (unsuccessfully, due to the rope restraints) to put his face in his hands. "You really need to learn when not to speak."

"Eloise, I have to agree with Frank on this. Why would you tell her that?"

"I'm sorry," she said. "But it's not like everyone didn't already know you aren't really together anymore."

"If everyone knows, it's because you told them."

"Not on the set," she said. "I meant me and Trent and FJ know."

"How do you know?" Frank asked.

"Because we know both of you. We know you were determined to get this show for us. We also know Maddie agreed to *The Family Frugalicious* because she thought it was in the best interests of the family, not because it was best for herself."

Tears I thought I wasn't going to allow myself to shed began to roll down my cheeks.

"And no offense, Dad, but after everything that's happened this last year, I wouldn't have blamed her if she'd refused." Her voice cracked. "And that's from someone who was falling hard for a mur—"

"Ivan had us all fooled," I said, hoping to be of some comfort despite it all. "And, as your dad said, he did come down to Mexico with the best of intentions. Just like I did when I agreed to do the show."

"Me too," Frank added.

"All I know is something's gotta give," Eloise said, going back to sawing the rope attached to her left wrist. "Assuming we all live, that is."

THIRTY-ONE

It took hours, or what felt like hours, for Eloise to slice through the rope so she could untie me. Together we freed Frank. We ate our peanut butter and jelly sandwiches for strength, and decided on a strict rationing plan for the items in the first backpack, which, to Ivan's credit, was filled with energy-dense foods like dried fruit, nuts, and beef jerky. While he was also kind enough to load the second backpack with useful items— a flashlight, Advil, bandages, first-aid cream, a mini water purifier and, as a small salve for Eloise's wounded heart, a bag of Hershey's Kisses, we were determined not to stay put for very long.

After a brief discussion, Frank semi-relented about whose rights and lefts were the most right by claiming he'd misunderstood at first and that we were both saying the same thing because the backward direction of left, right, right, left, straight, was in fact, straight, right, left, left, right. That issue settled, we decided to chart our way out of the cave.

How we would get off the island was another problem entirely, but we all agreed it was a much better one than being stuck in a cave, given the choice.

The more vexing problem, we soon discovered, was that there were at least ten tunnels leading into the cave.

Seeing as Eloise could only remember that we appeared "somewhere in the middle of the water" we decided to start exploring in pairs, and then charting and marking the various exits.

"Number one is a dead end," I said, having explored a hole just beneath the ledge, which not only seemed to be in the wrong location and felt a little too large, but turned out to be a crater that lacked any tunnels.

Frank marked the spot by scratching a large NO on the rock wall above for future archeologists to mull over.

Two holes later, one of which had a promising straight-right combo before dead-ending, the light filtering into the cave through cracks in the ceiling gave way to darkness.

"I didn't want to have to spend even one night in here," Frank said, fumbling for the flashlight.

"But it may not be our last, so don't waste the batteries, even for a second."

"I won't," he said locating a small camping blanket that Ivan had included in the supplies backpack.

"Ivan told me he discovered this cave," Eloise said as Frank and I huddled together under the blanket on either side of her. "Do you think he's the only one who knows about it?"

"I don't want to think about that," Frank said.

"Do you think there's a chance anyone could be looking for us yet?" she asked.

"I don't know what to think," I said. "No one knows to suspect Ivan of anything."

"And we paid that man at the dock not to say anything to anyone about us taking the jet ski."

"Even if he did, there are so many islands," Eloise said.

"The boys know we came out here looking for you and Ivan," I said.

"Why did we insist they stay put and not talk to anyone?" Frank moaned.

"Because it seemed like the only way to keep them safe."

"There's no way anyone is going to find us in here if Ivan doesn't send someone," Eloise added unhelpfully.

Frank said, "That's why we'll find our way out first thing in the morning."

"Yes," I agreed.

"Definitely."

The cave grew silent enough to hear the quiet symphony of slow drips and droplets of water.

"I'm scared," Eloise said.

"Me too," Frank said.

"So am I…"

———

"Maddie! Dad!" Eloise whispered shaking both Frank and I awake from a surprisingly sound slumber given that we were huddled together under a single blanket on a mattress made of rock.

"What?"

"What is it?"

"Listen to that noise."

There was a new and distinct bubbling sound echoing through the cavern.

"What is that?" Frank asked, fumbling for the flashlight.

"Do we even know what kind of creatures live in cenotes?" Eloise's voice cracked. "I mean, other than small fish?"

"That's all I saw," I said. "But look …"

I pointed to a faint light deep beneath the water.

"Please don't let that be an electric eel …" Eloise said. "I hate—"

"Electric eels are the least of our problems," Frank said, flipping on the flashlight, locating both the scissors and the clippers, and handing them to us.

"You think it's him?"

"Who else could it be?"

"Why would he come back?"

"I don't know, but as soon as he rises to the surface, Maddie will clonk him with the clippers. Eloise, you hold the scissors to his neck until we tie him up." Frank and I had somehow swapped roles, and he was now the calm one while I fretted.

"But what if I knock him out and he has a concussion and can't remember how to get us out of here?" I asked.

"Let's see exactly where he's coming from. That way we'll know how to get out of here even if he's incapacitated." Frank shined the light on the bubbles and pointed. "He's definitely coming out right there—from the middle of that back wall."

"I'm ready," I said, leaning toward the water, the clippers poised over my head.

That was when I noticed a second person emerging from the tunnel.

"What is—"

"What do we—"

Before I could say the word *do*, a head broke the surface of the water.

"*Policía!*" the first diver shouted. "No one move."

We all froze, makeshift weapons in hand. A second diver rose to the surface.

"*Hola!*" he shouted, and lifted his mask. "It's me, Felipe."

"Felipe?" I said, stunned.

Eloise dropped the scissors and burst into tears of joy.

"I had a feeling this was where we'd find you," Felipe headed toward us. "Thankfully you're all alive."

The policeman continued to search the cave with a flashlight. "Where is he?"

"Gone," I said, the adrenaline giving way to a huge flood of relief. "Long gone."

Felipe shook his head. "I knew we should have come here first."

"Does anyone need medical assistance?" the police officer asked.

"We're okay," I said. "Thank you for rescuing us so quickly."

"I can't tell you how grateful we are," Frank said, offering both men a hand out of the water.

"How did you know about this place?" I asked.

"I grew up playing on these islands," Felipe said. "I know all of them, which is why I was brought along to help."

"But Ivan told me he discovered this cave," Eloise said.

"That gringo?" Felipe snickered. "La Caverna del Oro has a long and colorful history as a vault for Mayan treasure, a pirate hideout, and, for a few people I know, one of the most thrilling romantic spots they've ever brought a significant other."

He looked so wistful that I suspected he counted himself amongst the lucky. I myself felt the luckiest I'd felt since, well, the last time I'd been rescued.

"When Enrique told us that no one knew more about the history of this area than you, I never imagined your knowledge would be critical to our lives," Frank said. "Thank you again."

"At your service," Felipe said with a smile.

We took turns hugging him as the police officer continued to check out the cave.

"How did you figure out that Ivan killed Alejandro?" I asked.

"We didn't," the police officer said.

"Like I told you, the whole situation made no sense at all," Felipe said. "Alejandro was a difficult guy who dealt in some rough circles, but no employee would dare hurt him. As for the bigger players, they'd go after someone higher up in the de la Fortuna family."

"Then we figured out that Ivan attacked Geo," the police officer said.

"How?" I asked.

"A guest at the water park found the underwater camera lodged between some rocks on the opposite shoreline of the inlet."

"That's incredible," Frank said.

"So was the video of Ivan exiting an alternate tunnel and grabbing Geo from behind," said the officer.

"He confessed to killing Alejandro," I said, "because of a time-share deal gone wrong."

"Murder, attempted murder, and kidnapping," the officer said. "That's going be a pretty hard rap to beat."

"Did you catch him yet?" Eloise asked.

"They hadn't when we left to come out here," he said. "But how about we get you back so we can find out?"

"I can't think of anything I'd like to do more," I said.

"Follow me," Felipe said. "I'll lead the way."

———

After an infinitely less terrifying series of rights and lefts, none of which I paid any attention to, we were once again blessed by a beautiful starlit sky. We retraced our path, now moonlit, back to the rocky natural harbor and onto an awaiting boat.

It wasn't until we were well on our way back toward the mainland that I thought of one more unanswered question.

"Felipe," I asked reveling in the ocean breeze for what felt like the first time in my life. "How did you know to look for us out here?"

"It was a little tricky," he said. "As soon as the police saw the tape, they started looking for Ivan. When they couldn't find him, we figured he might be with Eloise so we called, looked for you all over the resort, checked with people from your show, and finally headed toward your room with a master key. On the way, I ran into that young man who's been spending time with your sons."

"Liam?" I asked.

"He said he was supposed to meet the boys and was concerned about where they were. I explained to him that we'd found the tape and that we were worried about the entire family. He didn't know where the boys or Maddie and Frank were, but he did know one crucial detail."

"Which was?"

"He told us Eloise had gone off jet skiing with Ivan."

"How did he know that?" Frank asked.

"I think it might have been me again," Eloise said with a shrug. "I saw Liam and told him just before I met up with Ivan. Ivan told me not to tell anyone, actually, but I was so excited about it, I figured what the heck…"

I gave her a hug. "Thank goodness you did."

THIRTY-TWO

ALL I REALLY WANTED was to return safely and quietly to shore, hug my boys, and sleep in the comfort of an honest to goodness, genuine bed until I woke up with the last eighteen or so hours behind me. Seeing as the local *jefe de policía* and company were already at the hotel awaiting a debrief about our island adventure, I knew it would be a while until my head could be reacquainted with the divine softness of an actual pillow.

The very last thing I wanted was a huge welcoming committee, but, to no surprise, we arrived to a lineup of everyone from Antonio to Zelda, as well as various onlookers, the local news, and all three *Family Frugalicious* camera crews (no doubt being paid double overtime for working in the wee hours of the morning), all poised to capture our triumphant return to the Hacienda de la Fortuna.

Ignoring the cameras and the crowd, we rushed off the boat toward the boys, who'd been waiting for us to pull in at the end of the dock.

"Do you realize how scared we were?" FJ asked hugging me tightly. "We couldn't even leave the room or ask anyone where you were."

"We ate everything in the mini bar," Trent said, looking pale and weary despite his tan. "Right away."

"I'm so sorry," Eloise said, embracing her brothers. "This was really all my fault."

"How was it your—"

"All that matters is that you three are back safe and sound," pronounced Anastasia, making her on-camera appearance with tears running down her face for dramatic effect. "And that the network is committed to doing whatever it takes to catch that murderer."

The onslaught of eager, concerned onlookers descended upon us from there.

"Please allow me to be the first to thank you and express our sincere appreciation on behalf of the Hacienda de la Fortuna for everything you've done and been through," Enrique said, wearing rumpled clothes and a day's worth of beard. "We are so grateful that everything can now return to normal."

"I apologize for having had to be so secretive, but now you understand," the mayor said, standing with both Elena and Benito. All three looked like they'd grabbed whatever outfit was nearest their various beds and rushed over to be part of the fanfare. "My family is forever in your debt."

"Alejandro was so complimentary of you," Elena said to me. "If only he were here to know how right he was about you and your incredible family."

Benito hugged us. "I wouldn't have made it in jail for even for a day."

"Thank you," Antonio said. "I am now free to work with the mayor to make my brother's dream expansion a reality without the fear that paralyzed all of us around here."

"The *jefe de policía* is waiting to take your statement," a police officer said, gently guiding me toward the walkway leading to the hotel lobby.

Two of the other officers who'd been part of the search effort fell in to help push through the growing circus. As we walked, we did our best to acknowledge but not comment on the nonstop remarks and questions being fired in our direction:

Why? Why did he do it?

Everyone loved that jerk. He needs to be locked away forever.

To think there was a serial killer on the loose...

Did he give any hints who he was planning to kill next?

Only Frank stopped to address a local TV reporter.

"How does it feel to have escaped such a clever, ruthless killer?" the reported asked.

"Indescribable," Frank said. He seemed to be poised to say something more, when something else caught his attention just inside the lobby.

Or rather, someone.

"Dude," FJ said, also spotting Liam and waving him over from where he stood with Face, Hair, Body, and their significant others.

"My mom told me they found all of you and to come down to the lobby," Liam said rubbing sleep from his eyes. "So glad you're okay."

"You saved our lives," Eloise said.

"Me?"

"My man, you're a hero," Trent said. "No one but us knew that Ivan had taken Eloise jet skiing out to the islands."

"And Mom and Dad made us stay in the room and forbid us to talk to anyone," FJ said.

"Which was really pretty dumb when you think about it," Trent said.

"It didn't seem dumb when we thought we were dealing with a murderous cartel," Frank said. "We wanted to keep you boys safe."

"Liam, you saved the day by telling Felipe where Eloise and Ivan went," I said. "If it weren't for you, we'd still be trapped down in that cave."

"Indefinitely," Eloise said.

"So, thank you," I said.

"You're welcome," he said dubiously, and a little pink in the cheeks.

"Yes," Frank said, "thank you." He glanced at FJ for a split second, and then stepped over and gave the boy a hug.

———

While sleep seemed nowhere imminent, we soon found ourselves in the relative quiet of a conference room with only the local chief of police, a translator, and Philip, our personal chief of police/bridegroom, firing questions at us.

The chiefs (as well as the boys, who insisted they be allowed to sit in) questioned us about every detail, starting with the note I found on the door and all the way up to Ivan's promise he would send help as soon as he got wherever it was he was planning to go.

"Any hints as to where he might have gone?" El Jefe asked.

"No idea," Eloise said, "But he did tell me he loves to surf in Costa Rica."

"Don't we all," El Jefe said, jotting a note.

As soon as he was satisfied that we'd covered as much as there was to know, he showed us four seconds of tape in which a man was clearly grabbing Geo's leg and misdirecting him. While his face wasn't visible, the sea turtle tattoo on his right forearm definitely was.

Ivan.

"And you say he killed Alejandro because of a timeshare dispute?" Philip asked.

"A timeshare sold to him under false pretenses," I found myself saying. "He came down here to try and settle things amicably, but Alejandro wouldn't budge."

"We've definitely seen our fair share of skirmishes over timeshares," the translator said for El Jefe.

"But no murders?" I asked.

"I suppose it was bound to happen."

"I'm surprised it hasn't happened sooner given the sales tactics and impossible-to-understand fine print."

El Jefe shrugged. "Just the way it's done."

"Maybe it should be done differently," I said.

"That's not my call," he said.

"Ivan told us he only ever planned to confront Alejandro, not kill him."

"But he took the law into his own hands, then tried to deflect suspicion with the attack on Geo. Not to mention that he left you to die in a cave."

"He left us food and a water purifier and even a first-aid kit," Eloise said.

"Which we'd have gone through pretty quick," Frank said.

I had no choice but nod in agreement.

"I can't believe Ivan did all that," Trent said. "He seemed like such a super-great guy."

"Tell me about it," Eloise said, tearing up.

"His real name is Evan Matthews," Philip said. "He is twenty-nine, divorced, comes from Orange County, California, and has no prior criminal record."

"His name is really Evan?" Eloise said. "I can't believe he didn't even tell me his real name."

"What a shame." Frank shook his head. "Ivan—I mean, Evan—was planning to be a lawyer."

"He looked too young to be married and divorced already," FJ said.

"He looks much older with a shaved head," Eloise said.

"He shaved off those cool dreads?" Trent asked.

Frank nodded. "He's all but unrecognizable, which will make him a lot harder to catch."

"But we will catch him," El Jefe said. "Of that, you can rest assured."

———

The only thing I wanted to do was rest, but the moment we finished answering questions about Ivan/Evan the kids were sent off to sleep, but we were escorted across the lobby to recount our story once more for the *Family Frugalicious* cameras.

We arrived just in time to hear Sara, Susan, and Sally and company wrap up their end-of-the-night-recap with some final thoughts about our rescue and their overall experience:

"This whole week has been unlike anything I've ever experienced," Sally said.

"It's been quite a ride," Sara said, looking moony-eyed beside groomsman Dave.

Susan sighed.

"I keep telling Susan that despite it all, we've made out like bandits," her husband Michael said. "All of us were way more involved in the whole reality TV aspect and everyone got timeshares for a song."

"Good point," Sara said. "I suppose all's well that ends well, right?"

"True," Sally said. "But do you think our sacrifice scene will be cut now that all the other drama has happened?"

———

"I have a surprise," Anastasia said as the sisters were cleared out and we assembled on chairs to recount the pertinent details of *all the other drama.*

"They've found Iv—Evan?" I asked.

"He's still at large, but he won't be for long." She smiled. "Not after we tie reality TV in with real life in a way no one has ever tried before."

"And how is that?"

She smiled. "How does a worldwide manhunt for Evan in connection with the show grab you?"

"The ratings would be monster," Frank said.

"Don't you think?" Stasia gushed.

I couldn't stop thinking about some of the things Ivan had said as part of his confession.

My plan was to come down and fight him in court and/or the court of public opinion.

Why are these outfits allowed to lie and manipulate people?

Why hasn't anyone stepped up to stop this kind of unethical behavior?

I stopped one man. I just wish there weren't so many Alejandros out there, eager to bully people out of their money and happiness for the promise of paradise.

Evan would eventually have to deal with the ramifications of his actions, but in that moment I realized what had been bothering me even more than my experience as a hostage in the midst of yet another murder. "I think we have a major problem."

"What do you mean?" Anastasia asked.

"What is our show really about?" I asked.

"Our family sniffing out good deals and the best bargains for other families in a slice-of-life reality TV format," Frank said as if I had the intellect of a below-average kindergartner.

"Do you agree, Anastasia?"

She nodded. "With some interesting subplots thrown in for good measure."

"Glad to hear you admit that, which I'd love to discuss when I had a bit of sleep," I said. "In the meantime, I believe we're going to scrap this whole episode."

"What in the heck are you—" Frank said, abruptly stopping mid-sentence. "Evan—"

"Evan what?" Anastasia asked.

"Oh man," Frank said, putting his head in his hands. "I didn't think of that."

"Think of what?" Anastasia asked.

I steeled myself for what I knew I had to do. "You know how our experience in the timeshare department was pleasant and pressure-free?"

"That's how they do it here at Hacienda de la Fortuna."

"Really?" I asked. "How much research did you do?"

"We looked into timeshares," she said. "You saw it."

"Can I possibly see your phone?"

She handed it over, I Googled "Hacienda de la Fortuna Horror Stories," opened the first site, and handed it back to her. "Read."

She began to read.

"Ivan, or whatever his real name is, snapped because of how horribly he was treated after being pressured to buy a timeshare, lied to about the cancelation policy, and then threatened for months on end."

"Can any of this be substantiated?" Anastasia asked, still scrolling through a conversation thread filled with complaints against Hacienda de la Fortuna.

"I met a couple this weekend dealing with a similar issue, and there are apparently many, many more," I said. "Even if these folks are the exception and not the rule, how can we air an episode on budget destination weddings and the lure of timeshares with a side dish of murder when—"

"When the murderer killed in a blind rage over the way he was treated at the timeshare office?" Anastasia said finishing my sentence.

"I can't in good conscience recommend people come down to this resort, much less suggest they take the timeshare tour," I said. "In fact, I don't believe I can keep the timeshare given to us."

"But ..." Frank said. "There has to be some way we can ..."

"You're right," Anastasia finally said, but looking as if all the blood had drained from her face. "We have a major problem."

THIRTY-THREE

I WAS SENT OFF to bed with no idea what Anastasia planned to do, whether Frank had anything to do with whatever it was she planned to do, or what I was supposed to do.

When I awoke the next morning, Frank was nowhere in sight. Unsure what was going to happen beyond the fact that we were due to leave in a matter of hours, I set about getting the kids up and getting us packed to go home.

I zipped my suitcase, opened the safe, and had just removed my computer and the timeshare paperwork I planned to leave with Antonio or Beti in the vacation sales office on my way to the lobby, when the door to our suite squealed open.

A camera crew filed in.

"What's going on?" I asked, not at all sure I wanted to know the answer.

Stasia directed the crew to set up. "I spent the rest of the night researching, and you were absolutely right," she said, trailing the crew into the living room. "We had an enormous and costly potential disaster on our hands."

"Had?" I asked.

The next thing I knew, Frank, Anastasia, Elena, Enrique, Antonio, and, miraculously, Geo appeared in the doorway.

"You were released from the hospital?"

"I did a little strong-arming of my own."

I wasn't sure if that was supposed to be funny, but everyone seemed to be smiling, if a little tightly. And then the man I recognized as the CEO of Hacienda de la Fortuna joined the group.

"What's going on?" I asked.

"You ready?" Anastasia asked the cameraman.

"Ready," he said.

"Lighting?" she asked.

"We're good."

"Everyone else ready?"

Everyone nodded but me.

Anastasia stepped out of the shot. "And action."

"Evan Matthews needs to pay for what he did to me," Geo said.

"And me," Elena said, tears instantly spilling from her eyes and down her cheeks.

"He will," the CEO said, "but we can't discount his message."

"No, we can't," Enrique said, nodding in agreement.

"What is going on?" I asked, quite certain that Anastasia would yell *cut*.

Instead, she gave me a thumbs up.

"We've been in meetings ever since we got word about Evan Matthews's motives for killing Alejandro," the CEO said. "And I, for one, can't live with the idea that he was driven to murder by sales tactics we, unfortunately, were employing with far too much regularity."

"Are you serious?"

Everyone nodded.

"From here on out, the Hacienda de la Fortuna is going to be the model of aboveboard sales tactics for the timeshare industry."

"Really?" I asked.

"I never want to see another criticism leveled at our resort, particularly where vacation ownership is concerned," the CEO said. "We are in the business of making dreams a reality, not causing people murderous nightmares."

"Thank you Mr. and Mrs. Frugalicious," Elena hugged us. "My husband's death will not be in vain."

"Cut," Anastasia said.

"Is that all you need?" the CEO asked with no trace of the warmth he'd shown a few seconds earlier.

"That's it," Anastasia said.

"Okay then," he said. And just like that, he was gone, along with Antonio, Enrique, and Elena.

"'Okay then' is right," I said to Anastasia, Frank, and Geo, who remained in the room. "What just happened here?"

"They're a tough group, but they're shrewd business people," she said. "The bad publicity associated with their underhanded timeshare sales techniques would have destroyed them. As soon as I met with them and laid out the situation, they quickly agreed to the solution I thought up: we tell our story just like it happened, they come clean, at least for the foreseeable future, and rebrand themselves as a no-haggle timeshare outfit."

"Like the new 'modern' car dealers?"

"Very much like that. They get the *Family Frugalicious* stamp of approval as well as the increased traffic from people who want to come to their beautiful resort and are interested in vacation property, but are afraid of the high-pressure tactics," she said. "And we get kudos for straightening their crooked ways."

"And killer ratings," Geo chimed in.

"They didn't seem as happy about their future prospects as you guys are."

"I wouldn't necessarily say that," Geo said, pointing out the window and down to the semi-private courtyard below our room.

Elena held Enrique's hand as they stood together beside the fountain.

"Apparently they've been in love since they were kids," Anastasia said. "Until now they had to pretend otherwise because they could never be together."

"That's so hard," I said.

"Not all that much harder than pretending to actually be in love with someone you're not," Anastasia said.

Frank and I made real eye contact in the first time in I didn't know how long. Neither of us said a word, even though everyone in the room likely knew what was going on with our marriage.

A big fat nothing.

Anastasia noticed our look and flashed her bright, white grin. "The good news is, I think we may have that worked out a solution for that too."

"You have?" Frank said.

"What is it?" I asked.

"I figured things were rocky even before Eloise slipped and said something, so when test audiences started saying they want more about Maddie and her struggles in the aftermath of Frank's issues, we added the Alejandro element to spice things up."

"I knew it had to be a setup! He was awful, Stasia."

"But awfully charming when he needed to be."

I felt my cheeks color.

"No one believed you'd truly fall for his smooth talk, but if you had, you know I'm always up for a totally killer B story."

"As in my love life or lack thereof?"

"Not for long. Think of the ratings when we announce your split, and the newly single Mrs. Frugalicious starts dating! We'll do a whole episode on bargain dating websites, finding bargains to keep the cost of dating down. And bargain shopping together…"

"We may not be together," Frank said, "but I, for one, hate that idea."

"Oh?" I asked.

"I *really* hate that idea," Frank said.

"Maybe so, Frank, but you know what I always say," Anastasia said.

"I don't think I do," he said.

"All's fair in love, war, and reality TV."

ACKNOWLEDGMENTS

Mrs. Frugalicious and her latest adventure would never be possible without the support of Terri Bischoff, Nicole Nugent, Beth Hanson, and the rest of the fantastic gang at Midnight Ink.

Thank you to Josh Getzler and Danielle Burby at HSG for the all-around agent brilliance.

A huge thank you to my friends, family, and fellow writer pals for all the encouragement and continuing support. Specifically: Ben Le Roy, Becky Stevens, Cary Cazzanigi, Keir Graff, Jess Lourey, Mark Stevens, Jennifer Kincheloe, Melisa Ford, Chris Jorgenson, Suzanne Proulx, the Joffe/Hull/Moskowitz clan, Rocky Mountain Fiction Writers, and, of course, the Dog Park Gang.

Lastly, but mostly, to Brandon Hull—thank you for making everything seem (and then somehow be) possible.